Queen Crow

J Bree

Queen Crow
Queen Crow #3
A Mounts Bay Saga Novel
Copyright © 2021 J Bree
Cover Designed by Bellaluna Cover Designs

This book is licensed for your personal enjoyment only.
This book may not be re-sold or given away to other people. If you would like to share this book with another person, please purchase an additional copy for each recipient. If you're reading this book and did not purchase it, or it wasn't purchased for your use only, then please return to your favourite book retailer and purchase your own copy. Thank you for respecting the hard work of this author.
All rights reserved.
This is a work of fiction. Names, characters, places, brands, media, and incidents are either the product of the authors imagination or are used fictitiously. The author acknowledges the trademark status and trademark owners of various products referred to in this work of fiction, which have been used without permission. The publication/use of these trademarks is not authorised, associated with, or sponsored by the trademark owners.

Queen Crow/J Bree – 1st ed

ISBN-13 9798541849028

*To my codependent, noodle-loving friends.
Who are out here saving lives, and I don't just mean my own.*

Prologue

Atticus
Two Years Ago

The second I meet the Wolf's eyes across the hallway as the elevator doors shut, I know that this is the moment I've been waiting for since I'd heard from Luca that she was attending Hannaford.

This is the moment that I have to kill the girl to keep Avery safe.

I meet Luca's eye from across the room where he's been watching this entire evening unfold, nodding to him as I step forward to wait for the next elevator. I check the security cameras on my phone and watch as they all walk into their hotel room together. Avery looks upset and Ash is snarling at the Wolf, so clearly she's let them know.

I wait until I get up to their floor before I call her, sure that she'll leave me to go to voicemail but when she does actually answer, I don't give her the chance to talk her way out of this. "Which room are you in? We need to talk."

There's a pause like she's considering this but when she speaks, her voice is as steady as ever, the immovable Wolf of Mounts Bay. "We're leaving. We're going back to Hannaford. Avery is under my protection and if you want to discuss the parameters of that protection with me, we can do it at the next meeting."

Like that would ever stop me. "Open the door, Wolf."

She hangs up on me and it's a full minute before the door opens, the Morrison kid staring me down with that moody arrogance he's perfected. I step past him without acknowledging him, now isn't the time for playing pretend, and the moment he has the door opened for me, he stalks back over to his friends, flanking the Wolf alongside Ash.

Avery is sitting on the living room chair, her back straight and a look of scowling betrayal on her face. I have to contain the snarl I want to let out at the little slum assassin for meddling in her life. I shouldn't have let Luca talk me out of killing her.

I've never been able to see why he's so soft on her.

All I see when I look at her is a *threat*.

No one should be able to get into the places she can without help or detection, and the trail of bodies she's been able to leave behind her isn't just impressive...

It's disturbing.

Ash is staring at me with that same furious loathing he

always has for me, except this time he's practically vibrating with rage and bloodlust. Morrison is also ready to throw himself into a fight, rocking back on his heels as he shifts his stance in preparation.

I need to play this right.

Stepping forward and inclining my head at the Wolf respectfully is the right thing to do, but she's too perceptive not to see what this is about. She's always seen too much, always been a little too smart for everyone else in the Twelve to get a handle on her.

It still is astounding that she sides with the Jackal.

"I already told you we're leaving," she says, her voice pitched low and even, as though she's projecting an older, more formidable version of herself.

She's seventeen, for fuck's sake.

I keep my eyes fixed on hers as I kick the door shut behind me, using my peripherals to check for the Butcher, because nothing would shock me less than that psychopath stalking out of the bathroom right now.

When it's clear we're alone, I get right to it. "I'm not leaving here without her. Name your price."

It's like a match to Ash's temper, instant ignition as he snarls, *"She's not for fucking sale!"*

It's a calculated move for me, a test to see not only what they know about her, but how it is that she'll treat them here. If she offers me Avery, she's dead. If she doesn't... Well, I'm leaving here with her, so she's still dead.

Killing a seventeen-year-old girl from the slums isn't even close to the worst thing I've done.

Except the Wolf holds up a hand to stop Ash from lunging at me and taking a swing, the shot he's been waiting for years to take. Miraculously, his eyes break away from me for a second to glare at her. Even more interestingly, Morrison instantly stiffens like he's getting ready to jump in between them and I've never seen him side with someone over Ash. Never, in over a decade of friendship.

There's a staring contest for a second, everyone watching and taking bets in their heads over what the fuck is happening in the air between them, before Ash crosses his arms and swings back to seethe in my direction once more.

Avery and the Wolf share a look and I don't like that at all. I don't like that they have their own language, that Avery trusts her enough to establish that level of communication.

"How much? How much is she worth to you?" Lips says coolly.

It doesn't make sense with how she's acting, but I don't have the time or patience to speculate right now. It's all about the negotiation. "Three favors."

She pauses, as close to a reaction as I'll ever get from her, and then she slowly shakes her head at me. Her eyes are calm and steady on mine, and I want to strangle her for this moment.

Fuck it, she's dead anyway, I might as well find out how deep her loyalties lie. "Six, but I'll have your word that you will never tell the Jackal about her."

She instantly freezes.

I'm expecting her to grab her phone and call her psychopath friend, the man who is singlehandedly attempting to murder me at every opportunity. The man who loves nothing more than being *the Jackal*, running all of the drugs and destroying as many lives as he possibly can.

I need to get Avery the fuck away from them all.

The Wolf looks me over in that slow, assessing way of hers and whatever she sees is enough to make her decision, taking a single step forward. I shift my own stance, just enough that I'm ready if she launches herself at me, and instantly her eyes narrow.

The mood in the room gets malevolent.

Her words, when they come, are a low rasp, saying the last thing I'm expecting from her, "You're in love with her, aren't you, Atticus?"

We never use our names, not ever.

"I told you, I'll—" I start, but she cuts me off.

"She's not for sale. Not to you, not to Matteo, not to anyone. Either admit you're here because you have real, genuine feelings for her, or leave. And to be perfectly clear, there is *nothing* I wouldn't do to keep her safe. I'll risk the Twelve if I have to."

It's a declaration of more than friendship, of a loyalty that runs deeper than just some schoolyard bullshit.

My eyes swing down to land on Avery because this has to be a play, some tactic to use her as a pawn against me, but again, that betrayal in her eyes cuts me to fucking ribbons.

I'm a second away from pulling a gun and killing the Wolf for messing with her head and turning her against me when Avery says, "The Wolf is my family, Atticus. I'm not leaving with you."

Family.

Avery has never had family before.

From the moment Alice was murdered in that fucking mausoleum of Senior's, she's had Ash and no one else. Even I have had to keep myself at arm's length from her for years, just to keep her safe from my family and her father.

Ash doesn't react to her claiming the Wolf as her family, and he's the most protective, possessive brother I've ever met.

Maybe I won't kill the girl.

It's a risk to Avery's safety, but she's already made her choice for now.

I turn to face the Wolf again. "You can't let Matteo know about her, or what she means to me. He'll fucking destroy her. It's bad enough she's with you."

It's as though all of the fight has been sucked out of me and I sink down in the armchair in the corner of the room, rubbing my hands over my face.

When will the mind games and careful moves end? When will I have Avery safe, alive, and *mine*?

"You don't need to explain to me what that man does to innocent girls when he has an agenda," the Wolf whispers, and it hits me once again that she's Avery's age. She's a teenage girl, orphaned and alone and without someone like me watching over her.

All she's had is the Jackal.

The self-loathing that happens when the black-hearted Crow slips away from me sets in, a dark chuckle slipping out of me. "I guess I should remember that better than anyone. I was there when he snapped your leg with his bare hands. What were you, twelve years old?"

Morrison takes her hand and tugs her into his body, trying to comfort her for trauma from long ago. His closeness to her is confusing because with the way Ash trusts her, I would've guessed they were dating.

She clears her throat. "Thirteen. I was thirteen and I had just won the Game. He told me he wanted to teach me how to deal with pain, but really, he was trying to break me in. Nothing he hates more than a female he can't break."

And yet he doesn't hate her. "Well, he didn't break you, did he? Here you stand with two Beaumonts and the richest kid in the country. You've inducted the heir to the O'Cronin family into your fold, and let's not forget the Butcher. I'd wager *this* wasn't Matteo's plan."

She chuckles and sits on the couch, pulling Morrison down with her, and Avery moves over to them immediately. Ash is slower to move over to them but when he does, he slips his hand to rest on the Wolf's thigh.

I have no fucking clue what to make of them. "I was under the impression you were with the O'Cronin kid. That's what Matteo thinks anyway. I heard a rumor of… more but I thought that was just his delusions."

The Wolf starts to *blush* and Avery scoffs at her, irreverent to her status and infamy. "Seriously? We're in a life-threatening situation and you're getting all shy about your harem of obsessed boys?"

Morrison nudges Avery's leg with his shoulder and cackles at her. "Leave her alone, she's used to being a badass under pressure."

The Wolf of Mounts Bay has a harem and Alexander Asher William Beaumont, the scowling and savage boy who can't even handle sharing his sister with the world, is one of them.

This is incomprehensible.

So is Avery thinking that her life has *ever* been in danger from me. "This isn't a life-threatening situation, Avery. As long as you are safe, I'm not going to do anything. The last time I saw the Wolf, I knew things had changed between her and the Jackal, but I couldn't risk being wrong. I couldn't leave your fate up to chance because the Jackal would do things to you that I've spent *years* making sure your father didn't fucking do."

My words mean nothing to her though, and she just stares over at me like I've lost her trust for good.

I won't feel bad for this, not for coming here ready to kill for her, or for keeping her in the dark about who I've become. It's saved her life over and over again, and that's all that matters in the end.

Even if she hates me.

The Wolf cuts in to our staring competition. "It's Lips, and I'm not Matteo's protégé or girlfriend or whatever it is that the Twelve think. He sponsored me for the Game and he's helped me out, but he's also done things to me that I can't ever forgive or forget. I went to Hannaford to figure a way out. That's what we're doing, we're finding a way out of all of this."

I nod and rub at my chin, thinking through a thousand new avenues this potential alliance could open up for me. For Avery. For building an empire so big and safe for her that she becomes untouchable.

Avery hesitates for a moment and then asks with her usual commanding tone, "You were at the meeting with Lips and Harley, do you think the Jackal is going to continue to send people to kill him?"

I shrug, easily able to slip into a business conversation with her. "He's in less danger now that he's under her protection. He was on very limited time with his grandfather before then, despite my efforts. Matteo can't just kill him, he has to find some sort of betrayal or dishonesty to be able to take him out. He doesn't just answer to the Wolf if he does, he answers to the Twelve. He's a big player, but he's not the biggest, and definitely not bigger than us all."

"And what if he continues to try to kill him stealthily?" Avery continues. "I'm sure you're aware he's spiraling and recruiting."

Well.

I guess the little Wolf hasn't been so open with her family at just how far she went to stake a claim on Arbour. It was the first time I've seen her really throw around the reputation and power she's cultivated over the years, and it was impressive, to say the least.

When I grin and cock an eyebrow at her, she blushes like a maiden, jarring me once again with how *young* she is, and I answer Avery with a drawl, "Oh, after the Wolf's declaration at the meeting, the Jackal has been served a severe warning about touching her toys. The rest of the Twelve are much more aware of his… instability now. Those who have chosen his side are in as much danger as he is."

I finish with a sharp look at Lips but she shrugs it off, leaning forward in her chair and saying, "If I induct these three as well, would you be willing to back me up in the meetings if Matteo starts with his shit?"

It's simple and easy and exactly what I need from her.

It's the way to give Avery a name that isn't my own, isn't one her father or mine can use against her, and no one in the streets of Mounts Bay would ever go against the Wolf. Never and certainly not now that the Butcher has been inducted by her.

I stand and run a hand down the front of my suit jacket, a slow smile forming on my lips at how simple it is. "If you cut yourself off from the Jackal and start calling *me* when you need help instead of him, then I will take him on with you. Induct them, keep Avery safe from the Jackal and her father, and I will offer my help with *anything* from this moment onward. Whatever the cost."

That's *exactly* what I need.

Lips glances up at Avery and I'm shocked to see that's all she does. She doesn't make an attempt to convince her or manipulate her into anything, she just stares up at her and waits for her to make her own mind up about this.

One by one, I watch as they all agree to these terms. Avery is the first, always weighing up her options and making the best choices she can. Morrison is quick to sign himself over to the girl, a lovesick idiot following her to his inevitable doom.

Ash takes a lot longer.

I've never seen him show any interest in girls before. He's slept his way through Hannaford, sure, but he's never looked as though he's wanted to keep one around before.

He stares at Lips with the same type of obsession that the Jackal does. He stares at her like he would do anything to keep her tied to him, the same way Joey stares at him. If I wasn't seeing it all with my own eyes, I wouldn't believe it.

What magic has she cast over them all?

Finally, he squeezes her thigh with his eyes still cast away and Lips says firmly, "Done."

I look to Avery with a tight smile, her presence always demanding my attention whether she knows it or not. She stares back at me like I've betrayed her so deeply that she may never forgive me.

If that's the cost of keeping her alive, I'll gladly pay it.

I hesitate at the door, but I turn back to Lips because this has to be said. "Don't ever let her wear red again. She wears your color or mine."

And then I walk out, praying I'm not wrong.

Queen Crow

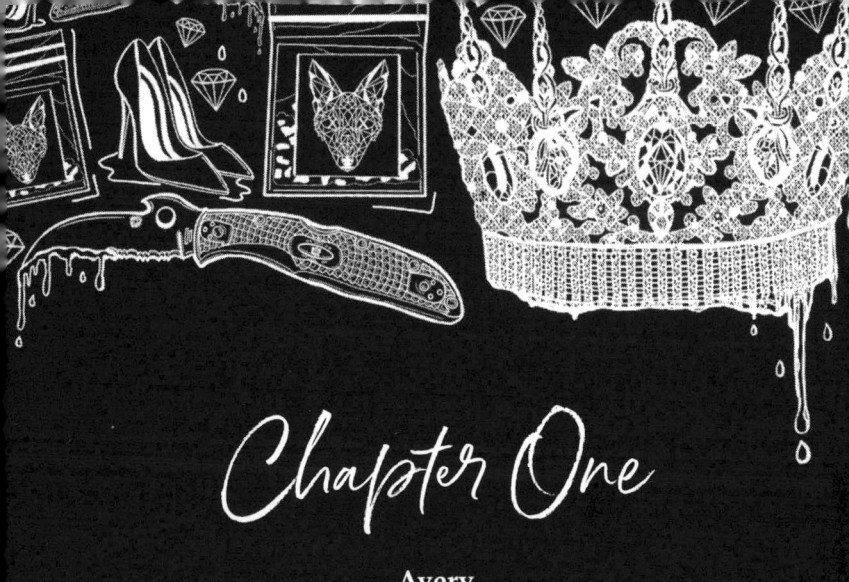

Chapter One

Avery

I stand there in the middle of Atticus' front foyer, covered entirely in blood, with the knife still dripping in my hands, and watch in horror as Ash throws himself at Aodhan.

Horror because I've seen my brother fight a million times before and there isn't a single part of him that is holding back right now. He's here to kill Aodhan, and fighting someone who doesn't want to kill you back will always give you the advantage.

"Ash, stop! ASH!" My voice is shrill and hysterical, but it does nothing; he doesn't even register that I've spoken, his fists just fly.

I'm about to do something stupid, ridiculous even, but as my feet start moving toward the brawl, the front door opens again and I see the greatest sight ever.

A furious looking Lips stalks through the doorway, looking me over quickly for injuries and when it's clear that I'm both alive and unharmed, she dives into the fight with absolutely no regard for her own safety.

She gets an arm around Ash's throat and a foot on Aodhan's chest, shoving them away from each other. It would be an impossible move, except that she hisses something in Ash's ear and he immediately stops, pushing up and standing, even with her wrapped around his back. She stays holding on to him for a second before she eases up and slides down his back, stepping around him so she's in position to grab him again if she needs to.

Aodhan pulls himself up, his lip cut and one of his cheeks swelling, but his eyes stay fixed on Ash even as he takes a step toward me.

Ash stares right back at him, his lip curled into a snarl. "Stay the fuck away from her."

I purposely step toward Aodhan, my voice still caught in my chest at exactly how *exposed* I am right now. A pair of yoga pants and a Kevlar vest, I might as well be naked for how far out of my comfort zone I am.

Lips glances around the room, taking in Bingley's corpse and the knife in my hand, and then she says, "Are you going to explain exactly what the fuck is going on now, Ash? Before we resort to homicide, we usually vote on that shit."

He doesn't react to her at all, his focus is entirely on the space between Aodhan and I. "There's no voting on this. He hurt Avery; he's dead. *I will fucking kill him.*"

I share a quick look with Lips, but whatever the hell he's talking about, she has no idea. How they've gotten back here without this conversation is also beyond me, but that's for a later, less fraught time.

Ash looks up at me and then says through clenched teeth, "I saw the fucking tape of him raping you."

Oh God.

I fall into a complete panic, every inch of my body beginning to shake, but Ash is still seething with the rage he's obviously been wallowing in since he saw that *fucking* tape.

His voice is almost shaking with unspent rage. "At the Jackal's lair. I knew something happened, I fucking knew it, and everyone told me to give you space. *Space!* I left you behind with that piece of fucking shit and I will never leave you again. Fucking *never*."

His eyes lock onto Aodhan again, but Lips shuts him down quickly. "You go for him and I'll be throwing myself into the fight. Look at me, Ash. I've never been more serious about anything in my life. You're here about Avery being hurt, right? You're the only one hurting her right now."

She's not getting through to him, I can see it clearly, and the knife in my hand slips away from my fingers to land with a heavy *thunk* on the marble floor.

I can't lose either of them.

All I've been doing for weeks is losing; people, power moves, my sanity and privacy. I can't do this anymore.

"How the fuck can you say that to me? *I saw the fucking tape, Lips.*"

"I heard you the first time, Ash, but you need to look at your sister. *Look at her.* Look at what you're doing to her. Because you're doing this right now, *not* Aodhan."

His eyes flick over to mine and finally he sees me, roaming over the blood and carnage all over me before his eyes meet mine.

A sob breaks out of my chest, rattling me, and he moves so quickly that he's just a blur before I'm pressed into his chest. "Are you hurt? What happened? Where the hell is that fuck Crawford?"

My sobs get even worse and then I'm breaking the hell down because his arms have always been my safe haven, but this is all wrong. He's not my protector anymore.

Aodhan is.

Atticus is, just the second he comes back to me and wakes up.

Is this what growing up feels like? Because part of me doesn't want it, I never want to lose any part of him because we've only known safety together, but part of me knows that this was the whole point of staying in Mounts Bay while they travelled together.

We needed to find out who we are as adults, without hiding in each other.

"Floss, whatever has happened, I'll fix it. I'll kill him right now and we'll destroy any evidence of the tape."

I press my hands against his chest to push him away, the tears pooling in my eyes at his soft tones; his gentleness and need to protect me always brings down my guard, but I can't get lost in that right now. "Whatever you think you saw in that tape, Ash... it wasn't what actually happened."

His eyes narrow at me and I take another step toward Aodhan, preparing to throw myself between them if I need to.

Aodhan immediately moves to my side, coming back within arm's reach of Ash and his rage again.

Lips senses the same danger as I do and stalks back over to us, holding out her hand to Ash. "Show it to me. I really don't want to watch it, but Avery told me what really happened; I'll prove to you that it's not what you think it is."

I would rather die than watch it, but I also really, really don't want Lips seeing it either. "Can we just forget about the tape?"

"Only if you agree that O'Cronin dies," Ash snarls at me, and Aodhan instantly slides in front of me again.

"Don't talk to her like that. Brother or not, I'm not fucking standing for it."

Lips' face clears and her eyes flick to mine. He's already won her over, but I can see the approval shining through her face at the move. She's never been someone to stand behind others, but when her guys all made their obsession for her clear, they'd also protected her as much as they could. It was their love language from the moment they'd found each other, so she has an appreciation for it that others might not.

Ash doesn't feel the same way. "Move the fuck away from her before I choke the life out of you."

Aodhan doesn't move and he doesn't raise his voice, his tone as clear and steady as it's always been. "I'm not going to let you destroy your sister right now, no matter how angry you are. I know what it must look like and so I'm not going to get pissed at you for going for my throat, because she's your sister, but I'm not going to let you take that shit out on her. Stop and take a breath. Let Lips watch the fucking tape and find out who's messed with it, because I went into that room to die for her. She was in control the whole time; if you can't wrap your head around that, then that's a you problem. She doesn't owe you an explanation, be grateful you're getting one."

The adrenaline sucks out of my body all at once, the knife forgotten at my bare feet as I lean forward and press my forehead against his back. I squeeze my eyes shut for just a second, letting him hold me up for a moment.

I'm exhausted.

Atticus is in the hospital with a hole the size of my fist in his chest. The Twelve are still sizing us all up and looking for an opportunity to strike at our family. There's the Graves kids to find and protect, Amanda Donnelley to sort out, and Randy and Holden Crawford.

Bingley's corpse is still leaking on the ground at our feet.

Tears fill my eyes and then the door at the end of the hallway opens and Luca walks through, armed to the teeth and with blood splattered all over himself as though he took on the entire group of intruders on his own. His eyes flick over the entire scene, including the hand prints around Aodhan's throat and the bloodied mess of my legs.

"Avery, are you okay? The house is clear."

We discover that Luca's voice is also a trigger for Ash's seething rage, whatever moment of quiet that Aodhan's words had forced him into now completely gone as he turns on Atticus' second with a snarl. "Where the fuck were you? Where *the fuck* is Crawford? I'll kill him too. Forcing Avery to stay in this fucking mausoleum and then leaving her to fend for herself against *your* enemies? I will fucking destroy you—"

Lips side-steps back around him to push herself against his chest, making it clear that she's not about to let him fight his way through all of the anger in him tonight.

It's going to be a long night.

Luca ignores him completely, his eyes dropping down to Bingley before they snap back to me. "Are you hurt? Do you need first aid?"

A watery sounding sob bursts out of my throat. "Well, after a night of being rescued from the Collector's son, watching Atticus take a bullet to the chest for me that I'm sure will kill him, and killing Bingley myself after an attack... Ash seeing a director's cut of the Jackal's tape might be the thing that pushes me over the fucking edge."

It's very clear to me that Ash knew very little of what has been happening with me in the last few days because he turns to stare at Lips like she's stuck a knife in his back, and I immediately wish I could take back those words.

Too late now.

Luca immediately tries to back me up, his first mistake is thinking that Ash has a rational bone left in his body today. "Amanda Donelley sent him the edited version? Fuck. I've seen it. I saw the original; it's not what it looks like. I was also there—"

Lips isn't quick enough to stop Ash from launching himself at Luca, taking him to the ground and reminding everyone that he is in fact the son of Joseph Beaumont Sr, no matter how different he may seem. Luca doesn't have time to reach for a weapon or even get his hands up, and no matter how much he struggles, he can't dislodge Ash.

He might actually die.

"Jesus fucking Christ," Aodhan mumbles as he moves to wade into the fray, but Lips shuts him down with a stern look and a shake of her head.

"Ash, I will get involved if you can't control yourself. This is your last warning before I join in, and I'm not sure you want that."

He doesn't.

He really doesn't, because if there's even a tiny chance that she might get hurt, he'll lose his shit and none of us will be able to talk him down. It was her arms around his neck that had pulled him off of Aodhan without too much fight. I've always hated seeing him like this, mostly because I don't like seeing him getting hit, but there's something very *Joey* about this complete loss of control over himself and that is terrifying. I know they're not the same, I know this is all for me and keeping me safe, but my brain just sees the manic need for vengeance and freaks the fuck out.

He hesitates for a second at her words, some sense finally filtering in, and Luca takes the opportunity to get out from underneath him, flipping him over and pushing up onto his feet again.

There's another pause, like we're all holding our breaths to see what will set him off next, but he pulls up onto his feet again, walking back over to pull me away from Aodhan and back into his arms.

Luca looks over at me and when I give him a curt shake of my head, he tips his own back at me, stalking out of the room to give us privacy once again.

For a second there, I'd forgotten I was in charge of all of this for now... until Atticus is back.

If he lives.

I feel like I can't take a breath, my lungs will never fully fill again, and then the door opens again, startling me for a second before I realize that it'll just be Harley and Morrison getting here a little too late to help.

"What the fuck happened here?"

I stiffen in Ash's arms at the completely unfamiliar voice, and he growls under his breath as Lips snaps, "I told you to stay outside until I told you it was safe. You're going to end up dead if you can't *listen* and follow instructions."

I pull away from my brother to get a look at the guy who's standing there staring around at all of the blood with a weird sort of detached interest. "Who the hell is that?"

Ash mutters back, "Another fucking Graves kid. Grimm owes us a fuckload of child support right now, because he's a nightmare."

The kid spins on his heel to grin over at Ash, and I get a proper look at him through the mass of dark curls on his head. It's easier now to pick them all out because I know to focus on his eyes first. The smudges of kohl only make the bright depths of the blue even more striking. The rest of his face is different to Lips' but there's a little of Colt in him, maybe some of Senator Blakeley if I squint a little.

He looks young, some baby fat still in his cheeks, and there's a faint scar running down one of his cheeks that's still a little pink, not quite white yet. He's more olive-skinned than his siblings and only a head taller than Lips, which makes him shorter than any of the guys in our family.

He's also dressed in fishnet stockings under a pair of shorts with a tank top, wrists full of bracelets and leather cuffs, and a thin leather strap wrapped around his throat twice.

I have no idea who he is.

A *ninth* Graves child? We need Grimm in a shallow grave and we need it to happen yesterday, before there's a whole legion of children Lips feels responsible for.

I give Lips a look and murmur, "Where the hell did you find another Graves kid?"

She glances over at him and grimaces. "Meet Noah."

Her words take a second to register before I blink back at her. "Noah. Your dead brother, Noah?"

"That's the one."

I turn to look at him again, but he's so different from the terrible black and white photo I have pinned on my wall back at the mansion that I almost want to ask her if she's sure. "What the hell happened?"

She groans quietly and rubs a hand over her face. "I found Wyatt, the cop. I spoke to him a little, but the second he heard I was from the Bay, he freaked. Wanted nothing to do with me. Fuck, I thought Harley was going to murder him for how he spoke to me. It took me a few days, and after I got back from sorting Colt's problem out... he told me about Noah. He needed some help wrangling the asshole."

Ash snaps, "We should've asked ourselves then if we really wanted to take him on."

I shoot him a look, but Noah finally takes some interest in what we're saying and rolls his eyes at us. For a second, all I see is the sassy teenager we'd had appear in Lips' hospital room last year. Despite the age gap the resemblance between him and Poe, it's uncanny.

"Am I supposed to give a fuck about drug lords and the slums of the Bay? This place isn't to my taste."

Lips rolls her eyes at him and then floors me by saying, "The only thing that *is* to your taste is dick. Wyatt gave you to me to take care of; you can either shut the fuck up and live here nicely, or we can find you a nice basement to hide out in."

He looks over at Bingley's corpse and then back at Lips. "You do this shit a lot, huh? I should've fucking known."

No.

It's been a long night, an endless week, and I don't care who he is, no one speaks down to Lips like that in front of me. "Your sister is the Wolf of Mounts Bay. She took on the Jackal, the Lynx, and every other slum lord in this city to keep her family safe, because that's who she is. If you disrespect her in front of me again, I will show you exactly what happens to people who attack our family."

He goes very still, taking in every inch of my blood-soaked image, because I still haven't even managed to wash my hands, *oh my fucking God*, and the fact that he's eyeing me warily while happily giving the Wolf lip?

He is so out of his depth here.

"Lips has been soft on him," Ash mutters grumpily, and Lips shrugs at me.

"I'm doing the best with what I have, but Noah is a lot fucking harder than any of us expected when we took him in."

I glance back over to where he's crouched down, looking over Bingley's leaking corpse, and it's never been so clear to me that we're in a lot of trouble with these Graves kids.

Too much trouble.

Chapter Two

There's nothing I want more than to climb into the shower and scrub the filth of the night away from my skin, but I'm also stronger now than I was before—I can handle this moment.

I won't be moving the body though.

"What the fuck did Atticus do to him?" Lips murmurs as she crouches over Bingley, looking over the damage that I did.

I can't think about that soft *plop* of his innards on my foot when I'd yanked the knife out of his gut, except now it's all I can think about, and I immediately start retching again.

Ash's arms tighten around me and he snarls at Aodhan, "Deal with it, I'm taking her to get clean."

Aodhan's eyebrows almost hit his hairline and there's about to be another argument that I can't handle right now. "I'll go wash up by myself. I don't need hand holding."

And then I walk out without waiting for their arguments or protests because now that the adrenaline has left me, I'm no longer upset about the way things have gone.

I'm furious.

I duck into one of the downstairs rooms so I'm close to where everyone is, just in case. I'm pissed, not stupid, and if Amanda fucking Donnelley didn't get what she wanted from us tonight, then I'm sure she'll be back to take another swing at us.

I can't take the scalding hot, four-hour shower I want, but at the very least, I can clean away the blood from my skin and scrub at my foot until the first three layers of skin are gone.

I forget about what clothing I'll have to put on when I get out, but when I unlock the bathroom door, wrapped up in a towel and prepared to rummage through the wardrobe until I find something to get me through the next hour until I can pass out, I find Lips sitting on the bed waiting for me, her eyes on the ceiling.

She looks as exhausted as I feel.

She holds out her hoodie and a pair of yoga pants to me. "I left Ash and Aodhan to clean up, and I called Illi to tell him what went down… and that we're home. Harley and Blaise are still a few days out."

With a quick glance at the door, I drop the towel and pull the clothes on, grateful that they're clean and smell like family, the same soap as I use because Lips is as sappy about that stuff as I am. She's just a little more discreet about it.

"Are you sure Ash isn't murdering Aodhan right now? We should probably babysit them both until Ash gets over this… so until the end of time, then."

She shrugs at me, her eyes respectfully away from me, because if there's anyone on this Earth who understands what it's like to feel exposed and on display, it's Lips. "Ash will get over it. He honestly thought we'd left you behind with a rapist, he was frantic. He just fucking disappeared; I've chased him halfway across the country with Noah dragging me down, but Ash wouldn't listen to me. He wouldn't until he saw you."

I slump down onto the bed next to her, tears in my eyes, and then I take a shaky breath. "Lips… Atticus was shot."

She hesitates for a second, like she's figuring out what the right thing to do here is, before she puts her arm around my back and pulls me in close to her side. "Illi told me. He told me everything. I'm sorry and whatever I can do, I will. We're going to sort everything out and, fuck, if Atticus needs a new kidney or lung or something, I know a guy. We'll get him good again."

I snort at her attempts to cheer me up, because of course she has a spare organs guy on speed dial, but it's a watery sound thanks to the tears now streaming down my face. "I swear, I've been a complete badass since you've been gone. I haven't cried and I've only stress-cleaned once a week, which is a record for me."

She huffs out a laugh and murmurs back, "That *is* impressive. I've cried since we left. Enough that Harley has broken half the bus over my moods, growing up is fucking hard."

Focusing on her issues is much easier than dealing with all of the trauma and bullshit of my life right now. "Why have you been crying? I'll kill someone for you. I've done it now, I will definitely do it again for you."

She pulls back and then falls back on the bed, sighing dramatically. "No one told me it would feel this empty. I thought surviving high school would mean that life would become easy, and it's really not. I have six brothers and a sister. I have a crazy fucking asshole of a sperm donor. There's still a million people who want me dead. It's never really going to... end, is it?"

Okay, so she's having an existential crisis and none of the guys are equipped to deal with this at all. No wonder she's been a mess, although I doubt she's *actually* been a mess. I'm sure her eyes watered once and Harley was such a dick about it that she never showed another emotion again.

Fucking idiot boys.

I lower myself down on the bed next to her, staring up at that same white ceiling as if it has answers for us. "It's been a little like that for me too. I had all of these expectations about what my life would be like without Senior and Joey, and this is not what it looked like. There was a lot less blood and manipulative sex tapes in those fantasies."

She cringes and catches my hand in hers. "Tomorrow morning, I am going to find that cunt, Donnelley, and skin her alive. Nate gave me some pointers. I didn't realize I would ever use them, let alone so soon, but that bitch is dead."

I shrug. "She's not exactly an easy target. There's a lot of... bullshit I have to update you on. I'm just... really fucking glad you're home."

She nods and squeezes my fingers with hers. "Me too. We might've needed that time away, but fuck is it good to see you. I'm never leaving again."

I chuckle at her. We should really get back out there to the guys, but there's also something vital about this moment of quiet. We had three years of these moments in our shared room at Hannaford, and now I find myself craving just sitting in the quiet with her.

Knowing she's there for me, no matter what.

We lie there in silence together for another minute before I break it, still incredulous about Noah. "You have a kid brother who is both gay and a complete asshole."

She groans and covers her face with both of her hands. "He's also fucking *obsessed* with Ash. Like, trails-after-him-all-day-drooling levels of obsessed. He refused to stay behind with Harley and Blaise because he wanted to follow... never mind, I'm not going to scar you with what he's nicknamed your brother."

A giggle bursts out of me at the very idea of Ash navigating that sort of situation. "How has he been hiding all of this time? Why? How the fuck did some kid fake his own death?"

"Fuck knows. He won't tell me a thing. He doesn't trust me at all, but Wyatt was at his wits' end over it all. He's too... straight for this shit. He's a cop, through and through. It was fucking weird, staring at someone who looks so much like Nate but talks about what's right and legal. I would've bullied him in high school."

I laugh at her, ignoring the banging on the door because it's the same noise I've grown up with, a very impatient Ash demanding attention. "You weren't a bully though, that was my forte."

"If you two don't get out here soon, I'm killing everyone. O'Cronin, that Luca dickhead, and the fucking brat with his shitty commentary," Ash snarls through the door, and Lips turns to catch my eye, bursting into laughter with me.

Neither of us comment on the hysterical edge to it.

I wake up before my alarm in the icy-cold clutches of the nightmare tormenting me. Years of living in the Beaumont mansion have taught me not to scream or make a noise and Aodhan is draped over me. Even in his sleep, he's been stopping me from thrashing around and risking hurting myself.

I carefully move to grab my phone to check the time without waking him, just in case my panicked insomnia is kicking in again and we've only been in here for a couple of hours. There's already messages from Ash and Lips waiting for me, neither of them are sleeping well either.

Lips and I had to use every trick in the book to get Ash to agree to sleep here in Atticus' fortress-style mansion for the night. He'd only backed down when I pointed out how much work it would take to get us all back home, only for us to come back in the morning to deal with the aftermath of the shooting and Donnelley's attack.

"You should take the day off," Aodhan mumbles into my hair, his voice still rough with sleep, as his arms around me tighten.

I shift around until I'm facing him properly, the glow of the bathroom light illuminating his face enough that I can see the bone-tired lines on his face. We're all running on nothing, and I don't think that's going to change anytime soon.

"I can't, I'll go insane if I have to sit around here waiting for something else to happen. Lips is home. We'll figure this out together."

He makes an unhappy noise, a deep rumbling in his chest I've never heard before, and a smile surprises me as it stretches over my face. "I'm never going to get you to myself again now that she's back, am I? I wanna be jealous, but I signed on for this."

I giggle at his fake grumpy tone, mostly because I can tell he's putting it on. "She was willing to manipulate the shit out of my brother last night to save you, you should love her just for that alone."

He smirks and leans forward to kiss me. "I'm team Wolf for the relief I can feel in you now that she's home. And for the record, she was going to throw down with him for you, not me, which I can also get behind. I've always respected her, you know that. I might just be a little bit put off by how much your eyes light up when you talk about her."

I laugh at him, a quiet sound but one that instantly has me feeling guilty thanks to everything that's wrong with the world right now. Jack is dead. Atticus is dying. Ash saw that fucking tape and now he's going to be insufferable until we get the damage under control.

"It's almost noon; I need to get moving. If you let me go, I can leave you to get a little more sleep while I get ready."

He grumbles again and then when he moves to get up, sweeping me into his arms as he goes, I'm a little embarrassed of the noise I make, the squeak flying out of me and probably rupturing his eardrum with its shrillness. "If I'm being forced to get up, then the least you can do is let me shower with you. I won't hog the water."

I giggle and wrap my arms around his neck. "You wouldn't dare because you already know I'd kick you out for messing with my routine."

He huffs out a breath at me and sets me down in the bathroom, stepping out of his boxer shorts and getting the water running for us both, like a gentleman. I try not to look around the room because there's still evidence of the horrors of the night before, little splatters of blood and his clothes are still in the bin in the corner. I'd checked last night, but there aren't any cleaning supplies for me to sort this place out.

Aodhan would have freaked out about it if I'd have started

scrubbing everything down, he probably would've called Lips and Ash from down the hall to come help, and then there'd be a whole new fight to deal with.

An hour later we're both clean and dressed, looking a million times better than we did last night, and I text Lips to meet us in the meeting room. We'd once attended a Twelve meeting there, and she knows the way well enough.

Aodhan spends some time on the phone with his cousins, planning out the work they need to get done for his contracts with the Boar down at the docks. I have no intention of meddling with his business and I do my best not to eavesdrop too much on the conversation there, but I also don't trust the Boar at all, and I'd like nothing more than to destroy his business and give it all to Aodhan.

That man watched his niece go through hell without a word, not to her or to her brother who would've come here, guns blazing, and killed anyone who ever dared blink in her direction threateningly.

I might be appropriately terrified of the Devil, but I also respect his love for his sisters a hell of a lot.

When we arrive at the meeting room, Lips, Ash, Illi, Luca, and Noah are already there waiting for us. I'm shocked to see Illi, but when I raise an eyebrow at him, he huffs at me.

"I'm still on paternity leave, but I'm not leaving you all in danger, and I'd rather be here for this. Odie and Johnny are safe, Harbin has already promised a grisly death for anyone who so much as walks past the warehouse."

I nod approvingly, because half of my workload is now about taking care of all of these kids we're now somewhat responsible for, and then I steel myself for what's to come.

"Luca, can you bring in the men I requested, please."

He nods without a word and walks out, silent and very obedient.

"Well, that's just fucking weird," Illi drawls, and Ash nods.

"I bet he's a fucking sub. Atticus probably has a torture den filled with whips and leather somewhere in this shit-hole."

Aodhan tries to hold back his scoff and laughter but he can't and I elbow him. "If anything, I'm jealous he's been so well trained. You lot could learn a thing or two."

Lips slaps a hand over her face as she cackles. "Now all I can see in my head is Luca in a gimp suit and I'm traumatized."

Gross.

My eyes flick over to where Noah is sitting in the corner on one of the chairs he's pulled over from the table. He's on his phone, messing around on there, which raises more questions for me because who would text with a dead boy? Wyatt? Is he such a great brother that he checks in with him?

Aodhan slips a hand around my waist, ignoring the way Ash's eyes narrow at him, and leans down to murmur to me, "Are you going to be okay dealing with Luca?"

The door opens again and six men file in slowly, all of them wearing the suits and fresh haircuts that the Crow's men are known for. I nod to Aodhan as my eyes meet Luca's. I might never like Luca after what he was forced to do, but I can get through this. I can get through anything I need to if it keeps our family safe.

I pull out my phone again and check over each of the guys, just to be sure that we have the correct men before the bloodbath begins.

The men all look calm enough, assuming they're here for a job and not the job itself. The only one smart enough to look at least a little wary is Lips' informant, he obviously knows a little more about what happens when the Wolf arrives somewhere than the others do.

Luca presses the door shut and then says, his tone firm and commanding, "On your knees."

He says it a little too convincingly to believe he really is a sub, and Lips meets my eyes with the slightest of smiles on her face. This is definitely not the time or place for the two of us to be having these sorts of silent conversations, but when have we ever lived by the rules?

The men all move to their knees, hesitant but obedient, and Luca zip ties their wrists without any trouble. Illi moves behind them, his gun already in his hands. I'm glad he's chosen to go with bullets, my stomach can't take another slasher blood-soaked scene right now.

Luca meets my eye again and I nod, stepping to the side so that I'm as far away from the splatter zone as possible. Aodhan moves in front of me, and when Lips steps over to join us, Ash follows along, his body only half covering hers because he's learned not to try to block her entirely by now.

Luca waits for another minute and then says, "If it's not already clear to you, you've been made. We know that each one of you has sold out information on the Crow to his allies and his enemies. One of you even had him shot."

Illi points the gun at the back of the head of the first guy and pulls the trigger, the silencer muffling the sound to a small pop. One by one, he takes the men out.

The guy on the far end panics, his eyes peeling back as he jerks around to try to plead with Lips, "I've only ever been loyal to you! I've never given anyone else information!"

She stares down at him with the same cold apathy that she gives everyone in the Bay. "You're a snitch. You've done great work for me but allegiances change, that's part of the game. If you were willing to sell to me, then you'll be willing to bend for someone else too. You played your part and now you're dealing with the consequences, take it like a man."

I almost smirk at her words, because men never take anything with any sort of pride and humility, but I hold it together as Illi works his way down the line.

I'm right.

He dies screaming.

Queen Crow

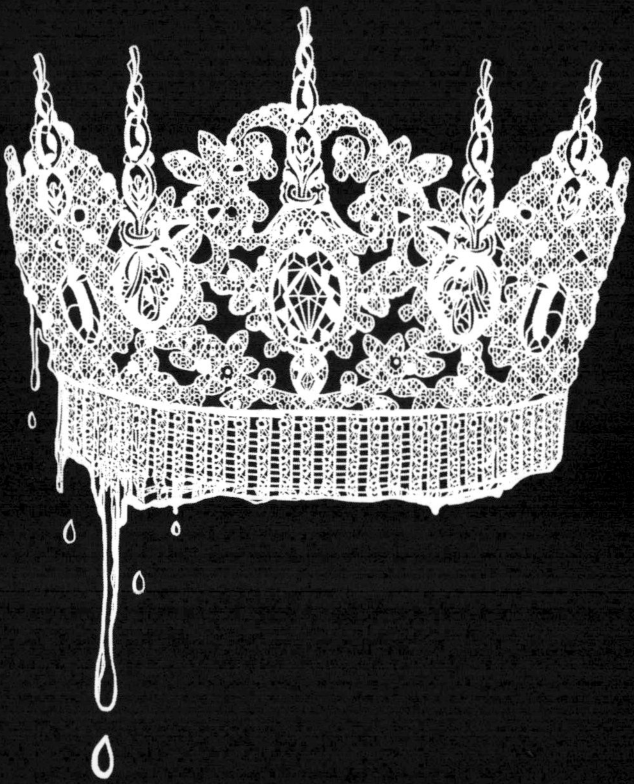

Chapter Three

After we deal with the informants and spies, Aodhan leaves to head to the dock for work, kissing me irreverently in front of Ash and Illi before heading out. Illi laughs like this is all a very amusing game to him, and Ash gives him a death glare that would get any other man a cleaver to the throat.

It takes three hours to collect enough information from Luca and from trawling through Atticus' laptop to make some very vital business decisions on his behalf. The instability of the Bay is a threat to us all and not something we can just wait out.

I also get every last piece of information he has about everyone on my murder board, ready for any insights of his that may help us take care of all of the threats coming our way.

Then I climb into one of Ash's favorite Ferraris, the custom built one with the full backseat that is a one-of-a-kind creation just for him that I surprised him with for our sixteenth birthday, and we head back home.

There's something insanely comforting about having Ash

and Lips home and, while I miss Harley and Morrison because their absence is very obvious in the tension in Lips' shoulders, I already feel a thousand times better.

Until I think about Atticus attached to dozens of machines, all of them keeping him alive… for now. My brain can't stop adding that little nugget of information in to completely destroy any sense of peace I might have.

Luca had arranged for a live security feed into the hospital room for me that I watch religiously. When I'm scrubbing the dishes after our late dinner together—French toast and ice cream because we needed comfort food and the one thing Noah and Lips seem to share is their sweet tooth—Lips watches it for me without question or judgement.

Ash is less understanding.

"I think this is proof that you're starting to get over him. I don't like O'Cronin, but I'll tolerate him after what Illi said. I'd pick him over Crawford any day of the fucking week."

I roll my eyes at him and stare him down from where I'm scrubbing the oven. "What is proof? That I'm not at the hospital with him now? I don't have that luxury, Ash. This isn't high school, there's an entire fucking city to keep in line, and without him at the helm of the Twelve, there's unrest."

Lips nods but Ash is still pissed off at her, throwing her a filthy look that I'm not happy about as he snaps, "And why is that your responsibility? Just fucking leave them to rot."

I take a deep breath, mostly because I know this is all coming from the part of him that will never accept that he cannot protect me forever, not from living my life however I want to. "I stepped up so Lips could take some time away. Now I'm stepping into Atticus' shoes so he doesn't lose everything after he took a bullet for me. Did you want me to ruin your little touring orgy getaway by not helping out Lips and forcing her to stay behind? Or am I supposed to spit in the face of the man who rescued me and took a bullet to the chest for me? Because I am not that girl, Ash. I'm not going to turn my back on my friends, no matter how much you want me to."

He doesn't like that at all, mostly because I'm speaking rationally and he's not in that place right now. He's in the hyper-vigilant, freaking-the-fuck-out place that I was really hoping the time away would sort out.

He stalks out of the kitchen and I already know he's either heading for the gym or the garage, neither of those places is nearby so I can breathe for a second without the rage-filled cloud in the space anymore.

I shut the oven and strip my gloves off, packing away my cleaning supplies and washing up, even though there's another hundred things I'd like to disinfect and scour before my head hits my pillow tonight. Lips watches my every move without comment, handing my phone back to me and then following me into the theatre room so we can sit and watch a movie together, even though we'll both be too busy with the shit in our heads to actually pay attention to a fucking thing on the screen.

Noah is already there, snoring on the couch. He's wearing one of Lips' old sweatshirts that hits him mid-thigh. I have no idea if he's wearing booty shorts with it or if he's just free-balling on my freaking couch, but I tear my eyes away from him before I wake the little brat up.

"So Wyatt didn't trust you at all and then just… handed your brother over to you?" I murmur, and Lips sits right next to me on the plush sofa and tucks her arm in mine.

"I think he was out of options. I get the feeling there's a lot of shit going on in his life that shouldn't be happening with a cop, if you get what I'm saying. He was a total nerd but… jumpy. I left him with my number, told him to call no matter what happened, but he looked at me like I was a monster. It was fucking weird."

I scoff at her too loudly, and Noah groans in his sleep, turns, and then the snoring starts up again. We both wait a second before I murmur quietly, "He's a cop who just found out he has a crime lord for a sister, I'm sure that's it."

She pulls a face. "It was more than that. It wasn't me he was against, it was the Twelve. Fuck, I'm not explaining this right. He was totally open to knowing me and he didn't give a shit about me being a Mounty or what I'd done to survive. He told me Noah had done some shit too, it was only when I mentioned the Twelve that he freaked."

Huh.

I mean, it still makes perfect sense to me, but Lips is never wrong, not about this kind of thing. Her gut instincts have kept her alive in the worst of situations, and I'd be an idiot to just disregard this feeling of hers just because she can't explain it fully.

"I'll look into it. There's some other avenues we can explore with his background, and I know someone who can keep an eye on him."

She nods and sinks back a little more in the seat. There's still a tension in her that hasn't really left since she got home and I can't help but prod at her to fix it. "Are you worried about Harley and Morrison? Or is this Ash's temper tantrum?"

She groans. "Both. A lot of shit happened on tour and once we've dealt with all of this shit, I'll fill you in. You've got enough on your shoulders right now without the guys' bullshit. And mine."

My eyes dart back down to the phone screen right as one of the nurses enters Atticus' room to give him more medications. It doesn't matter that I've seen it happen a dozen times today, I still feel that icy dread in my chest as she starts filling syringes and poking his IV lines.

If one of those is poison, there's no saving him. If the dose is off, he's gone. There's a thousand different ways he could be taken from me now and even with this security camera feed, there's no stopping it.

"He's going to be okay, Aves. You and Luca have vetted, cross-vetted, and terrorized every person around him right now.

If they can't keep him alive then, well, no one can. You've done right by him," Lips whispers, her fingers threading through mine.

Tears well up in my eyes because it doesn't matter if she's right, he's still in that bed because of me, and dying isn't an option here.

Right.

Distraction.

"Tell me something. Anything. Something small about the tour that will distract me enough that I won't self-destruct."

She hums under her breath quietly, a habit she picked up from me, and then smiles softly. "I've never seen the guys relax that much or be that happy. They all still fought like crazy and were absolute assholes over the littlest things but… Ash was so calm and relaxed. He was really fucking happy, Aves. If we can get the Bay under our thumb and wipe out the bullshit again, you're not even going to recognize them anymore."

I want that. Desperately. I want us all to be happy.

A text message flashes on the screen from Aodhan, telling me he's heading back here a little after midnight, and Lips smirks at the smile on my face.

"He's worth the tantrum from Ash. We both knew he was going to be a nightmare no matter who you ended up with. But at least with Aodhan, we know it's all worth it."

He is.

But so is Atticus.

Two days later, Harley and Morrison arrive home to Ash as a full-blown alcoholic and Lips being her own version of a nervous wreck about it. It's hard to pick out, because she's so quiet about it, but she stops eating and sleeping, spending most of her time on her phone or following me around, making sure I'm not about to throw myself off of the roof over Atticus.

The moment the alarm sounds to say there's a vehicle in the driveway, it feels as though the entire house takes a deep breath.

I buzz them in, swiping the bourbon from Ash and shoving him toward the front foyer, just in time to see Lips rip the door open and stalk down the front steps like a woman on a mission.

I then have to look away from the make out session in my driveway so I don't lose my lunch.

"They're like this all the fucking time, aren't they? It's like watching horny teenagers go at it, fucking gross," Noah whines, and I have to bite my tongue to stop myself from pointing out that they are in fact horny teenagers who fought and bled for the right to live.

They've earned this, and he can shut the fuck up about it before I slit his throat over it.

I also don't point out that his utter obsession with my brother is both obvious and disturbing. He's been a creepy little fuck, following him around all day and begging for attention. It wouldn't be so bad if it wasn't his sister's boyfriend, his sister who has taken him in and protected him from whatever the fuck is going on with him.

He should not be chasing after her boyfriend.

When Harley finally lets Lips go, only for her to be swept up into Morrison's arms and pushed back against a bus like it's been six months since they saw each other and not five days, he stalks over to me and pulls me into a bone-crushing hug of my own.

"What the fuck have you gotten into, Floss?" he murmurs against my hair, and I almost break. Almost.

I will not cry.

I will not cry, god-fucking-dammit.

"Your fucking cousin is what she's gotten into, and I'm still not sure he's going to survive," Ash snaps, and Harley pulls back from me to look over Ash.

"You've been a complete fucking nightmare, haven't you? You'll never learn, asshole."

Ash scoffs at him and turns on his heel, stalking back into the house and I'm assuming he's heading straight for the alcohol. Noah trails after him and I curse under my breath about it.

Harley keeps his arm around me, reluctant to let me go, and my stomach drops at having to face this all over again.

"Please tell me you haven't seen it," I whisper, and he huffs at me.

"What, the tape of two of my cousins fucking? No, thanks. Lips gave me the general rundown, that's enough trauma for me, thanks, Floss."

Well.

That's surprisingly reasonable of him.

He looks down at me as we head back into the house together and sighs at me. "I would've probably lost my shit as badly as Ash has, if I had seen it. I'm not blaming him, I'm just fucking glad I'm not in that boat. Lips said you're okay, and I'm not about to drag you back down to the depths of miserable you were when we left by making this about me. Ash isn't thinking clearly enough to do the same. I'll beat the shit out of him tomorrow until he gets it, once he sobers up a little."

And that's why I have always loved Harley, why he's always been my family from the very moment we met him. He's always been the balance, even when he was going through his own version of hell, he always has done what he can for me and Ash.

He's also loved nothing more than taking my side when Morrison and Ash used to gang up on me, if only so he could take a swing at one of them in my honor.

It's why I'm not mad about him stealing my best friend half of the time.

When we get to the kitchen, we find Ash there already with a glass in his hand and Noah perched on one of the stools, chin propped up on his fist as he stares dreamily at my brother.

Harley ignores them both and says, "Where's Aodhan hiding? I needed to talk to him about the funeral. He's refusing to let me help pay for it, and I might snap his fucking arm off and beat him with it if he doesn't change his mind."

Noah rolls his eyes so hard that I'm surprised they don't fall out of his head. "The Irish fuck? He only drops in for booty calls and then slinks out in the morning, like he's scared to face us all in the light of day."

Jesus fucking Christ.

Ash slowly lowers the glass and turns to look at me, but Harley saves the day by smacking Noah in the back of his head right as Lips and Morrison join us.

Lips immediately groans, "What's he done now? Seriously, would it kill you to just try to get along with us for once? You've gotten the easiest ride I've ever fucking seen and you're still being a dick about it."

Noah gives her a look that sets my teeth on edge immediately and Harley shifts his stance like he's going to choke him the fuck out. Ash drains the last of his drink and then stalks back out to find the rest of my stash of alcohol. Lips follows him with a frown, and I already feel a headache over this entire mess.

We're never going to know peace again.

Morrison can't let anything go and as he comes over to give me a very sedate and formal half-hug, he drawls, "He's a jealous little brat, spends all of his time whining about who Lips has in her bed."

Noah shifts that derisive look over his way and says in the most scathing tone, "You look like you want to spoon after you fuck, so no, thanks."

I manage to keep my face straight at the look of outrage on Morrison's face because, really, I'm absolutely positive he's the little spoon post-coitus with Lips. Harley doesn't even attempt to school himself, he just throws his head back and roars with laughter, oozing the type of joy he's only found since he's had our Mounty in his life. It's good to see the joy that Lips was talking about up close.

"And why is it that you're obsessed with my brother? How does he look to you?"

Noah smirks at me, the kohl smudged under his eyes making the blue of his irises pop. "He has big dick demon energy. He would definitely slit my throat after rearranging my guts, and that's too fucking hot."

Kill me.

Just fucking kill me.

Morrison chokes out a sputtering laugh and Harley drawls, "Oh look, there's the Graves in him."

Lips stalks into the room with a bad attitude, comfortable enough to actually show it because it's only us at home... us and her new kid brother. "If I find out you've survived all of the shit you've had thrown at you only to be taken out at a dick appointment, I will buy a ticket to hell to kick your ass, Noah. Right after I bleed the asshole who fucked you out. Can we just agree to no guys for, like, another year, at least? We need to put you under the same fucking rules as Poe."

He stares at her in disgust. "Be fucked, you're going to be

getting railed by three guys every night and telling me to cross my fucking legs? If you want me to stay home, then share that one with me."

He jerks his head in the direction of Ash, who looks like he might slit Noah's throat sans fucking if this conversation doesn't end soon.

Lips stares the kid down, calm and steady. "Wyatt left you in my care. I'm the only thing stopping you from getting your ass murdered, so you might wanna shut your mouth because I've left a long and bloody trail behind us, all people trying to fuck one of my guys."

There's a minute of quiet, not even enough for me to relax and make a plan of what I'm going to get done today, and then Noah starts up again.

"It just seems very selfish, all of that good dick going to waste."

Lips shoots me a look, because we both know how this is going to go and she's feeling bad for whatever details I'm about to be subject to.

Morrison is the one to snap back, and I'm sure it's because he's still smarting at the spooning comment. "Why? You're upset she's getting great dick from not one, but three guys who would kill and die for her? Because I can tell you right now, none of us are missing out. Besides, she has three holes and can go all night."

Lips groans quietly next to me and Harley tucks her a little closer into his side. Honestly, it could've been worse, the things they usually come out with are truly obscene.

"Just start talking about murder, the only thing that can distract him is planning out gory deaths," Lips says, looking at Ash's bourbon with longing.

"Fine. I have a long list of people who need to die."

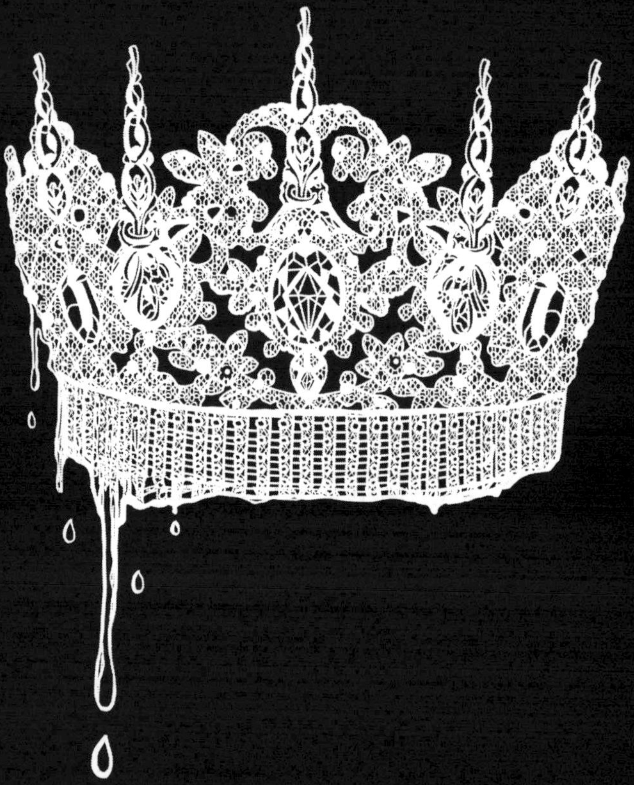

Chapter Four

It's a surprisingly cold morning as I step out of my Rolls Royce, tucking my phone into my purse and looking around the parking lot. It frustrates me that there's no valet here, no priority parking at all, and we're forced to be sitting ducks from here to the hospital doors.

The wary look on Lips' face tells me she feels the same way.

"Stay in the car, Noah; you can't be seen and there's security cameras everywhere in there," she mutters as she shuts her door, ignoring his immediate cussing at her orders.

He hasn't learned a thing about how things work around here.

"Let's just get you inside, fuck the little brat and his attitude."

I nod and take the lead, mostly because I know where we're heading, but also because Lips is better at standing back and assessing situations. She's only a half-step behind me, not really trailing along, but it still feels good to have her at my back.

She's one of a very select few I trust to watch it.

We skip the security line at the front door, one of the Crow's men ushering us through without a word spoken. I watch everything around us obsessively, not at all for our safety, but for Atticus. I want to know that they're doing their jobs correctly, thoroughly, with the utmost care, because if they don't and I lose him?

I'll kill them all.

"I fucking hate hospitals. I can't believe Harley wants to work in one," Lips mutters, and I shrug.

"He used to want to be a doctor because of Aunt Iris, but now I think it's changed. I think he wants to make sure that he can do more to keep us all safe and alive. We need a trusted medic, who better than one of the family to do it?"

She nods, and we step into the elevator together. "It makes sense, and he's definitely smart enough to do it. The insomnia will help too. It's just the time commitment. He's going to be in college forever and then med school, residency? Jesus. I want to go to college but not for the rest of my fucking life."

I scoff at her dramatics, stepping out of the elevator, and the humor instantly seeps out of me at the sight of the ward Atticus is in.

I had the entire floor cleared for him.

There's men in suits everywhere and the nurses all look confident but on high alert, the way you do when you're the best at your job but also are sure you're about to take fire and have to find cover. Everyone turns to watch us both walk out of the elevator and down the hallway to Atticus' room.

They all know who I am.

They all know Lips too.

There's a lot of lowered gazes and dipped heads in our direction as we walk past everyone, a lot of signs of respect from everyone around us. It would normally have me gloating and enjoying the moment, finally having the respect that all of my time and efforts deserve, but here it just feels hollow.

There's sympathy in the nurses' eyes too, all of them sure we're going to lose him.

I want to scream.

Lips' hand slips into mine as we step into the room, dozens of machines surround the bed and tubes are coming out of every part of Atticus' body. I want nothing more than to crawl up onto his chest and weep, but now isn't the time for that. If I break down, then I can't accomplish anything else today, and Atticus is relying on me.

He built his empire for me and I will not let it fall.

I pull up a chair at his side and grab his chart, flipping it open and then immediately regretting it as I see every last one of his vitals listed out hourly from the moment he came out of surgery.

He's a mess.

Lips takes the seat on his other side, perching carefully as she takes in the entire room. I already know she's looking for any little possible signs of tampering or foul play, anything to say that we've missed something and Atticus' life is at further risk.

She's got clearer eyes than I do right now.

I read the chart over and over again, and time comes to a standstill. Lips doesn't say a word or attempt to rush me along, she just sits there and waits me out.

There's a reason I would kill and die for this girl.

Eventually, the silence twists and distorts into something smothering and I break it, just to keep myself from screaming. "The last time I saw him, before he came for me and got shot, he told me he wouldn't share me."

Lips nods, her eyes still on the rise and fall of his chest. My eyes just keep scanning over his chart as though the words 'he'll live' will suddenly appear if I stare at it for long enough.

"I was so angry at him, so frustrated that even now I wouldn't get to have him because… I love Aodhan. I love him and I love Atticus but—is it really fair of me to ask them to share?"

Lips takes a deep breath, blowing it out slowly, her eyes still on Atticus as we watch him breathe together, as though if we look away, he'll stop. "I still have doubts. Not about the guys or how much I love them but—they don't deserve to have to share. They should each have someone who will only love them the way they only love me. They deserve marriage and kids and the whole picket-fence life that they don't have to navigate and negotiate. They can't have that when they're sharing me."

Tears fill my eyes again, stupidly. "They would never give you up. All three of them will happily share and negotiate and fall into a big pile in your bed as long as they get you. They love you that much."

Lips nods slowly. "Yeah, I'm really starting to believe that. Aodhan has already said he's down, no matter what. I guess you just tell Atticus again that you're not giving him up and he has to decide… it's not a great choice, but that's just the way it is. Who knows, you might just date them both and then move on, find someone else."

I nod, but we both know that's highly unlikely. Neither of us are the casual type, and I know that both of the men I've fallen for are the forever type as well.

We wouldn't have been drawn to each other if they weren't.

I look back at Atticus' face and I try not to freak out about how wrecked he looks. He's still as handsome as ever as long as you don't linger on all of the signs of mortality on him: the dark hollows under his eyes, the bloodless color of his lips, and the sallow tone of his skin.

The nurse walks in and startles just a little when she sees us both sitting there with him, then she pulls herself up straighter and rolls her shoulders back as though she's preparing for the biggest assessment of her life.

She's right.

"I'm here to give Mr. Crawford his antibiotics and painkillers. I can talk you through it, if you like?"

She doesn't sweat or shake under my sharp glare or Lips' cold, apathetic stare. I give her a point in her favor as I nod, and then we listen as she explains the changes in medications.

His condition hasn't changed at all, which isn't necessarily a good thing. They were hoping for improvement by now, something to show he's fighting and doing better.

Instead, we're at a stalemate.

I want to scream, the impotent rage inside of me brewing with absolutely nothing that I can aim it at. There's nothing, absolutely nothing that I can do about this, except wait. Wait and continue to pay the best doctors and nursing staff that money can buy to take care of him while I pray that it'll be enough.

It has to be enough.

Two hours later and the wind has picked up even more as we stand together in the Mounts Bay cemetery.

The black skirt suit I'm wearing is trimmed with a delicate white lace that is handcrafted, painstakingly sewn on by an artisan in Paris, and staring down at it is the only way I make it through the graveside ceremony and burial of Jack O'Cronin without bursting into tears.

I don't have any feelings of shame about doing so, but Aodhan and Harley are struggling to keep themselves together and I can't break down and send either of them over the edge.

Lips' hand is cold in mine.

She's dressed all in black as well, dark sunglasses over her eyes, and a stern sort of look on her face as she keeps an eye on everything happening around us. Ash and Blaise are both standing with Harley, though my brother is keeping an eye on us both like he's ready to storm over here and murder anyone who dares to attempt to talk to us.

And then there's Noah.

Lips' baby brother is smoking a cigarette two steps away from us both like he couldn't give less of a fuck about Catholic funeral decorum. He's also wearing torn up fishnet tights and a Grateful Dead tee that is more holes than fabric. He looks like an adorably fierce Mounty street brat and there's a part of me that admires that in him.

Right up until I notice that the sunglasses he's wearing are a pair of mine.

I wait until the priest has finished his Bible passages and starts to throw some dirt onto the coffin before I threaten the little asshole.

"If you scratch them, I will end you. Chanel doesn't make them anymore, why couldn't you take my Diors?" I murmur, and he huffs at me, flicking the cigarette on the ground and stomping on it.

Lips shoots him a look and it's impressive to watch him blanch and pick it up without even seeing the death in her eyes.

"You have more money than God, according to Lips; you can get a new pair made. These ones suited me best, my blood is too rich for the cheaper ones."

Lips groans quietly and rolls her eyes, squeezing my hand. "He asked me for an allowance last night, as if I'm his goddamn mother. I told him to earn it but his ideas for that make me want to murder something, so that's not going to happen."

The priest turns back in our direction and I seal my lips shut again. I'm not religious, but I do try to be respectful of these sorts of ceremonies, especially when they mean so much to people I love.

Aodhan planned this entire service out for his cousins, and Harley also cares deeply about giving Jack the burial he deserves. They've argued for days about the expenses, and I'm not entirely sure who won, but they're standing together now, shoulder to shoulder, and it's good to see them supporting one another.

The moment the priest ushers Aodhan forward to throw more dirt onto the coffin, I have to pat my eyes dry. Ash shoots me a look but I wave him off. This isn't about me, I don't want his overprotective dramatics to make a scene right now.

As Harley steps up to take his turn, Lips leans into my side, supporting me as she murmurs into my ear, "They've done a good job. They've given him a much better burial than most get down here. He's with his girl again."

I nod and try to clear my throat as we watch each of the O'Cronin family say their final goodbye to Jack. "I should've done something. I should've spoken up or dragged him out. I'll never forgive myself, I don't care what the guys say."

"This is all about guilt?" Noah scoffs, and Lips pulls away from me to pinch his wrist between two fingers. It looks like nothing, like she's gently grabbing him to stop him from tearing me down, but I see the wince and that wide-eyed terror he has with her sometimes when he oversteps the mark.

She's a flick of her hand away from breaking his wrist.

"This is about loyalty. This is about Jack doing everything for his family and making the ultimate sacrifice. If you learn nothing else from me, Noah, learn this; I would do anything to keep my family safe. You need to decide if you're a part of this family or not, and then get your shit together. If you're in, it's all in."

She lets go of his wrist and he clutches it to his chest, glancing around like he's worried everyone is watching him being disciplined by his sister and laughing at his expense. He doesn't know us at all.

Because despite everything we've hissed at him or snapped at him whenever he's run that mouth of his, we're all also very aware of who and what he is. There's no way that any of us would joke around in that way with this very obviously broken child. God, there's only two years difference between us but also a thousand years of life. Sure, he's had to fake a death for some reason, but his trauma couldn't ever touch his sister's.

Two years ago, Lips was killing crime lords and being stalked by the Jackal, Senior, and the Devil himself. She was being tested over and over again, and every time she came out of those trials stronger.

I can't imagine this brat surviving anything.

The moment the music starts up again, Aodhan turns to come over and collect me, his eyes still rimmed in red even as his face is stern and gruff looking.

Men always have trouble with emotions, but there's no shame in grieving your blood, your best friend, the man who would have happily given his life for you and yours. Jack was all of those things.

He was also desperate to be with his girl again.

"We're heading back to the compound for the wake now," he says needlessly, because I'm already on top of the entire plan for the day, but it's easier to talk details right now than the hard stuff.

Lips squeezes my hand one last time and then jerks her head at Noah. "We'll meet you over there."

She hesitates for a second, always touch-shy, but then she leans forward to give Aodhan a squeeze. "You did him proud, all of you."

Aodhan gives her back a single pat and nods his head, swallowing roughly without a word, but if anyone in the world understands this sort of thing, it's Lips Anderson.

We all walk together to the cars, Ash coming to my side as a show of support. Aodhan helps me into the Impala, waiting until I'm buckled in before he shuts the door behind me. There's a small moment between him and Ash, just the tiniest passing of respect between them that I would've missed if I'd blinked, and then Aodhan is sliding behind the wheel and getting us on the road back to the compound.

I love my brother.

No matter how he reacts to things, no matter how much he hates the idea of me belonging to a man who might hurt or disrespect me, he has only ever loved me and protected me. He's lived and breathed for me even in the darkest days we've faced together.

I start to weep again because Aodhan has lost that, over and over again. His sister, his cousin, his best friend. Everyone has been ripped away from him.

We pull up outside his house and I wait dutifully for him to open the car door for me. He pulls me into his arms the moment I stand up.

"No more crying, Queenie. That part is over with," he says, and I pat my eyes with a silk handkerchief. He huffs at the sight of it and I smile, even through my tears.

"No more death. I can't handle any more of it," I croak, and he nods, pulling me into his arms even as the wake begins to get loud around us. There's people everywhere, bodies coming and going from the houses regardless of who they belong to.

"I can handle that. I can definitely get behind that. How did Crawford look? He'll be back glowering at us all in no time, I'm sure."

I glance around, but Harley parked the Escalade two houses

over and they're all piling out slowly. "He's not any better. He's not any worse though so... I guess we can be hopeful. What exactly is happening here? This looks like a house party, not a funeral."

"It's an Irish wake. The drinking is part of it."

I look around, there's a quiet moment for us both with everyone else busy with each other so I step into his body, sliding my hands under his coat and burying my face into the warmth of his chest. "It's a stupid part of it. Why would you want the grief and the hangover mixing? That sounds like torture."

He huffs out a dry laugh and it's a sad sort of noise. "That's probably the point of it. The Irish are a morbid lot when death and religion come into play. You should head home, get clean and tucked up into that big princess bed of yours. I'll come 'round tomorrow."

His words are rough with an accent the longer he's here with his family, it's a little too charming for the day of Jack's funeral for my tastes. "It's just a bed, you need more pillows for aesthetics."

Harley scoffs at me as he stalks over to us, handing Aodhan a glass of something that looks distinctly home-brewed. Aodhan pulls away from me to take it, sculling down half of it without taking a breath or pulling a face at just how strong it must be.

This is the part of Harley's childhood that I never had a window into, not until now, and it's weird to be locked out of something when it comes to him.

"Everything you do is princess-flavored, Floss. That's kind of your thing. I can find you a cocktail if you're going to stay and do this properly."

I look around again at the family, all of them rowdy and loud and entirely inappropriate for any sort of funeral I've ever attended before. It feels like family. It feels warm and loving and like everything we all need.

Codladh sámh, Jack.

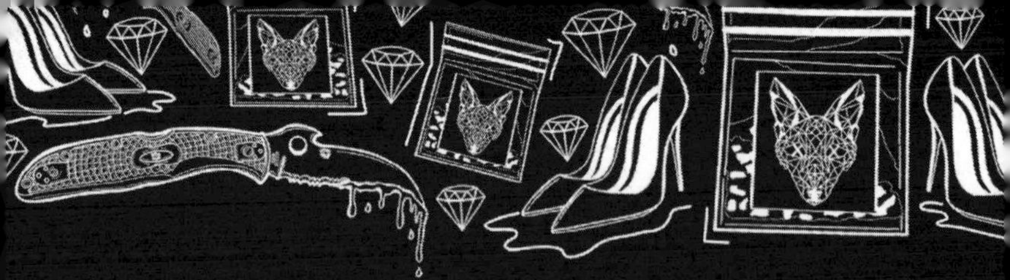

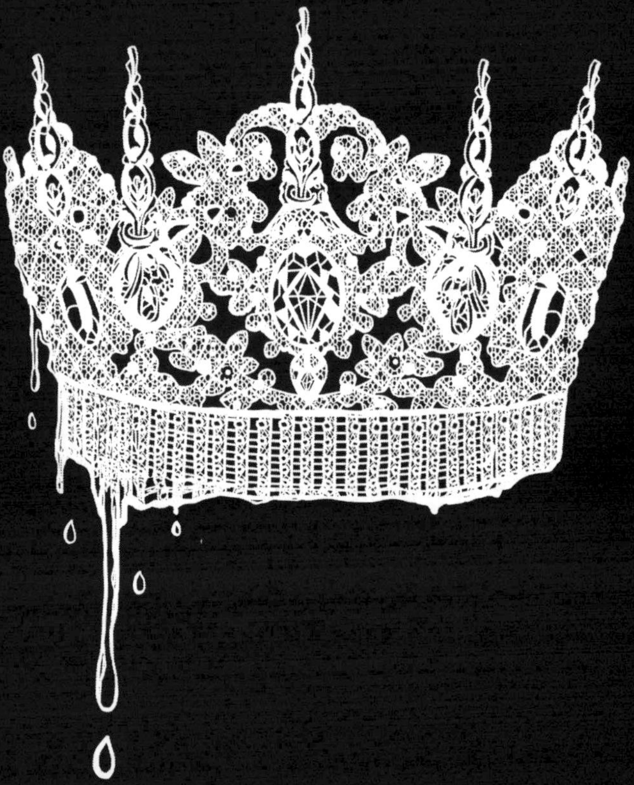

Chapter Five

I lose two days to Jack's wake.

I've never seen Harley get that drunk before, and there must be something extra in the moonshine that was passed around because even Ash passed out from it.

Lips is the only one who didn't over-indulge.

When I wake up, somehow in my own bed, two days later, I find her perched on my bedside with a giant cup of coffee and a stack of blueberry pancakes.

My favorite.

She holds a finger to her lips, which confuses me until I try to move and find out that Aodhan is in the bed with me, an arm slung over my naked body.

I have zero recollection of ending up back here or how we both are naked, but I'm glad that Lips is the only one coming to get me. She grins at me and leaves me to get up, wrapping a robe around myself and trying not to wake Aodhan with my groaning.

When I get out into the hallway, she hands me the coffee and waits while I gulp it back like a dying woman. "Marry me."

She scoffs at me. "Your brother would fight you for my hand. He's told me that before, drunk off his ass."

I giggle, because of course he has, and then I take the plate of pancakes from her as well. "You're the best. Are we going to plot some murder together, for old times' sake?"

"Of course. I'll grab coffee refills, head down to the dungeon."

I roll my eyes at her ridiculous name for my panic room basement, but she doesn't need to ask me twice. Another coffee is exactly what I need right now, and dammit if she doesn't know how to make it exactly right.

I pick at the plate of food on my way down, mentally promising myself that I'll vacuum the moment my head stops throbbing like a fucking wound. The marble floors are icy on my bare feet and I curse myself for not grabbing slippers.

It's difficult to open the staircase entry with one hand and limbs that don't want to cooperate, but I get it working, cursing under my breath, right as Lips arrives with two cups of coffee.

Cups is an understatement, they're more like buckets.

"You should really drink more often because this is kind of adorable," she says, all sarcasm and dripping wit.

I glare back at her but when I take one of the cups from her, she grabs my elbow so I don't land on my face as we head down the stairs together.

As I flick the lights on and then regret having eyeballs as the sharp pain slices into my brain, Lips sits crosslegged in front of the murder wall. She leaves her coffee on the ground next to her as she leans back on her arms, squinting at each photo the same way I have for months, as though it will somehow suddenly tell us what to do here.

I pull up a chair to sit next to her, mindful that it's been two days since I had the chance to vacuum down here and I don't want to end up covered in dust.

We sit there in silence, the only noises are of coffee consumption, and we just stare at the tangled mess I've found myself in. My eyes keep drifting back to the same three photos.

Noah.

Amanda Donnelley.

And Bingley Crawford.

An hour later there's the sounds of life happening at the top of the stairs, groaning and laughing, then Harley and Aodhan join us. Aodhan kisses my cheek before finding another chair to pull up and sit with me.

Harley crouches down to kiss Lips but when he notices how focused she is, he leaves her to it, slumping back on the couch with another groan. He sounds exactly how I feel but I just take a sip from my now stone-cold coffee.

"Fuck, do you remember when our murder boards fit on a whiteboard and it felt like too much to handle? This is too fucking much," Harley grumbles from the couch, and I ignore it. Aodhan does too, his eyes on the Crawfords like he's trying to find some clue in the photos that will fix all of this for us.

Honestly, I hope he does.

I'm still trying to come to terms with the fact that not only have I killed Bingley, but that Atticus was the one hiding him away all of this time.

Why keep him alive? If he was already keeping the ruse of Bing being overseas, living his best life and sampling all of the underage prostitutes his heart could desire, why not just kill him and be done with it?

I never realized Atticus craved torture or control in this manner.

Does it make me a monster that I don't even care about that? That it's only the motivation questions that are eating me, not at all that he actually did it? Maybe that's the Beaumont in me.

Finally, Lips speaks, "Okay. I have some solid ideas. Aves, do you want my help here or am I just subbing into your plans?"

Aodhan jerks around to give her a look as I giggle, my voice still wrecked from the moonshine and Irish wake. "No, Lips, I need your help. You already know what I have ready, if there's anything you can add here then *please* do."

She turns back to the wall and says, "I have some leads in mind. I have a few for that cunt Amanda and there's some people we can leverage for the Crawford situation. Atticus always did focus on a very different brand of information than Illi and I do, but there's some crossover I can take advantage of. Let's go with the shit we can take care of without Illi for now, leave him with Odie and Johnny for as long as we can before we have him back on the streets."

I agree wholeheartedly with that plan. Honestly, if I thought we could retire him altogether so he was at home with them forever, that would be the plan, but he was born here, the Bay is in his blood, and there's no walking away from that.

Lips has tried enough that I know that for sure.

Aodhan rubs at the shadow of a beard on his face, he clearly rolled straight out of bed and came looking for us without a shower and shave, and says, "Just tell me what you need and I'll do it. I'm sick of chasing our asses with this."

Harley nods approvingly, his eyes on his little Mounty. "What are you seeing up there that we're missing, babe? What does the Wolf see that the Butcher can't?"

She shrugs and points at Amanda. "I see a daughter. Cartel don't usually spare much time for grown daughters unless they're selling them off. Women don't matter, not unless they're wives, mothers, or grandmothers. They have to contribute first, give some part of themselves away before they have a chance to have a voice. What has Amanda given away?"

I scoff. "She's given herself away a million times over. She probably bartered with information to get out of a marriage."

Lips shrugs. "Doesn't matter. Her father is where we go for her. We get everything we can on him and then we go to him.

Once she's dealt with, we take out the Crawfords. Randy, then Holden. Fathers can be very fucking tricky if they lose their heirs."

We share a look and I nod. That's a reasonable enough plan. Aodhan looks between us and then shakes his head with a grin. "I have no doubt you're going to get this sorted out, but you're giving me nothing to go on here. Dig up some information and that'll do it? Sounds too easy and easy never wins out."

Lips grins back at him, then turns back to the wall. "Oh, I plan on killing a lot of people in this plan. As many as I can, really. I need to remind everyone what I can do if you threaten my family—it's been too long."

Harley scoffs at her. "It hasn't been that long."

I lean into Aodhan a little more, finding comfort in the firm planes of his chest. He also smells amazing, not at all like the moonshine or the smoke from the bonfire that had been lit at some point.

When we hear the others waking up and banging around up in the kitchen, we finally head back up so I can cook something greasy to soak up some of the hangovers. Lips grabs my hand and points out Lauren's photo to me.

"We start with her. We might need Illi for that one though, he's more recognizable than I am. Or maybe we can borrow Harbin for the night."

I nod, happy to let her make some decisions for a day or two without much input. Whatever she has, I'm happy to give it a fair go.

Ash is savage but less grumpy than before, kissing Lips and dragging her over to sit in his lap at the breakfast bar. Aodhan helps me to pull out pots and pans, then ends up in an argument with Harley about muscle cars that I couldn't care less about.

Morrison slumps into one of the other stools and groans dramatically, only looking alive when Lips runs a hand through his hair and murmurs gentle words at him like he's terminal, not just hungover. It's loud and messy and everything I've ever wanted for us all.

It doesn't matter how packed my murder board downstairs is, it feels like home again. If Atticus were here too, I would be the happiest I've ever been.

When Noah arrives in the doorway wearing one of my robes, he snaps, "Is someone dead or are we standing around in here screaming for no fucking reason?"

Ash swings around to throw an icy glare at him. "That could be arranged."

We still have a little ways to go before it's a *peaceful* family environment, but when I shove a plate of bacon at Noah, he takes it with a mumbled 'thanks' and heads to the dining room without another word.

Ash drives the Ferrari like he's hoping we all die in it, a giant, fiery ball of flames on the six o'clock news style of death. He usually leaves that sort of recklessness up to Morrison, but he obviously needs to let some steam off.

It doesn't help that Lips is sitting in the front with the only other five-point harness and I'm stuck in the back, sliding around like a freaking pinball. I don't say a word, even though I wanted to threaten everything he loves in this world, because I'm a fucking saintly sister sometimes.

Lips curses him out on my behalf and threatens to bite his demon dick off, which is disturbing but very funny, mostly because he looks at her like she's betrayed him deeply. Harley and Morrison have taken to calling him 'demon dick' just to get a rise out of him, and once I made them all swear to stop listing off reasons why the name is apt, I've been able to laugh along with them.

Harbin is already waiting outside the mansion when we arrive.

He's alone, Roxas nowhere to be seen, and I'm grateful not to put up with the idiot for once. Lips shoots me a look every time I talk about how much I hate the asshole, so I wouldn't be surprised if he finds himself at the pointy end of her knife sometime soon.

Lips slides out of the car before Ash has a chance to open the door for her, but for once he doesn't snap at her, he just opens mine and helps me out.

"Thanks for meeting us here, Harbin. We didn't want to pull Illi away for the night."

He shrugs from where he's leaning on the seat of his bike, a cigarette hanging out of one corner of his mouth, "No problem. I'm skipping church with the Boar to be here, so no skin off my ass."

Lips chuckles and holds out a hand to him. "Thanks for talking to your boys about Poe. I'm still not a hundred percent about the Unseen down in Mississippi."

He nods slowly, his eyes flicking back up to the mansion. "You know my stance on it. The Callaghans are better than most and if the heir is chasing her tail, then she'll be fine down there."

Huh.

I look over at Lips, but she just looks angry and kind of murderous at that comment. Not at him, just at the world, because of course her baby sister has caught the eye of some dirty biker.

Of course.

Harbin chuckles as he puts the cigarette out and straightens. "Yeah, he did some digging to try and find out about who her sister was too. I shut it down fast, and the Boar did too, so your secret is safe for now. I can't wait to see his face when he finds out about the infamous Wolf though."

I pull my phone out and double check the information there, just to brush up on the finer points here that we need to hit, and then I gently nudge Ash from where he's still staring Harbin down with vicious murder.

"Let's get this over with, I want to get back to the hospital."

He glances down at me and nods, keeping his mouth shut about Atticus now that Lips has reamed him over it, I assume. She was vehement about getting him on my side, no matter who I chose.

Lips gives me a nod and then we walk right up to the house, through the side gate, and into the kitchen door. No alarms blare at us, no sirens or security, and that's one of the many advantages of having the Coyote on our side and on our payroll.

Technology means nothing to him.

The kitchen is the picture of new money. Everything in it is flashy and oozing dollar signs, none of it about class or ease of use, and I hate the man even more.

The color palette is also abhorrent.

"I'm down to help if you wanna smash some plates in here, Queen Crow."

I startle at the name, no one has used it outside of Atticus' men, but I shake my head at him. "I'm here to do a lot more damage than some plates."

As Lips pulls herself up to sit on the countertop with a complete disregard for the place, Ash glances around and then pulls out his phone, tapping away at the screen as he sends out a text message. He's not usually this involved, but the time away has set some things very straight in his head.

Lips is the Wolf, she will always be the Wolf, and if he truly wants to keep her safe, he needs to find his own place at her side as an asset. Harley decided that medicine is his calling, his way of contributing.

Ash was never cut out to just be the muscle, he was always going to be more active than that.

There's a crashing noise from upstairs and then the sounds of footsteps, frenzied and thumping, as Police Chief George Drummond makes his way into the kitchen, wearing nothing but an old pair of boxer briefs.

I want to gouge my eyeballs out at the sight of him.

"What the fuck do you think you're doing in my house? I'll have you all on charges for this!" he roars as he steps up, a gun in one hand, but when he finally gets a good look at who it is he's facing, the blood drains from his face.

I'm not sure if it's Harbin, strapped up with an entire militia worth of weapons, or Ash, who looks almost identical to Senior, who has him shitting himself but as always, he's misidentified the real danger because Lips and I are the ones holding his life in our hands right now.

We decide if he lives or dies tonight.

I look around the kitchen, my face its usual cold mask, and say, "Is this how you treat your houseguests? Your hospitality is certainly lacking. I'm here on some unfinished business we need to get straight. I don't have your daughter, Drummond, and I'm not sure if she's still alive, but for a price, I'll get her back for you."

He's sweating, his eyes on Harbin like this is his worst

nightmare come true, and Lips swings her legs from the counter top. It's such a small and careless movement to the eye, but she's making sure this asshole knows his life means absolutely nothing to us.

Either he's useful and alive, or a liability and dead, leaving his daughter without anyone looking for her. She's so close to just being a statistic, a number we all hear about on the news of the hundreds of thousands of women that go missing every year in this country.

"You know who has her?"

I incline my head. "I ran into her at a party. She has made friends with someone no girl ever wants to know. You should be prepared for the amount of damage she'll have, the therapy you'll need to pay for."

He grabs a tissue from the box on the counter without an inch of shame as he dabs it over his forehead, muttering, "Fine. Fine, I'll work for you like I did for your father. It's not so bad, and if we keep it as business, then everything will be different this time around."

I chuckle and share a look with Lips. "It'll definitely be different this time around, Drummond. For starters, we're not paying you. This isn't a job—I'm not putting you on a bribe roster. You owe me a lot of money, and you'll be paying this blood debt until you die. If you're lucky, I won't pass that debt on to Lauren when you're gone."

His eyes flick around the room and the gross, gaudy new

riches of this place have never stood out so much. A Police Chief salary isn't going to cut it to keep this place. I already know what his finances look like; I know all about his wife's shopping addiction and the holidays they love taking. I know he drinks and gambles too much.

I know he's drowning under this mortgage without Senior's blood money.

"If I'm going to be an informant, I'm going to need compensation," he says, frowning and growing a backbone now that we're talking about money.

Lips smirks and swings her legs a little harder. "You mean your life isn't compensation enough? What about your wife? Is her life enough?"

He has to dab at that sweat of his again as it starts to run down his temples. "Do you have any idea how much I'm risking by doing this for you?"

Harbin scoffs and Drummond startles, looking over at him again and almost shitting himself when the biker speaks to him. "He's not worth it, you should just replace him. There's enough decent candidates to cut him out."

Drummond starts to shake and then snaps, "I'll do it. Just get out of my house, and I'll do whatever you want."

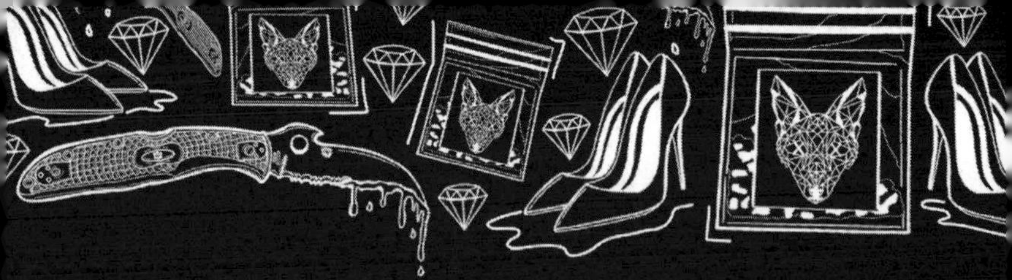

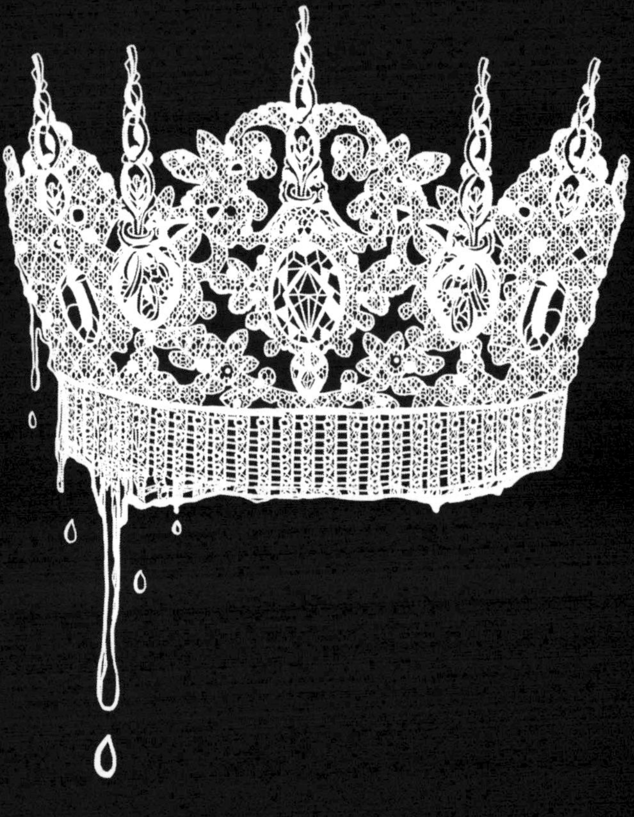

Chapter Six

I'm convinced that the reason the Twelve drag the Game out for months is so they're able to take out each other's sponsored candidates before the Game even starts and start petty little wars with each other.

There's no other reason I can think of to spread the fights out so much, and I find myself frustrated beyond all belief the evening of the next Game. I want this to be over, I want it to be the last time I'm forced into a space with the other members and their little followers for at least the next six months, but there's still one more session to go through after this. I'm ready to just wipe the board clean of them all, start fresh with a new group of people who are all firmly under our thumb.

We should start something new, start an institution of the Bay with only our family so that we own the streets with no other competition.

Something to consider once things quieten down and Atticus wakes up.

I ride over to the warehouses with Aodhan in the Impala, enjoying the subdued quiet as I work on my phone. There's a respectful air around us, like we're both so far on edge that we're holding ourselves on the line for each other alone. His hand rests on my knee, only moving when he needs to change gears, and I do my best not to disturb him with my tapping on my phone as he gets his head into the right space. I understand the need to prepare for whatever it is that tonight throws at us.

The last time we came here, my heart was ripped out and stomped on, thanks to the Bear and his manipulations killing Jack. It's different this time around, and not only because Atticus isn't here.

No.

News of me laying down the law with the rest of the Twelve has spread and when I step out of Aodhan's Impala, there's a lot of eyes on us both. I'm so used to the attention now that it barely does more than register with me but Aodhan isn't a fan, his protective instincts kick into overdrive and he tucks in close to me.

Then Ash's Ferrari pulls up next to the Impala and the rest of my close family piles out—suddenly the eyes are anywhere but on us.

No one touches the Wolf.

I was clear about that. Illi was clear as well, and every person who has heard even a whisper of what took place here in the city last year knows what it means to cross the Wolf and her people, and now the Bear has been taken out for crossing that line.

They're all terrified and rightfully so.

Lips acts as though it isn't happening, stepping over to slip her arm into mine and nod respectfully at Aodhan. "Let's get tonight over with, I already hate everything about it."

I nod and scan the crowd quickly for any signs of Lucy or Luca, the only other two people that count right now, but they're nowhere to be seen.

As we move through the crowd, it parts like the Red Sea, eyes dropping as they all move away. It's weird seeing such large scarred and tattooed men looking so subservient and respectful, but nothing in this city talks quite like blood and violence.

"Jesus fucking Christ, what have you done while we were gone to have them all acting like this?" Harley murmurs, and Aodhan smirks back at him.

"She's put the fear of God in them all... and she's reiterated the power of the Wolf. They all know they're on notice."

Lips meets my eyes with a quirk of her eyebrow, as close as she'll come to a grin while we're surrounded by crime lords who are intimidated by us and their loyal followers who are equally quaking in their biker boots.

The Coyote comes over to stand with us, looking a little less insolent and boyish now that Atticus isn't here to protect him from the fallout of his words. Viola is with him, which is rare these days, but she's looking happier and healthier than I've seen her since her father was killed.

I'm strangely happy about it.

I don't understand their relationship at all because I would rather die a grisly death than ever touch Jackson and his unwashed, greasy self. Lips always laughs at my assessment of him—something clearly went terribly wrong with her during development because she doesn't think he's actually that bad.

He is.

I don't care what she thinks.

"You need to come visit us, we have some shit for you," Viola says, her voice quiet enough but she sounds smug, which gives me hope that it might actually be good information.

I raise an eyebrow at her as we watch Luca arrive, wearing his usual dress pants, a white tee, and a jacket thrown overtop. He meets my eye across the room and dips his head in a sign of respect, clearly so everyone can see it, and I nod in return.

The convoluted politics of the Bay are even more important when you're a woman, especially a young one, because everyone doubts that you deserve it. Lips has used those biases to her advantage a million times, but I can't hide in them.

I have to break them to keep Atticus and his empire safe.

Aodhan's hand slips into mine and I thread our fingers together, giving him the only comfort I can right now with so many eyes on us. As the newest current member of the Twelve, he can't afford to have any doubts or infractions against his name.

Not that I would ever let anything happen to him. Oh no, I

would use every last one of my resources, and then I would work my way through all of Lips' and Atticus', until I had wiped all of Aodhan's enemies from the face of the Earth.

That's kind of my specialty.

As the warehouse fills up with more bodies and the air gets thicker and hotter around us, I check the time, ready for this night to be over with. We're already running behind schedule and I want to bleed someone out for it. My impatience is palpable, like a thick cloud around us all, and Aodhan squeezes my hand again. "We're waiting on the Viper and the Fox. No surprise they're the last ones arriving."

I shoot him a look but he's too busy watching the small group of contenders. Without the Bear's men, who are now ineligible thanks to his death, there's only eight left. Nine, once Lucy arrives.

I start to feel a small pit of nerves in my gut that she's not here yet. I might not count her as a friend or really even an ally yet, but she's still who we've backed, and any attack against her is only a step away from attacking us.

We can't let something like that go.

"Fucking finally. Your girl isn't exactly proving to be reliable, is she?" Jackson says, his voice a low drawl, and Viola digs her elbow into his gut. I glance over to the door and, sure enough, Lucy is stalking through the crowd as it parts for her. Her blonde hair is pulled up into a high pony and the red lipstick is like a bright slash across her face. She's dressed the same as she always does, jeans and a leather jacket with knee-high boots that look as though she could murder a man with the heels.

Well, she's already proved that she can.

"She's not someone we want to get on our bad side, Coyote, or else we'll be hiring a food taster for the rest of our lives," Viola snaps back at Jackson, and I shoot them both a look of disapproval for talking so openly and *loudly* in this stupid warehouse.

I grab Lips' elbow and move forward a step, meeting Lucy's eyes from across the room and motioning her over to us. She doesn't smile or react to the sight of us other than a slight inclination of her head, respectful with this many eyes on us.

I'm still happy with our choice, she's been a great competitor and proved our adeptness at choosing another member of the Twelve. I want to smirk at the looks of fear and respect already in the eyes of the men around us, the quick turn around in attitude from the earlier Game is enough to give you whiplash.

I thrive on it though, there's nothing I love more than watching their little minds explode at the idea of the dangerous, bloodthirsty, and deadly women that are here to own this city.

The men can't be trusted with it.

"Lucy, this is the Wolf of Mounts Bay, your sponsor," I say the moment the blonde stops in front of us. Lips nods at her, sizing her up in her own subtle way, but Lucy just stares back at Lips for a second and then curses under her breath, glancing away like she's scared to look at her any longer.

I share a look with Aodhan because she's never acted like this before, never once flinched at meeting a member of the Twelve or even the Butcher, but now she's freaking out?

Seems suspicious.

I'm not the only one who thinks so either. Ash immediately steps up to stand with Lips, his hand by his side flexing and ready to strike the moment he needs to.

Lucy glances at him without any remorse or concern and then drops her eyes back down our feet. "It's a pleasure to finally meet you, Wolf. I hope you find my efforts in the Games satisfactory."

Again, she's being stiff and formal, and it's not just weirding me out… it's a warning sign.

I have to stop myself from jerking Lips away from her, shoving her behind me and into the safety of our family, surrounded by a giant wall of men who are all not only twice our size but also wearing their fair share of Kevlar.

I insisted on it and, thanks to Atticus, they agreed to it.

Lips just stares her down, no sign of the discomfort that's killing me on her face, before nodding. "Just make sure you win. You're the only person to carry my name in the ring, I don't want my name sullied by your incompetence."

Sweat beads at Lucy's forehead as she nods and steps away from us. I've seen her walk into these fights with nothing but that cool, calm exterior of hers, confident in her ability to take on any competitor, and she's sweating over Lips' displeasure?

I need to figure it out.

I will never sleep soundly again until I do.

From across the room, the Viper stares me down with loathing, snarling and turning away when I give him a scathing smile back. Lips chuckles under her breath like she's in love with me, which only gets her guys grumpy and insecure. It's funny how much less worried I am about this now that they're back.

I shared the load of what was going on with Illi, Aodhan, and a little with Atticus, but there's something fundamental about my family that means I can relax a little with them here. Lips will help me navigate the Twelve, who are currently only eight, and I trust the guys to watch our backs.

There's also the fact that I'm no longer worried about keeping three people alive in a Game that only two can win.

It's a cruel twist of fate that we only have two people left but three spots open, my heart is bleeding for Jack and for Aodhan and Harley.

"Alright, let's get this fucking show on the road! Some of us have better places to be," the Boar calls out, a group of bikers behind him jeering and calling out in agreement.

At this point, if you've seen the fights once, you've seen everything you need to. I'm just about to mentally check out when the Boar walks up to Luca, pulling a gun out of his belt with a smirk.

I glance at Aodhan and while he doesn't look worried, he does shift so he's covering me a little more.

"Right or left?" the Boar says, and Luca shrugs back.

"Doesn't make a difference to me."

The Boar scoffs and then lifts the gun, shooting Luca through the calf. It's obviously a low caliber gun, the bullet going in and out as neat as a pin, and Luca barely grunts at the wound.

One by one, every last one of the competitors are wounded, most of them choosing which leg to take the bullet in. Lucy goes last but she doesn't flinch, the blood running down her leg completely unnoticed.

The Boar turns and calls out over the talking and groaning in the room, "Kill your opponent before you bleed out."

"Well, this is new," I murmur, but Lips just clears her throat a little.

She glances at the guys before she mumbles back, "No, it's not."

Jesus H. Christ.

The Coyote looks over at Lips and pulls his shirt up a little to show me the scar on his stomach. "They're lucky the Boar's the one doing the shooting; the Jackal used to insist on it being in your gut. The Wolf and I have matching scars, twinsies."

And now there are three murderous looking guys standing around us, poised and ready to rip someone to shreds at the very idea of Lips being in that ring while bleeding from her stomach, thanks to the Jackal's obsession with her.

Luca wins his fight in under a minute, efficient and brutal, walking with barely more than a limp to grab a seat afterwards and bind up the wound.

Lucy takes a little longer, but there's none of her usual showmanship, she just takes the guy out and gets out of the ring, sitting with Luca and allowing him to wrap her up as well.

I lose interest in the rest of the fights, mostly because none of the men are who I would want sitting at the table with the Twelve, but they're also not a threat to us.

None of them are a ticking time bomb.

Queen Crow

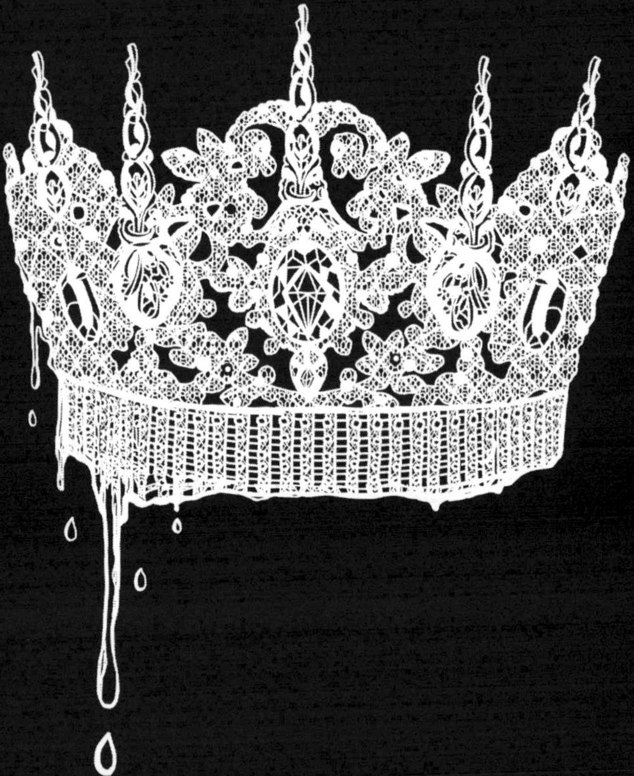

Chapter Seven

As if there hasn't been enough fighting and bloodshed for us all this week, there's an argument the afternoon after the Game about who is taking Lips and I over to the Coyote's bunker for the information debrief.

I end it by calling Aodhan to come pick us up to leave the guys behind.

Harley and Morrison accept this easily enough, bickering on their way back to sleep off their hangovers, but Ash is relentless in his anger at this entire mess we're stuck in for now.

I'm fairly certain that Lips bribes him with sexual favors to leave us alone, but I refuse to question or comment on it. Some things are better left alone.

We stand out on the front steps together, muttering between us away from the meddling ears of the guys, and I spot the tour bus still sitting like an eyesore in front of my garage, the one that's full of Ash's cars. There's scratches down one side, as though it side-swiped a building, and one of the back lights has been busted.

"When exactly is Morrison planning on moving that ugly thing? It's bringing down the value of the entire neighborhood sitting there. What the hell happened to it anyway?"

Lips winces and then looks over at me for a second like she's assessing me. Not in a way that pisses me off, not at all, because it's a very protective sort of look, like she's planning out killing everyone who has ever dared to look sideways at me, as a tribute to our friendship. It's why she has always, and will always, be the best friend I could ever have hoped for.

"We haven't gotten it completely unpacked yet. I'll get it sorted as soon as we have a second to breathe."

I nod as the Impala's lights hit the front gate, Aodhan leaning out to key in his code and use his thumbprint for the two-factor security I now have. "There's no rush if it's your things; if it were Morrison's, I'd be marching back upstairs and waking the petulant asshole back up."

She scoffs out a laugh, the rough tones of it singing to me after months of not hearing it in person. "Even Ash got pissy at how messy he was on the bus. There was an incident with a jacket being used as... you know what, you don't want to know. I'll sort the bus out, I just need to figure something out first."

I'm not sure what she could have to figure out but I nod and step forward to the Impala, stopping only when Aodhan gets out and frowns at me for daring to think about opening the car door for myself.

Lips makes this ridiculous cooing noise at us both, like we're adorable or something, and I glare my most severe glare at her. It bounces off of her, probably because she became immune to them in our freshman year of high school, and she slides into the backseat, laughing.

Aodhan raises an eyebrow at me, his wolfish grin melting my panties as he opens the door for me. I lean forward and press a quick kiss onto those lips. "I need new friends. After all of the boy bullshit I've put up with for her—"

"You threatened your brother's dick for two years! You told Harley last week that if you caught him looking at my ass again, you'd stick your knife through his eyeball," Lips calls out, and Aodhan laughs as I slide into the front passenger seat.

"Of course I did! But that's beside the point, I did that to them, not to you! I feel betrayed."

She rolls her eyes at me, pulling out her phone and very probably texting those idiot boys to moon over them because she's just as obsessed with them as they are with her. "I didn't say a word! I'm happy you're out here, living your best life and breaking Ash into a million pieces with your obsession with two men he has sworn to hate forevermore."

I turn to look at her in my chair. "Did you really just say 'forevermore' to me? Who the hell are you and what have you done with Eclipse middle-name-redacted Anderson?"

She glares at me, her best Mounty crime lord glare, as Aodhan slides in and tries his best to ignore the two of us sniping at each other. "Blaise keeps rubbing it in his face, I can't help that his dramatics have sunk in. Honestly, I'm so fucking sick of hearing about the two of you and having to remind Ash that Aodhan is off-limits. He needs a goddamn hobby or I'm going to kill him... or myself, really."

Now it's my turn to roll my eyes. "You need to spend less time with them, you really are getting dramatic. Besides, we can find him a hobby. It would be nice if it was of the killing-our-enemies variety."

Aodhan gets us out onto the road and flying down the highway in no time, his hand on my thigh only disappearing when he shifts gears. I spend the time looking through the security footage of Senator Blakeley, keeping an eye on Lips' oldest brother now that we know he's got a price on his head.

The more I look into him, the more shady people I find gunning for him. I know he wants to clean the streets up and rid the world of men like Grimm, but he's certainly making it hard to keep him alive for the rest of us.

I send a group of Atticus' men to DC to neutralize some more threats. I'm sure he'll hate that, but it only makes it a better plan.

When we arrive at the bunker, Lips gets straight out, smirking again at the way I wait around for Aodhan to open my door. I don't get the chance to snark at her for it, because the door swings open and Jackson stands there in a pair of old sweatpants and a tank top that has seen several lifetimes.

My skin immediately crawls.

"You're late."

I raise an eyebrow at him as Aodhan tucks me into his side. "We're exactly when we said we'd be here, don't be an asshole. Where's Viola? I much prefer her hospitality."

He smirks without answering and waves a hand at us to follow him. Lips walks after him like this is all nothing to her, but I have to take a deep breath before we step over the threshold, my eyes bouncing around at the dark space as we follow him down the stairs. It's cleaner than even the last time I was here, clearly Viola is doing a great job of upkeep, but it's still too dark and creepy for me to be comfortable.

There's also the smell.

I can't describe it, the electric smell of too much going on in here at once, but I just hold my breath as much as I can and let Lips take the lead.

"Your lead was too fucking good, Lips."

I hate the way he says her name, it's a little too gleeful for my taste, but she just nods back at him. "Jericho loves drugs too much not to know every last one of the cartel in the country. He's jumpy though, shit is getting harder for imports."

Jackson sits down at his desk as he snorts. "Yeah, and your brother dearest is the reason for that. This is all one twisted fucking web and right there in the middle of it is ol' sperm-daddy-o, Graves. He's one of Arias' buyers, you know? Loves pushing drugs out everywhere."

I frown, but Lips is the one to try to decipher his rambling. "Arias? Start at the beginning, Jackson, and give us the whole fucking story."

He smirks again and fills in the blanks. "Santiago Arias, the Colombian drug lord father of one Amanda Donnelley. Y'know, he's got a lot of business here that she tiptoes around? There's a whole lotta shit you can exploit here in this pile. It's good to have you back, Wolf. We needed your usual connections to get Queenie outta this shit."

Lips grimaces as takes the giant box of paperwork from him, glancing over at me. "I'll never be gone like that again. The cleanup isn't worth it."

We find ourselves in a church at nine o'clock on a beautiful Sunday morning.

Lips looks gorgeous in the relatively simple white dress, a blue diamond hanging around her neck in a halo of smaller blue diamonds on a delicate platinum chain. She's wearing a pair of simple Dior sling-backs that I got her for Christmas that complete her outfit beautifully. With her hair and makeup done by me, she looks unbelievably stunning, like a polished version of the perfectly gorgeous, but rough around the edges, girl we all fell in love with back in high school.

Ash almost disgraced himself when he saw her walk down the stairs. Harley and Morrison were also struck by her, but Ash always did have an obsession with dressing her up in the most luxurious things we could find for her.

The lace detailing gets to him and, while it's completely disgusting to think about *my brother* loving this outfit a little too much, I'm also always going to be happy and grateful that they found each other.

They all found each other.

I'm also in white, the diamonds around my own neck encased in the little ornate cage, and the white Louboutins have three extra inches on Lips' sling-backs. Every little part of my outfit and appearance has been carefully thought out and chosen for today because I never really thought that I'd be chosen to be a godmother, and certainly not by the biggest, most bloodthirsty heathen I've ever met.

Yet here I am, standing in front of a priest in the biggest and most prestigious church in Mounts Bay, with a handful of people I'm closest to on the planet, who also have body counts in the *thousands* between them.

"I can't believe you're doing this," Lips murmurs as the priest starts the ceremony. There's a faint sheen of sweat on his forehead and a tremble in his fingers, so clearly he's feeling the pressure. I almost feel sorry for him, it's not like this would be the easiest job to do with Harbin and Roxas standing at Odie's side with their cuts still slung over their shoulders, completely irreverent to the mood in the room.

I respect that.

"Odie wanted it and, honestly, I want Johnny protected. This feels more official," Illi murmurs back, waving a hand at the priest when he stumbles over his words at the interruption.

They both continue to talk through the ceremony.

"You think it'll take a baptism for me to kill for your son? That baby is my blood—anyone goes after him and I'll skin them alive."

Illi grins at her, his eyes still on the giant cross in front of us all. I'm a little surprised none of us have burst into flames yet.

The priest turns his back to fuss with the water for a minute, and Illi leans down a little to murmur, "I want him to know that we love him enough to dress him in that shit, stand in this fucking room, and give him godparents who would step up for him if anything happened to us. The other shit doesn't mean anything to me."

I smile and flick him a look of approval. He's a great father, exactly how we all knew he would be, even if it is still a little jarring to see him holding a little bundle of white baby blankets and beaming.

When the priest presses his hand on Illi's forehead, I almost lose my cool and dissolve into the fit of giggles bubbling in my chest. If looks could kill… and the priest knows it too, the sweating becomes a river down his temples as he freaks the hell out.

Lips stares him down with absolute blood-soaked murder when he steps over to her, and the priest is smart enough to not touch her, his hand hovering inches away from her head as he says all of the ancient and pretty words to swear us into this very holy duty.

I take the touching a little easier than everyone else, and when it's Odie's turn, Illi's hand rests over the cleaver strapped to his thigh and I hear the three idiots in the front row begin to wager if the priest is going to faint or not under the pressure in the room.

The faster we get this wrapped up, the better.

When it comes time for the baby to have the water poured over his head, Odie very gently unwraps the blankets and hands them to me. I smile at the perfect Dolce and Gabbana christening gown I'd had couriered to their warehouse apartment just for this occasion. I'm a little surprised that Illi is fine with his son being dressed in so much white silk and lace, but I'd done my research and knew that for our very chic and refined Frenchwoman Odette, this is the perfect outfit for this moment.

When the ceremony is over with, we all move into one of the separate rooms at the back of the church for refreshments. When Odie had called me for catering suggestions, I made the very adept call to cook for them rather than trusting someone else with the menu. Illi had immediately agreed with the choice, mostly because of the poisoning risks at outsourcing.

With all of us here, it would be too good a chance for one of our *many* collective enemies to attempt to take us out at once.

I'd baked the three-tiered christening cake as well, decorating it with dark blue brushstrokes and gold accents. It had taken me a dozen practice runs, and then three attempts the previous day, before I was happy with the masterpiece, and we are going to be eating cake out of the freezer for months before we run out.

The blindingly bright grin on Odie's face makes everything worth it as she cuts the cake and hands some to her husband, every pore of him oozing the type of male satisfaction that comes from a safe and joyful family.

I stand by and watch it all unfold, finding a little peace now that our hard work is getting us closer to clearing some of the bullshit from our overflowing planner.

Aodhan sticks with me for the speeches, only moving away when Odie approaches me with a grin and profuse gratitude for my help with today.

As though this isn't my forte and my utter joy to help her.

"Thank you again, this has been the perfect day and you've done so much for him already. It is a great honor to us both to have you and le Loup as his godmothers," Odie says in very rapid and happy French.

I grin back at her. *"He looks absolutely perfect; it's an heirloom piece for the Illium family."*

She blushes and grins, pressing her nose into his little blond curls and breathing in that delicious baby scent of his. *"We are very blessed to have you. I will never lose my gratitude for you all."*

"And I for you and Illi. You kept Lips safe and alive for us before we even knew we were missing her."

Oh God, I can't dissolve into tears here in the back rooms of this church surrounded by the most dangerous yet trustworthy criminal figures of the Bay.

Odie smiles at me with understanding, squeezing my hand before moving over to the group of bikers in the corner that are muttering and gossiping about turf wars and blood feuds. They accept her and the baby happily, barely changing the topics, but toning down the language just a little out of respect.

None of them look at her for longer than is strictly necessary, their hands carefully tucked away so there's no chance of even accidentally brushing her.

I glance over to find Illi and Ash talking a few feet away, their eyes on Odie as they pour out drinks from a hip flask of Ash's. I catch his eye and then roll mine at him as he salutes me with it.

Blasphemous shithead.

Lips sidles up to me, shockingly silent in her heels, and murmurs to me, "How serious is being a godmother, on a scale? Like… other than the shit I was already completely willing to do?"

I giggle at her. "You're supposed to be a spiritual guide for him, get him onto the right path to ensure the safety of his soul."

Morrison slinks in behind her, wrapping an arm around her waist as she blinks at me and then shrugs. "I was always planning on teaching him how to stab first, ask questions later. His *soul* is in great hands."

We both laugh at her and Odie glances over, making excuses

to the bikers to bring the baby back over to us.

When she holds the little bundle of cute out to Lips, I watch as she steels herself, reaching out to grab little Johnny as though she's handling a bomb with a hair-trigger. Morrison coos at the baby and her, murmuring little words of encouragement at how she's holding him, and it's clear he's been coaching her.

He's probably aiming to knock her up sometime soon.

"Don't get too comfortable, kid. I don't wanna see any Wolf pups for a lotta years," Illi grumbles as he walks over, pressing Odie into his chest gently and kissing her soundly on the lips. Watching them together used to make my heart ache because his love for her is one for the ages, and even though I'm happy for them both, it always made me feel completely and devastatingly alone.

My eyes drift across the room to where Aodhan and Harley are talking, their heads bent closely as they conspire together. I'm sure whatever it is they're talking about is going to be a headache for me and Lips to sort out, but it makes me happy to see them together.

To know the O'Cronins didn't ruin their relationship, no matter how hard they tried to.

"Stop mooning over him," Ash mutters, as sour as ever, and I shoot him a look.

"You promised. Do I need to remind you that he was ready to die for me? I decided—"

"Don't. I'll have to go find some washed-up Jackal junkie to bleed out if we talk about it too much." He knocks back the rest of the whiskey in his glass and subtly looks over to his girlfriend cradling the baby.

"Can you imagine the twisted family tree? No. Senior's DNA is going no further, not by me."

I don't say a word back to him, mostly because there's no need to start a fight at little Johnny's christening party. But also because I know my brother the same way I know myself.

I knew what he'd do if he found the tape. I knew his reactions to Lips in the dress, to Harley's family putting him in danger, to Morrison's father writing him out of his estate. I know every thought that he's ever had.

I know the deep and very secret longing in him to have a family that he can guard intensely, nurture, and love. He might not be ready to admit it, but I'm not worried about it either. He has a lot of time before Lips is even willing to consider kids to work through the trauma of Senior and our childhood of terror.

Lips notices his mood and glances over to me with a look, always a complete mother hen about her guys, but I give her a subtle shake of my head back.

No need to open that box of nightmares until we get there.

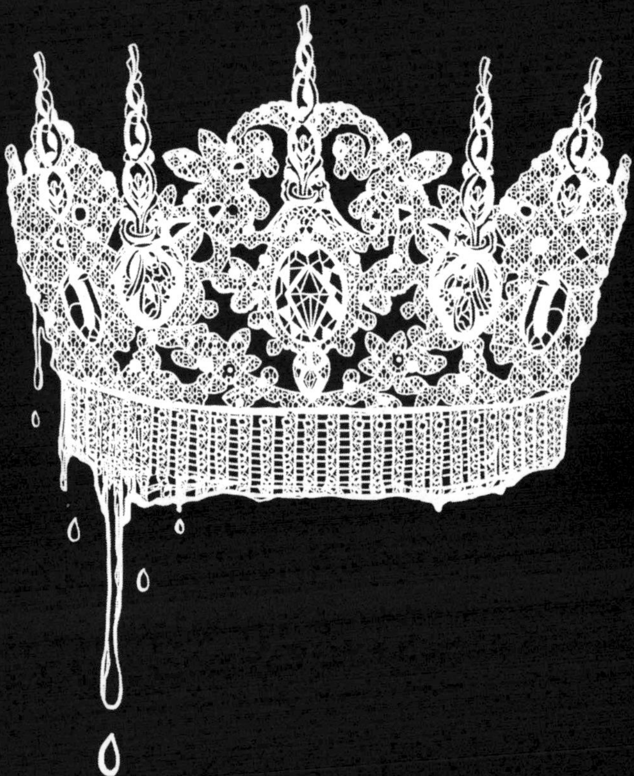

Chapter Eight

Lips and her guys leave the christening in the opposite direction of the ranch without a word about where they're heading off to.

When I slide into the Impala with Aodhan, my phone buzzes in my hand, a text from Lips that simply reads, *Don't wait up.*

"I need to stop in at the docks, are you in a hurry or can you ride along?" Aodhan murmurs, and I take the moment to lean across the seat to catch his lips with mine.

I feel as though I've barely gotten to be with him, no matter how much we've actually been around each other for the last few days. There's a distance there now and while it started with Atticus being shot, it's been made even worse, thanks to my family coming home. I needed space to figure out Ash and his anger, and Aodhan has been so good about giving it to me without just disappearing.

I just miss him so badly though.

"There's nowhere else I'd rather be right now," I mumble

against his lips, and he gives me one of his lazy grins, his eyes hooded but bright up close like this.

"Luckiest man alive, I don't deserve you. Let's get this shit over with so I can get you home, Queenie. It's been too long."

A shiver runs down my spine and I giggle under my breath, pulling back to sit against the old leather seats. It's not as comfortable as my car or as smooth a ride as one of Ash's, but it's become my favorite.

Harley would murder me if he heard me, his loyalty to muscle cars means that he likes the Impala well enough, but he'll never move past the Mustang that Joey destroyed. He'd sent a list of parts he needed to Poe last year and the deliveries have been coming in slowly. I'm fairly sure the original car isn't much more than an axle and a couple of bolts, but none of that matters to Harley.

He's set up one of the bays in Ash's garage, complete with a lift and every tool you could ever possibly need to put a car together, and he's ready to build the car back from the literal ashes with nothing but his own hands and some advice from Lips' little grease-monkey sister.

The thought of it has me smiling all the way down to the docks. I'm not as familiar with this area full of cargo ships and customs workers, but Aodhan directs the Impala through all of the check-in points without being stopped, the workers all waving him through on sight.

When he pulls up at the small parking lot by the water's edge,

I can pick out all of the O'Cronins in the crowd of workers, all of them peering over at the Impala now that the head of their family is here.

There's a lot of respect in those eyes and it calms something in me.

Aodhan unbuckles his seatbelt and leans over to kiss me gently. "I'll be half an hour. Do you wanna come down with me?"

I shake my head, facing my phone a little. "I have more than enough to keep me busy… and it smells out there. I'm fine."

He smirks at me as he climbs out, but I'm not wrong—the ocean smell is almost unbearable even after the door swings shut. I'm not cut out for south-side Mounty life, it's a well known fact.

Lips once told me that this place smells like home to her, which is both incomprehensible and unforgivable to me. I sometimes imagine digging her mother up just to spit on her for leaving her young daughter alone on the streets of this monstrous city.

I pull up the security cameras on Atticus' hospital bed to play in the background while I read through documents on Santiago Arias. Jackson is good at what he does and there's days of reading ahead of me, scouring through every little piece of his life until I find something, anything, to hold over the Cartel's head.

I'm still not sure exactly how things are going to go down, but Amanda Donnelley is still number one on my death list, no matter how evil and disgusting the Crawfords are… just so long as they stay the hell away from Atticus, which is exactly why I'm obsessively watching his security feed.

The half hour passes quickly, stretching out into an hour, then two. I'm not worried about it, not with one of Aodhan's cousins watching the car for him and waving a hand at me whenever I look up at him, a sign that there's nothing actually wrong. The docks are busy at this time of the afternoon, and I wasn't lying when I told Aodhan I had nowhere else to be.

The roar of engines catches my attention and I watch as a whole legion of leather-clad bikers ride into the parking lot. The Unseen patches are clear across their backs and I can pick out the Boar, Harbin, and Roxas clearly, but there's at least two dozen men here.

They all pull up and get off their motorbikes, some of them immediately moving off to the same area that Aodhan disappeared to, and I feel a small flutter of unease.

He's fine, he can take care of himself, but the hospital room is still showing on my phone as a stark reminder of what can happen to the men I love.

They're not invincible, no matter how strong and capable they are.

I keep my head ducked as though I'm working on my phone, but my eyes take in as much of my surroundings as possible, cataloging as many of the men as I can.

Which is how I find none other than Ruin Callaghan,

Poe's crush and the son of the imprisoned Coldstone charter president, standing there among the men.

What the hell is he doing in Mounts Bay?

He certainly doesn't look comfortable. To anyone without my skills of observation he probably just looks like a relaxed and confident biker, but I've watched enough security footage of him following Posey around Coldstone to know that there's a very fine sort of tension in him.

His man-whore of a cousin is with him, a phone pressed to his ear as he scowls around the docks like he's got issues with the whole world. Thomas Callaghan is a few years older than Ruin, he's covered in more tattoos, and has a nose ring that glints in the late afternoon sun. His favorite hangout spot is the strip club that the MC owns, and I'd rather set myself on fire than watch that man get another blowjob from a stripper there.

He's currently my least favorite Callaghan, which is saying something because Ruin's obsession with following Poe around is a giant pain in my ass.

I wonder if Nate keeps tabs as closely as I do? If so, Ruin is a dead man walking.

As the Boar finally spots me in the Impala and stalks over, I drop my eyes back down to the phone screen, watching Atticus' chest rise and fall like it's the only thing getting me through the day.

It might be. Somewhere in the back of my mind, it really might be the only reason I'm functioning.

"If it isn't the Queen Crow herself. What have we done to deserve your presence down here in the slums?" His voice is muffled through the car door, but I hear it clearly enough.

I subtly check that my gun is still within arm's reach as I roll down my window, ready to shoot the Boar between the eyes for making me let the smell in. "You've been looking into the Coldstone Unseen, haven't you? You wanna meet them or not, *your majesty*?"

The sarcasm is dripping from his words, but I give him nothing but a cold stare back. "I know everything I need to know about them, thank you."

My eyes meet Roxas' across the parking lot and he gives me the smallest, most subtle nod of his head, moving his cut just enough that I see how much firepower he's packing. It's a sign of loyalty, a sign that no matter whose tramp stamp he's rocking, he'll be getting me out of here if something is about to go down.

I wait until the Boar turns away before I give him one back, rolling the window back up and shutting them back out.

The Callaghans are both watching me, their eyes far more shrewd than any of the older and more experienced bikers around them. Thomas slowly lowers the phone, shoving it into his pocket and glancing at Ruin as they talk among themselves. They're too far away for me to hear anything being said, but then Aodhan finally appears again, a scowl on his face as he stalks past them and back to the car.

I don't say a word to him about it on the trip home, but I

make a note to add this little encounter to the murder board.

The house is still empty when we arrive back at the ranch and Aodhan pulls the Impala up behind the dented bus. I curse at the stupid thing under my breath, mostly about Morrison and his inability to keep his shit to himself, and Aodhan raises an eyebrow at me over it.

"Want me to tow the thing out? He's a rich asshole, right? I'm sure he can buy the house down the street and leave it there instead."

I tuck myself under his arm and shake my head, because I can't admit to him that the idea of any of them buying a house right now and moving out gives me the shakes. I need them here, in my space, the same way I need him here. Someday I'll get over the panic and fear of losing them all, but until then, they can be here with me.

They just need to keep Morrison's shit in line.

"Maybe I should just offer to clean it out for Lips? She's come home and hit the ground running to take out all of the issues that have cropped up, and if she hasn't got the time, then I'll help out."

He huffs and shakes his head at me. "You've got just as much on your fucking plate. I'll tell Harley to sort it out; if Ash catches wind of you cleaning up after them, he'll murder someone, I'm sure."

Ah, the joys of family politics.

I should just get over the bus being here, it's not that big a deal, but there's something about it sitting there in its state of disrepair that is itching under my skin.

We get back into the house and I turn the security alarms back on, checking through the log and seeing Noah stomp around the house in a tantrum thanks to being left behind for the christening.

He's such a brat.

"Are you hungry? I can cook us some dinner?" I say, but when I turn, Aodhan's eyes are glued to the long lines of my legs and the curve of my ass in this dress. I chuckle at him and he smirks back.

His phone starts ringing in his pocket, and he says as he digs it out, "I'm hungry but not for food. I'll be one minute, Queenie."

I roll my eyes, because there's no way he'll only be one minute, but a plan has already come together in my head for us both now, and I head up the stairs to my room.

What's the point of all of the lingerie I have if I'm not putting it to good use?

I'm absolutely right in that it takes him half an hour to find me, but when Aodhan steps through the door, his eyebrows hit his hairline as he takes me in.

I felt kind of ridiculous waiting in here for him, wearing nothing but the under-bust corset, suspenders, and my favorite pair of Louboutins, but the hunger and desperation in his eyes makes it worth it.

"What are you up to over there, Queenie? All of my favorite parts of you on display like that makes me think you've been planning this all day. In a church and everything. What would God think of that?"

I smile at him and step forward, his eyes dropping down to the way my chest bounces a little with every movement. He licks his lips, an unconscious action at seeing his next meal dressed up for him.

Men are such simple creatures sometimes.

"We're not all good Catholic men, O'Cronin. Some of us are heathens who love nothing more than sinning, especially when the outfits are this good."

His eyes are still on my nipples, budding up perfectly under his keen gaze. I let one of my hands drift down my hip, right until it meets with my pussy, already wet at just the sight of him and the anticipation of what's to come.

A soft groan rips out of his throat as my fingers start to move, my lips parting on a moan, and finally the control he has over himself snaps as he throws himself across the room at me.

It's hard not to giggle at how eager he is, how fast he crossed that room to get his hands on me, but then his lips are on mine and every thought disappears from my mind except *more, deeper, harder.*

He backs us up until his legs hit the bed, pulling me down

onto his lap and grunting when my hips grind down onto him, my bare pussy rubbing against his jeans.

I have to speak before I let him sweep me up into this moment and I don't get to try something out, so I tear my lips away from his. "Can you do something for me?"

He nods as he moves to kiss my neck, his hands running up my sides and stroking over every inch of my soft skin that he can. It's a desperate move, like it's been so long that he thinks he might have forgotten what it feels like to hold me close.

I almost cave and change the plans because his hands feel perfect pressed against me, the callouses dragging a little and giving me the most delicious friction. But I force myself to lean forward, pushing him down and pressing him back against the mattress as my body covers his completely. "Keep your hands at your sides. If you can keep your hands off of me until I tell you to touch me, I'll let you fuck me however you want the next time."

He smirks at me, squeezing my breast with one hand and tweaking my nipple before dropping his hand back down to his side. His voice is a rough rasp, all Mounty street kid as he murmurs, "You sure you want that, Queenie? I can think of a lotta things I wanna do to you right now, and at least half of them will probably be too much for you."

Too much?

That feels both insulting and like a challenge, one that I'm already fully prepared to take on. As long as it's not something gross… I'm not into feet or golden showers. Or sex in the kitchen.

Jesus Christ, what if he wants to stick something weird inside of me?

I can't imagine him wanting that so I say, "We need a safe word but sure, whatever you want."

The grin he gives me in return is lecherous, and I gasp as he pinches my nipple again, this time a little harder, until my thighs are clenching around his waist. I give him a stern look and repeat, "Keep your hand at your side."

He grins roguishly at me and moves it back down to the bed, all faux submission that is entirely too charming on him. I realize immediately that I should have gotten him naked before he was lying down, but it's easy enough to strip him with simple commands that he follows obediently.

Once I have his jeans and underwear off, I climb back up his body, hesitating for a second as I hold myself up over his dick because wanting to try this out and actually doing it are two very different things.

I clear my throat and just say it, "We haven't tried this position much since… well, I wanted to give it another go."

His brow furrows, but I don't want to spoil the moment so I lean down to kiss him again, one hand on his cheek as the other one wraps around his already-hard dick. He grunts again, his hands balling into fists at his side as he forces himself not to touch me, but after a few firm pumps of his dick, I pull myself up to sink down on it, taking him all the way down to the root.

It feels fucking amazing, none of the fear or shame breaking through, and when I plant my hands on his chest and begin to move, the look of adoration and worship in his eyes is almost too much, too real for me.

I stare at him though, I take it even as I roll my hips and take every inch of his hard cock as it pulses inside of me. There's something so fucking powerful about this position, about this man lying there and letting me take whatever I need from him right now.

I watch as the sweat begins to bead around his temples and his jaw clenches as he tries to keep himself under control, and I feel like the queen he's always calling me.

One of my hands drifts back down to my clit, circling and rubbing, and his eyes follow every movement as though I'm giving him the show of his life.

When I come, my pussy gripping his cock and milking it, he finally snaps, words tumbling out of him like he doesn't even know what he's saying. "I gotta fucking move. Queenie, lemme fuck you. I need you. I need to fucking move."

I nod, gasping at how quickly he's grasping my hips and holding me still to pump his hips into me, the wet sounds of him fucking me obscene as they fill the room.

I can feel another orgasm building, but when I try to touch my clit again, he tugs my hand away, surging up and over until he's back on top and pounding into me again. He tugs my hips until he's grinding into my clit himself, and when I shatter this time, he comes with me, roaring out his release.

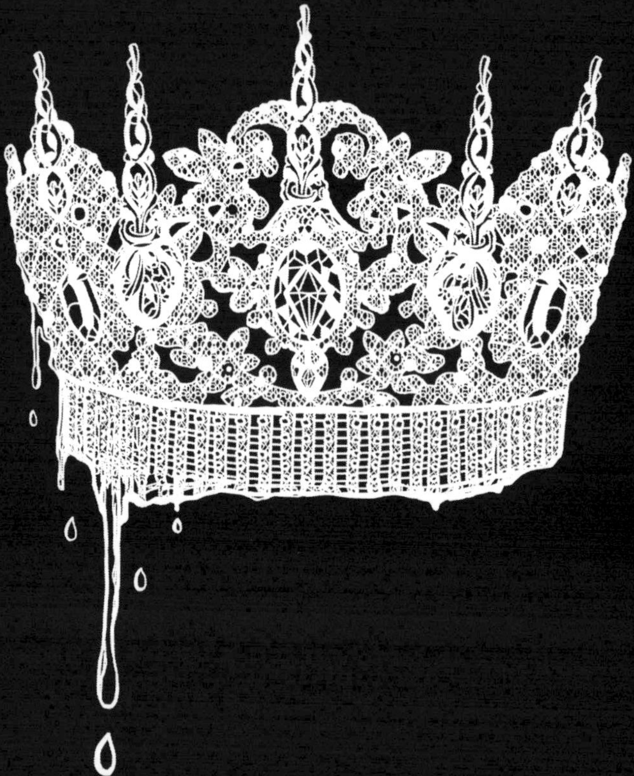

Chapter Nine

I spend the next week at the Crow's fortress dealing with matters I've barely gotten a handle on.

I have no choice but to spend my days over there, sifting through information with Luca while Ash or Harley snarl insults at him the entire time. It's informative and draining all at once, picking up the reins with no sort of information handover, and I feel like I'm fumbling around in the dark.

It also becomes clear to me that Atticus' influence stretches much further than I ever would have thought possible.

There are old gentleman's clubs in every major city in the world that he either has surveillance on or informants in. I suddenly have access to every president, prime minister, and congressman in the world. There is no political circle, both law-abiding or outlaw, that I don't have access to.

It's both amazing and very confusing.

All of this power and yet the Crawfords are still breathing. I understand what it means to be old money, Senior had access to many things that made him almost impossible to touch without far-reaching consequences, but with access to all of these people, why hasn't Atticus just taken them out?

When I question Luca about it, his eyes flick to Ash and then he shrugs, not at all eager to discuss it around the scowling and vicious man in my life who also doesn't love his boss. Okay, he absolutely freaking hates him, so I don't bring it up again, even though it's on my mind the entire week.

I learn a lot about the Jackal's nuclear bomb.

I also learn that it is *missing*.

"Jesus fucking Christ, of course it is! At what point was Atticus planning on bringing this to the table at the Twelve meetings? Or maybe just picking up the phone and telling me that there's a literal bomb missing that could take out the entire city?" I snap, and Ash is too busy in the corner on the phone to Morrison to add any snarky commentary.

Luca hesitates for a second before saying, "State. It's big enough to wipe out the state of California and do some damage to the surrounding states."

My stomach turns but I mask how sick it's making me by letting out my anger instead. "Right. So when Atticus said we were allies, he didn't mean that he'd let us know about that sort of potential threat? This is kind of important, Luca. I would have literally cleared everything off of my planner to help find it and get it defused."

He glances at Ash again and my temper just snaps. "He's

not going to disappear if only you keep looking at him! He's also here because there are massive trust issues between the Wolf's camp and this one. That's on you and Atticus, not us."

Luca shrugs and hands over another file that's overflowing with papers. "The two of you are breathing. Every last thing that the Crow did, all of it was for you and your brother. Sure, he was always going to put you first if shit really went south, but he got Ash out of the shit a million times as well. No matter the cost, no matter what he had to do, he kept you both safe. At some point, you two have to give him credit for it… and instead you're with O'Cronin and your brother is a snarling fucking dickhead about everything, even after he got his own member of the Twelve to keep."

Big mistake.

Big mistake bringing up my decisions and an even worse one to even gently mention Lips in a tirade. If looks could kill, Luca would be dead the second Ash's eyes swing his way, and I discreetly start looking for my phone under the papers to call Lips for a cleanup.

"Avery didn't ask for his help and she can make her own fucking decisions about what she does. If he thought building this pompous empire meant he earned her, then he's no better than her other buyers. Avery decides who the fuck she's with. Not you, not me, and not Atticus *fucking* Crawford."

It's not until hours later, on the trip back to the ranch in his Ferrari, that he snarks at me, "Well, I'm not fucking happy about you ending up with O'Cronin but if it has to be someone, then at least you didn't pick some coiffed, wet fucking blanket who can't even shoot straight."

And that is as much of an approval as Alexander Asher William Beaumont will ever give a man.

Whatever is going on at the docks keeps Aodhan ridiculously busy, and on the night of the final Game, I ride over to the forest at the edge of Mounts Bay with Harley in the Rolls Royce, ignoring his grumpy mumbling at the poor qualities of the luxury classic car. It's all just the typical boy bullshit I'm used to from him, he'd complained at me for months after he found out I'd bought it, but there's something very soothing about it as background noise as I work on my phone.

After all of these years of living in such close quarters, I didn't realize how devastating their temporary absence would be to me, especially his. There was never any doubt that losing Ash would be like losing a limb, but Harley had wound his way around my heart from the moment I saw him through that two-way mirror.

The others had arrived hours ago for set up and instead of joining them, I'd spent the afternoon at the hospital with Harley. He's a much less surly friend to have around at the bedside, sitting there quietly as I scour over the notes for any little inconsistencies or signs of foul play.

There's still nothing though, no little sign that he's going to come out of this fucking coma, no signs of him getting better or worse, and I start to believe that he's going to be stuck in this limbo forever, never really coming back to me, but existing instead as a shell of himself.

It's a fate worse than hell in my opinion.

"Who else do we want to win? I only know about blondie and the dickhead, the rest of them just look like wannabe gangsters and biker assholes," Harley says as we pull off the highway and start down the small winding road to the clearing.

I sigh dramatically, mostly because it's very frustrating to me that we couldn't hold off replacing the Bear until another round of the Game, giving ourselves another chance at picking out new candidates. "There's only six people left so other than our two, there's a couple of the Boar's men and one each from the Fox and the Ox. None of them raise red flags, other than the fact that we don't own them, so it's not anything worth worrying over. We just need our two to win."

He nods and scans the busy dirt road, leaning forward in his seat as if that will suddenly clear the path to where we're heading. There's too many people eager to see who's going to win this thing and take their seats at the table, too many people who want to see where the power is going to shift in the Bay.

There's been a lot of interest in who is going to end up running the skin auctions and the drugs now that they've been taken down. While I don't have as strong a stance on drugs as

Lips does, there's no way on this Earth that we're going to let the auctions start up again.

Not any of us, and for sure not the Butcher, the man responsible for killing the Vulture and shutting them down in the first place. If the third winner even shows an interest in taking them over, he's dead. It's that simple.

The Bay will not be known as the place to buy girls anymore, if it's the last goddamn thing I do.

When we finally make it to the clearing, Harley jumps out and comes around the car to help me out, waiting as I lock away my phone and check all of my concealment spots for the weapons I have on myself now. I'm also in Kevlar and wearing enough rings that if I have to take a swing at someone they're going to feel the worst I have to throw at them.

Lips has certainly rubbed off on me.

Then we walk through the forest together, using nothing but the moonlight to light the way.

There's men all around us, joking and talking among themselves, but falling silent if we get too close to them. Harley stays close to my side, glaring around at everyone like he's going to rip them limb from limb for breathing too closely to us.

When we get to the edge of the clearing, there's a check-in point, the same as last time, and even though there's no doubt of who we are, the guy standing there waves his UV torch over us anyway.

The Wolf on my wrist glows.

So do the snarling Wolf jaws across Harley's cheeks, and I enjoy watching the men around us gulp at the very sight of it, the mark not only showing he belongs to the Wolf but that she favors him.

He's hers to keep.

The guy waves us through, swallowing a little roughly but otherwise his confidence is unshaken. Harley smirks at me, and I have to rein in the scoff I want to give him.

"Nothing better than the whole fucking lot of them knowing she's mine. Nothing better than them all shaking in their fucking boots about the little Mounty girl of their nightmares, and she's all fucking mine," he murmurs, and I elbow him gently.

"Sure… yours and Morrison's and my brother's. Good thing she's just as fucking besotted as you are, you sap."

He grins and flicks the little platinum cage swinging around my neck, the forest-green diamond clear for everyone to see. "Must run in the family then, right? I wonder how he knew that blood diamonds literally make you squeal like you're about to… gross, never mind."

I laugh at the way his nose scrunches up in disgust right as we come up to find the large crowd gathering to watch the chaos of tonight's events unfold. We find Morrison standing off to one side with the other higher ranking flunkies, and we walk over to join him.

Ash is standing with Lips, both of them looking as though they've been dragged through the forest floor on their knees, the mud spatters reaching their chests. Ash is in a pair of dark jeans, biker boots, and a black tee that's stretched tight across his chest, like he has something to prove here. Without a doubt, Harley and Morrison will be giving him shit about it later.

Lips is wearing her usual Mounty wear, complete with her beloved cherry Docs that have definitely seen more than their fair share of bloodshed and gore.

I really should force a new pair onto her.

There's murmuring around the clearing, a shifting unease rippling through the men all standing around, and then Aodhan appears, stalking through the trees and looking as dirty as the others.

His eyes meet mine and he doesn't smile at me, not here in front of all of these witnesses, but when he inclines his head at me as a sign of respect, my heart flutters in my chest.

He's never seen me as anything but an equal and in this space, he's happy to show it to every last man, woman, and child of the Bay.

It's not fair of me to hold that over Atticus, not after everything he's done to help me over the years. The list of his sins in my name gets longer and longer the more I learn about his life as the Crow, but there's some part of me who will always crave this. Crave the open acknowledgement that I've built a name for myself and an entire ruthless empire of my own.

For myself and my family.

One by one, each of the remaining members of the Twelve

arrive until we're all standing around the clearing, just waiting for the final Game to start.

Aodhan comes to stand with me, his hand slipping into mine discreetly, and I appreciate it because a moment later the flare goes up, signaling the beginning. The last time we were here, I was so busy cataloging everything happening around us, trying to make out who was here and who could be an asset for us, that it didn't really soak in what was happening.

Lips was once buried in one of those graves, told to dig her way out, and kill anyone she came across to win her spot. Aodhan and Atticus too, of course, but there's something so much more horrifying to me about Lips doing it.

She was only a child.

Of course, they all underestimated her. Who's expecting a thirteen-year-old to be able to do the things she could? They also don't understand desperation or what happens when you're brought up in very specific conditions.

There's another timeline somewhere out there where Lips was brought up by parents who loved her, and that girl couldn't have survived this, but this Lips was starved and beaten and forced to take on the mask of a monster to make it out alive.

The crowd is restless, but there's too much fear in them still to worry about them. There shouldn't be any problems tonight, not after everything that has gone down in the last few months, but Lips still sidles up to me, carefully watching the crowd as much as she's looking out at the tree line for the first signs of the competitors. The guys all position themselves around us, close enough that they're able to dive in front of either of us if someone starts shooting, but far enough away that there's no mistaking who is in charge here.

No one needs to know that our family works with a democratic voting system, and while Lips might know more and have a greater say on most issues thanks to her experiences, she's still not our boss. Not the way they all think anyway.

There's the very clear sounds of fighting, grunting, and male screaming echoing through the night air, and my body breaks out in a very specific type of goosebumps. It's eerie, like the sounds aren't just from tonight and instead we're listening to the sounds of generations of competitors fighting for their survival.

Jesus.

Aodhan's hand squeezes mine again and I glance up at him, carefully keeping my face blank. He's scowling at the trees along with everyone else, focused entirely on whatever horrors are happening out there.

Everything changes tonight.

Luca makes it out first, dragging one of the other men's corpses with him and dropping it at the edge of the clearing as proof of death. His chest is heaving a little and he's covered in dirt and streaks of mud, but other than bloodied knuckles, he's unharmed.

Lucy is a close second, a bruise forming on her cheek and

her hands are torn up a little, but she's also in fairly good shape. Neither of them attempt to look at each other, let alone size each other up. There's no point, there's three seats open on the Twelve now and they're both being sponsored by allies.

It's everyone else who needs to die.

The other three men all arrive within seconds of each other, and they all go straight for Lucy. I wonder if Lips is the reason they've learned not to just leave the girl for last? Whether it was her strangling a man with her thighs and stabbing another that taught them the lesson.

It doesn't matter anyway, Lucy is ready for them, and even with the tiny limp she still has thanks to the last Game, she is more than prepared to take them on.

Luca doesn't hesitate to throw himself into the melee. They have to be careful to only kill two out of the three men, but it's not a pretty or skillful fight.

Two of the guys split off to take on Luca together, one of them viciously and the other one holding back a little, like he knows he's seconds away from a seat if he outlives the other two. Lucy gets her guy on the ground with a sharp jab to his healing bullet wound and then she sets about strangling him, holding him down long enough to find one of the many heavy rocks on the ground.

There's an audible crack as Luca snaps a neck, flinging the body away from himself right as Lucy lifts a rock without hesitation, slamming it into the asshole's skull, his entire body jerking as his brain is pulverized.

"She's good," Lips murmurs to me, loud enough that Aodhan hears and gives her a curt nod of approval.

He doesn't look at Luca, doesn't attempt to watch the man who killed his cousin win his own spot at the table. It's going to be a problem for us someday soon, the two of them forced to endure each other when there's so much bad blood, but for right now, all that matters is that Luca is alive and going to take a seat at the table as well. We're about to have six seats of our own, six people who will always vote together, and the Bay is ours. No matter what else happens here, we've accomplished exactly what we'd hoped for.

There's a moment of tense silence, only the panting of the three winners breaking through the quiet of the night, before the moment all of this violence and bloodshed has been for.

Lips doesn't hesitate to move forward, taking up the leadership role now that Atticus isn't here to do it. When she gets to Lucy, she says those same words that every other member has heard, standing there panting and covered in blood.

"Welcome to the Twelve. You're replacing the Lynx. Who do you choose to be?"

Lucy takes a deep breath, exhaling slowly before answering with a clear and steady voice, "I am the Scorpion."

I nod slowly. It's a good choice, appropriate for the poisons expert, and Lips takes another step down the line. Luca nods at her respectfully and she says again, "Welcome to the Twelve.

You're replacing the Jackal. Who do you choose to be?"

He's faster with his answer than Lucy, his eyes a little too fixated on Lips for my liking. "I am the Eagle."

The last guy is shaking a little, his broken arm still clutched to his chest, and when Lips says the words one last time, he replies, "I am the Hyena."

And then there were Twelve.

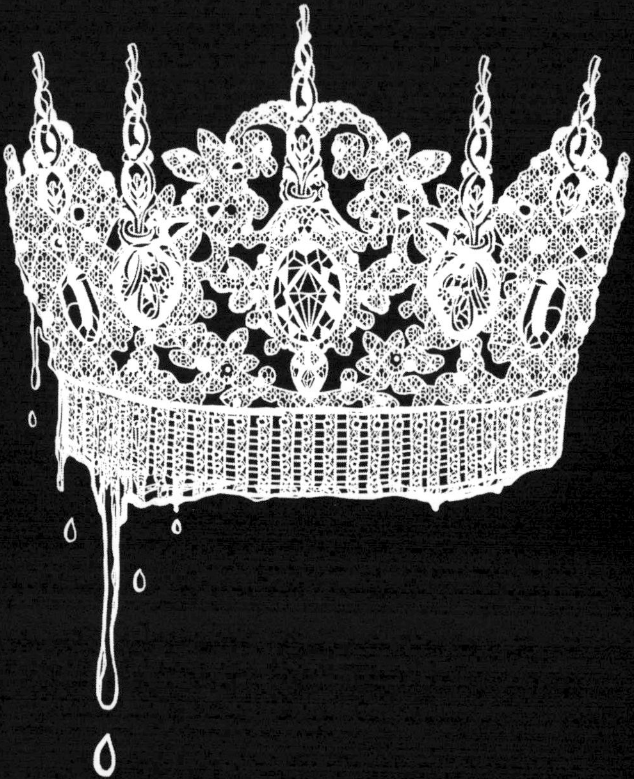

Chapter Ten

I start to think that Harley might gouge Luca's eyes out if he doesn't stop looking at Lips.

There isn't anything left to happen after the Wolf declares them all members of the Twelve, and we should be able to immediately move back to our cars and get the hell out of this haunted forest, but there's a tenseness in the air as the other, older members of the Twelve stare down the new members.

Aodhan shifts to cover me fully, surprisingly sharing a look with Ash as they both watch Luca speak to Lips quietly. Blaise is grinding his teeth and Harley is vibrating with anger, but none of us can hear exactly what's being said, only catching a glimpse of the savage look on Lips' face as she gives him a curt nod before stalking back over to us.

"We're done here. Let's get out of here and find somewhere to grab a drink."

I nod and step around Aodhan to link our arms together, knowing that this is a code for something else because we're not the sort to hang around down here in the city without a reason. Harley stays where he is for a second, staring Luca down with all of the pent-up rage he's had for him since day one. He might've held it all back for the greater good, but nothing triggers my cousin quite like someone staring too long at his little Mounty.

I'm very interested to know what's going on here.

We make it to the cars and Harley throws Aodhan the keys to my Rolls Royce and stalks over to climb into the Escalade with his little foursome of debauchery. Jackson climbs into Luca's car and they disappear down the dirt road until they're nothing but tail lights.

We're almost out of there after them, then Lucy steps up behind us, her motorcycle helmet in her hands already. We all pause for a second, the memories of Aodhan declaring his allegiance to Harley and killing his family in this exact spot drifting around us all. Lucy looks over to me, and then I watch as she draws herself up to face Lips as though she's facing her worst nightmare.

What the hell is going on here?

"I have a gift for you... one that you'll need to accept in person. I have it ready and waiting down at the docks near the Butcher's warehouse. I wanted to give you a sign of my appreciation for giving me the opportunity to sit at the table of the Twelve when no one else would."

Lips stares at her for a second, weighing her words and the look of her standing there shaking in her fucking boots. This can't be the same girl who ripped out a man's throat and felt his blood and life pour down her face and body only a few months ago.

"Sure. We'll follow you out," Lips says and then stands there until Lucy nods and walks over to her bike.

Are we about to walk into a trap?

She glances at me for a second and then turns to Ash, stepping up close to his body and murmuring, "I'm riding with Aves, meet us down there?"

He glances at Aodhan and then nods slowly. Harley slams his way into the Escalade, but Morrison walks over to join Lips in the backseat of the Rolls Royce, checking all of his guns on the way in an obvious retaliation to Ash's snarking.

Aodhan shakes his head at them, but none of us say a word until the car is started and we're following the lights of Lucy's motorcycle down the road.

"We're about to kill the newest member of the Twelve, aren't we?" Blaise says with a smirk, reaching out to grab Lips' hand across the seat.

I turn to shoot a look at him. "Probably, do you have a problem with that?"

He smirks at me, looking over at Lips with utter adoration. "I didn't think we'd be signing up for another bullshit Game this soon, but why the fuck not?"

I roll my eyes at him, because he's not the one organizing and attending them all so his opinion means nothing to me right now, but Lips is staring out of the window with a frown.

"What are you thinking, Lips? How are we doing this?" I say, and she hums under her breath a little.

"I can't figure it out. She was a great choice for you guys, didn't suck up or anything, but she proved herself. What is her deal with me? I've never met her, not that I can remember anyway. There has to be something and it's fucking annoying to not know it… and have no time to figure it out."

Aodhan pulls the car out onto the highway and checks his mirrors to be sure that the others are following us. "Right, so what's the plan? It's looking like one girl against the whole lot of us, but I'm sure this is an ambush."

I scowl at the road ahead of us, my phone back in my hand as I drum my fingers against the screen. "It can't be an ambush. She has no one, her family all hate her, and she has no real connections in the Bay. The few friends she has aren't notable. It can't be an ambush."

Lips shrugs in the back. "She might've cut a deal with someone without us knowing. There's a million fucking things it could be. We're just going to have to go in expecting the worst. We're all armed, covered in bulletproof vests, and we're together. We'll be fine."

I don't like walking into things unprepared like this, it feels like high school all over again, and I spend the rest of the drive on my phone looking for any signs that Lucy is about to throw a world of bloodshed and pain our way.

There's nothing.

Lips taps away on her phone too, and if I didn't already know that she's keeping in touch with Ash and Harley about our plans, then Ash's text with a list of demands to stay behind Morrison at all times is a dead giveaway.

Lucy drives past the turn off for Illi's warehouse but takes the next street so we're within spitting distance of him, Odie, and the baby. That makes me nervous as well for some reason, because if anything happens here, this close to them, I will rain hell down on every last Mounty in this stupid fucking city.

I share a look with Aodhan when he kills the engine and he murmurs, "Stay there. Let me and the other two check the place out first while you and Lips hang tight with Morrison."

Lips raises an eyebrow at him and he smirks at her. "We both know Harley and Ash will back me on this plan, just let us have a look before you two go in there and destroy this girl."

Ash pulls the Escalade in after us, and immediately he and Harley both get out, barely waiting for Aodhan before they stalk over to where Lucy is waiting. She glances at the car for a second and then shrugs, leading them into the old, rundown building.

Less than three minutes later, Harley walks out by himself.

"What the fuck is going on?" Lips mumbles as she climbs out, not waiting for him to cross the parking lot toward us.

Morrison curses and tears out of the car after her, glancing back as though he's keeping an eye on me as well, it's that same protective nature he's always had over me. I make things easier for him by getting out and following them over to Harley, sliding my phone into my pocket and running my hand over my gun again just to calm my nerves.

Harley waits for me to reach them and then says, "Well, it's not a fucking ambush. I'm not sure what the fuck it is except... she really does have a gift for you, babe."

Lips scowls at him. "What type of gift? Fuck, this is insane."

He blows out a breath and glances over his shoulder at the warehouse again as though he's waiting for a monster to come running out. "She's brought you someone from the murder board... he's not exactly in one piece."

What the hell?

I step forward so I'm at Lips' side. "Lead the way."

The guys flank us both, Harley's hand still resting on his gun, and we get inside the warehouse. It's built the same way Illi's warehouse would have been originally before he gutted it and built his apartment, but that only makes it creepier.

When we make it to the center of the room, right where the staircase is in Illi's place, there's a panel of the roofing tin that's fallen through leaning against one of the beams and obscuring the view a little, but when we get around it, sure enough, there's a man strapped to a chair there, a gag in his mouth.

Holden Crawford has seen better days.

I pinch my nose, the stink of him absolutely vile, and I want nothing more than to spin around and run out of here screaming at the sight of him. His feet are bare and blackened, his toenails have fallen off, and the bare part of his calves are purplish too. The veins bulging out of his neck are that same color, but it's his eyes that are the worst.

There's *stuff* oozing out of them.

I don't know what bodily fluid to even attempt to name it, but my stomach roils the moment I see it. It's disgusting. Utterly fucking disgusting, and there isn't a shower hot enough or long enough to get this out of my skin.

I'm burning *everything* I'm wearing the second I get home.

Lucy clears her throat, drawing our stunned and horrified gazes away from Holden. "He's dead. You can check it if you want, but I dealt with him tonight before the Game. I was going to leave him for later but… this seemed like the right way for him to die."

We all stare at his body for a second longer, as if he's going to lurch back up and take a swing at one of us, but there's no coming back from a death like that.

Lips is frowning at the corpse and, probably, at the why of it all. I understand the sentiment entirely because I am too. None of this makes sense. Except then Lucy speaks again.

"I met your brother. I was there when he killed my aunt."

Oh.

Oh *shit*.

Lips' face shuts down, we've been so careful not to let anyone know about her connection to Nate and now here Lucy is, already knowing everything about it. Aodhan glances down at me but keeps his face blank.

Lucy nods and glances around at each of us, choosing her cryptic words with care. "It was the most terrifying thing, but I spoke to him for a second, nothing major. When I met you, I realized... everything. It all came together. I knew then that the little show of loyalty I gave Queen Crow and the Butcher wasn't going to cut it. I still don't want in your family, I'd never assume to be added into that kind of thing, but—consider this a show of my allegiance. I'm not going to side against your bloodline, fuck, *his* bloodline. Not ever."

Lips stares her down for a second longer before she nods slowly. "That's a smart move. You're going to make it on the Twelve if you're thinking like that."

Lucy flushes a little at the compliment and then kicks at the corpse with the pointed toe of her shoe. "He deserved worse. You don't grow up around here without being able to spot this type from a mile away, but I made it as painful as I could. He was sniffing around after you all, asking too many questions down here so I assumed he was on your list."

Lips looks down at him for a second before nodding back to her. "You did good. You'll be a powerful ally and, where possible, we'll side with you too. Don't hesitate to call, Scorpion."

She gives us a sharp nod and walks out of the warehouse, climbing onto her motorcycle and taking off into the city right as the sun begins to rise.

Lucy leaves us with the corpse.

We already have Bingley on ice just in case we need his body for... well, honestly, I don't know what we'd need his body for but Luca had insisted, so I'd waved a hand in his direction so he'd deal with it before I puked all over the carpet at the thought of it.

"Another fucking popsicle, this is getting out of hand," Harley mumbles the moment Lucy is gone, and Morrison digs an elbow into his gut in retaliation.

Aodhan glances around the room, for what I'm not sure, and then he strips out of his jacket. "Is the clean-up kit still in the Escalade or am I calling into Illi's place?"

My eyebrows hit my hairline, but Harley grunts out an affirmative noise and heads back out of the room.

I'd very much like to leave as well.

There's a tense moment, then Lips turns to Aodhan. "We all agreed to not talk about my brother, but I don't want Avery to be put in a shitty position of lying to you later."

He shrugs and rolls up his sleeves, completely ready to help move Holden, and I've never been so horrified and impressed with my choice in man before. "I'm good. I'm aware you're protecting kids from Grimm and, as long as Avery is safe, it's none of my business who you share DNA with."

Lips shrugs and says, "I'm not talking about it here, there's no telling what ears are around, but if you ask me back at the ranch, I'll tell you."

Harley arrives with a black plastic tub filled with all sorts of supplies, including a body bag. I'm sure Illi was the one to provide them with that, but when he passes a pair of gloves to Morrison, I watch as the spoiled rich kid in him rears its head.

"Listen, I'm going to need Illi to get the *fuck* off of paternity leave right the *fuck* now, because I'm not doing any rotting corpse disposal."

Lips huffs at him, but Morrison waves a hand at her dismissively. "Look, Star, you need me to kill someone? I'm in. Theft, racketeering, blackmail, debauchery? Sign me the fuck up, but this? No. I'm not built for this. Who can I write a check to so I don't have to do this? Aves, let me walk you and Star out of here while the others sort it out."

Harley cusses him out and Ash has to get between them pretty quickly, but I keep my lips pressed tightly together, because there's no way that I'm helping with that corpse unless there's no other options here. I don't have a leg to stand on.

I would rather it be my rotting corpse, thank you very much.

It doesn't matter anyway, Aodhan is quick to help out and between the three of them, it's an easy enough job. Morrison turns green when it becomes clear that Holden is *leaking*, and Lips grabs an elbow on each of us to march us both out.

I vomit behind a bush.

Lips rubs a hand over my back and finds me a bottle of

water to wash my mouth out, but I decide that tonight is fucking cursed. Cursed!

The moment I have my stomach under control again, I tuck myself back into the Rolls Royce, my eyes on my phone so I don't have to watch them all drag the body bag out and stuff it into the back of the Escalade.

Morrison slides into the front seat, murmuring to me, "O'Cronin thought it was better if he has a bleach bath before he gets within three feet of you again."

"And that's why I love him. Next time Ash gets pissy over him again, remind him of this."

He chuckles under his breath, messing around with the radio station until something he likes comes on. "Lips already did. She's been quietly waging war with him for months over it, even while we were away. She loves you just as much as you love her, y'know?"

I smile, happy that he noticed, and say, "Illi's not going to be back at work for a while, by the way. I offered to babysit Johnny, but I don't think either of them are ready to leave him anywhere yet, not even with us. We're all going to have to pitch in and get our hands dirty."

He nods and gets us out onto the highway again, the sky a bright mix of all of the colors of dawn. "I wasn't lying, I'm not going to back down on anything except leaking fucking corpses. I don't think that's a bad thing, one of us has to stay human around here. Besides, are you going to touch him? Nope, didn't think so. Not unless your life depended on it, and I guess I'm the same, because that shit is fucking rank."

It is and I don't blame him, it's just good to check in sometimes.

We're quiet the rest of the way home, Morrison humming softly under his breath every now and then. I check over the security footage of Atticus' hospital room and pray that this isn't going to blow up in our faces.

Queen Crow

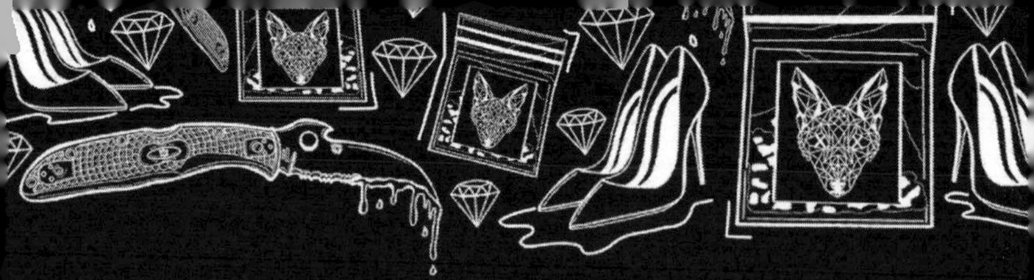

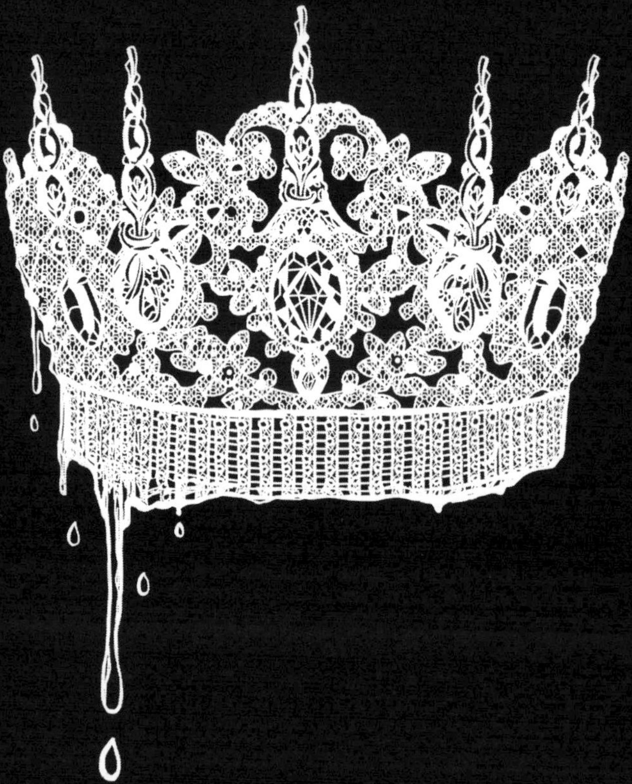

Chapter Eleven

Atticus

The beeping is constant.

Even before I have the energy to open my eyes, it's the first thing I become aware of. The next thing is the constant hum of machines and talking and life around me, everything is still ticking along even though I can't fucking move. I don't know how long I'm stuck like that, drifting in and out of awareness, but eventually my eyes actually open when I command them to.

Ash Beaumont is sitting at my bedside.

He isn't my first choice of people to wake up to, he doesn't even make it into the top five, but at least I'm not dead.

I have very patchy ideas of where I am and how I got here. I have no sense of how much time has passed, or what has happened since I've been out.

My last memories come flooding back into me as Ash leans forward in the seat, his eyes critical as he takes in the damage the bullet to my chest did.

Avery.

Avery was taken, locked in a glass cage, and fought her way out of there because there's never going to be a cage that could contain her, and then I got to her. The bulletproof vest. The call of everything being clear and then the gunshot.

Avery.

"She's alive. She's alive and well. I can already see you freaking the fuck out about her. It's a very distinct look you get and it's at least half of the reason I fucking loathe you."

I can't move anything except my eyes, glancing around the room again before I take him in properly. He's dressed casually in a pair of dark jeans and biker boots, a band tee with Morrison's tattooed face on it, and a leather jacket slung over his shoulders—he looks like a very polished version of a Mounty kid. All of his time with Lips and the other degenerates is rubbing off on him.

These little pieces of information mean nothing right now because I'm completely at his mercy.

If he wanted to kill me now, there's no stopping him.

His eyes are the same shade of blue as Avery's, but the icy-cold edge of them cuts into me the second he flicks them back over to me, his casual derision an insult to even the strongest man. "You have always been everything to her. I hate it. I hate that you're a Crawford and you have that sort of hold over her. If I could burn you out from under her skin, I'd do it. If there was any way to get rid of you without hurting her, it would already be done."

I barely have control over my eyelids, there's no way I'm going to be able to answer him, to tell him of all of the ways that I would destroy myself rather than hurt her.

Except I have hurt her.

I have and I just keep on hurting her with all of the ways that she grew up differently than I ever expected. Better, because this girl isn't some pretty little society girl. No, she's become the greatest asset any man in our world could ever ask for.

The Stag saw it and took her for himself.

"I thought she moved on from you. I wasn't happy with her choice, but an O'Cronin is a better option than a fucking Crawford. Except he's willing to share her, he knows that part of her will always belong to you and he doesn't want to break her. He was man enough to come and face me, none of this sneaking around and building fucking slum empires as though I'll be impressed by it."

He leans forward in his chair a little more, his voice dropping down lower as though he's telling me some great secret, "How does it feel to know that with all of your advantages, all of the money and connections you walked into the Bay with, that a little girl with nothing is more respected than you? To know that the Wolf is the one who came out of the war with the Jackal with the respect and fear of the Bay, and it's not you? Because I've watched them all, you know. I've spent all of that time in those stupid fucking meetings you insist on having, and they all watch her. The ones worth something, anyway. If you got unplugged from this machine and died right now, nothing would change in the Bay. The Wolf would still reign supreme, with Avery at her side."

I already know this.

The Wolf always did play the game of the Bay better than anyone else, she could walk the line between cold-hearted killer and merciful crime lord better than anyone I've ever seen. She built a web of loyal spies and contacts faster than anyone else on the Twelve through nothing but hard work and that very special brand of integrity of hers.

It's all of the reasons I let her live when she arrived at Hannaford Prep.

There's another beat of silence and then he stands, stepping around the seat with one parting statement, "My sister will be here soon to fawn over you. Make your decision about her and follow through with it, because if it drags on much longer, I'll slit your fucking throat."

He gets to the doorway and I force my voice to work, the thready tones and gasping are shameful as hell but I need to know. "Is this... your approval?"

He scoffs. "Over my dead fucking body will I ever approve. This is me saying that I love my sister enough to let her live her own life, and I will be watching your every move. At the first sign of you betraying her, I'll make Nate look fucking normal. I promise you that, Crawford."

It's a huge claim but if anyone were to turn into a monster for his sister, it'd be Ash Beaumont.

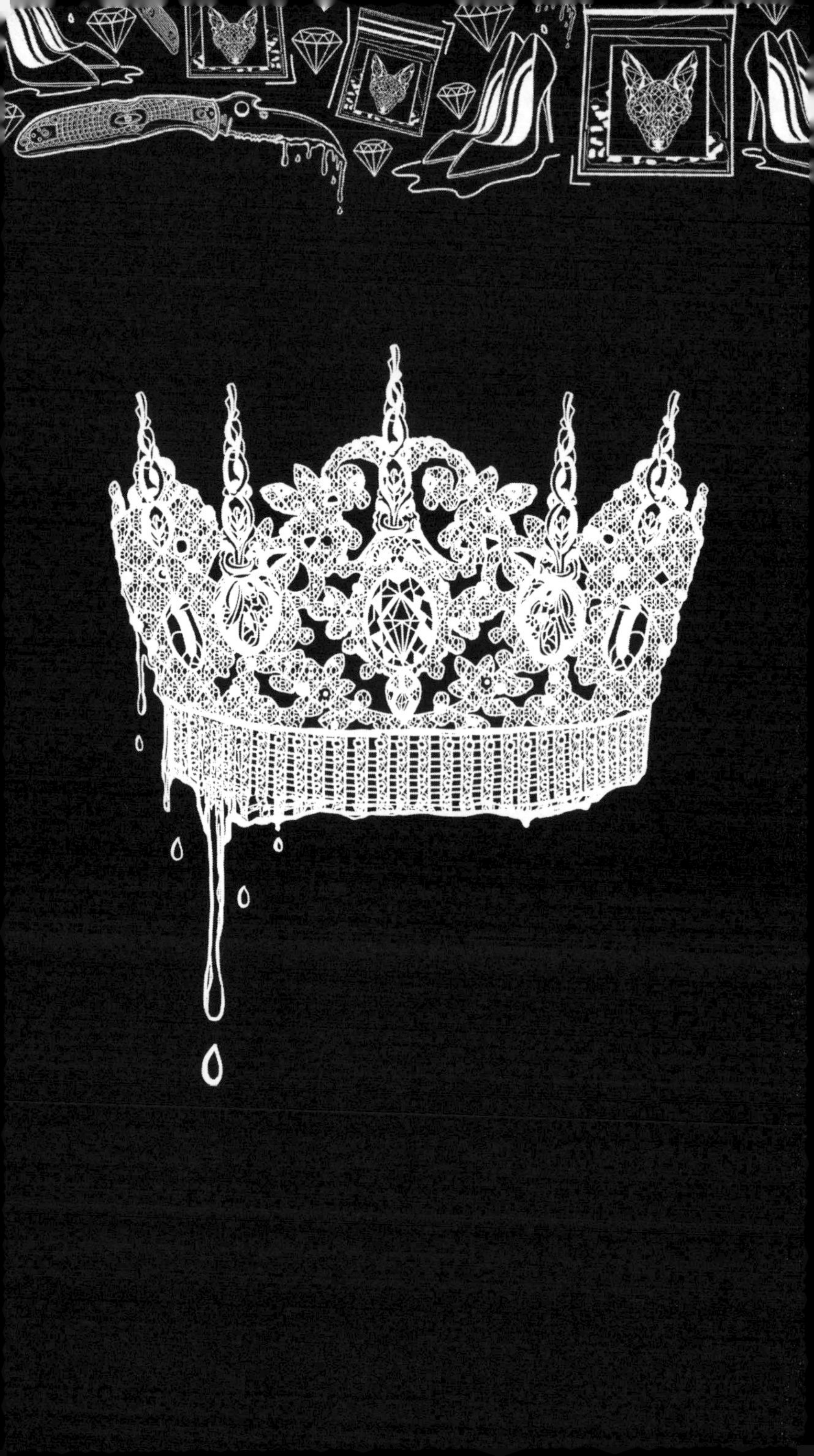

Chapter Twelve

Avery

Two weeks after Holden's death, Atticus wakes up.

He wakes up without me around because that's just who he is as a person. He couldn't possibly wait for me to be there, no, he just does his own thing. It's fine.

It takes him a full day to be able to speak to me, and then he is furious when I won't talk to him about how things are going in the Bay beyond, 'I'm handling it.'

He can't sit up without help and a lot of pain—there's no way I'm telling him about his brothers or Amanda's escalation. I'm also just a little bit terrified to speak to him about *us*, so I just keep my mouth shut for now.

Instead, I fuss over him and watch every little movement in the room as he recovers. He passes every test the doctors throw at him with flying colors, as though he hadn't just spent weeks in a coma. I spend days there in the room with him, working on my phone while he grunts and snarls at every little thing the nurses force him to do. I sleep on a chair in the corner for three nights before Aodhan comes looking for me and demands I go home to rest in a real bed.

Atticus looks at him as though he's a murderer, here to kill us both and wear our skin as suits, but I ignore it, kissing him on the cheek and heading home obediently with my Irishman.

I still check the security cameras obsessively, but knowing that he's alive is all I need right now. I don't need to think about the mess that our relationship is or all of the questions that are still unanswered, all that matters is that he's alive for those conversations to happen.

When I arrive back to see him the next morning, Luca is already there and there's a laptop on the table, both of them murmuring and planning together. I want to do some murdering of my own because he's supposed to be resting, but instead I flag down a nurse to get a report of how the tests are going.

There's been some concern about his heart and lung function that I've done enough reading on overnight that I'm practically an expert on the subject now.

The moment I have his notes in my hand, I dismiss the nurse and level Luca with my most icy glare. "He's resting. Anything you have can either wait or come to me."

Luca grins at me, shrugging casually. "I'm only giving him the small jobs. I haven't told him any of the good stuff yet, I thought I'd save it for you."

I eye him, his casual attempts at charming me aren't going to work, but at least I can look at him without wanting to scream and cry now, so... baby steps. "How very kind of you. Did he congratulate you on your seat at the fabled table of the Twelve yet? Did the two of you pick out your name together or was it a nice surprise?"

Atticus gives me another sour look but I grin back at him, unrepentant to the end. Luca glances between us both and then closes the laptop between them. "There's a gala Atticus was supposed to attend tonight. There's at least three notable figures due to be there that we were hoping to meet with."

I shrug. "You're the Eagle now, I'm sure that'll be enough to appease them."

"When I told them he was unavailable, they requested you by name... Queen Crow, specifically. What went down at that Twelve meeting has gotten around, they want to deal with you."

My eyebrows hit my hairline and I immediately look over at Atticus as though Luca is lying to me but he just grimaces at me. "Of course they want to speak with you. You have proven yourself and you're the one with all of the Twelve's ears. There isn't a single member who would deny you a thing... not even the ones who hate you because it would be a direct insult to the Wolf. Even without our alliance, I wouldn't piss you off either."

Oh.

Oh, I *like* that.

There isn't a thing about this that feels insulting because *of course* Lips would deal with anyone who dared to say no to me. Of course she would, the exact same way I'd destroy the city for her on a whim.

Having people realize this and take note of it though? I like it a lot. There's something about leaving the snake pits of high school and moving into the real world that has you floundering for a minute, figuring out how to be a whole person in a much bigger pond and finally, *finally*, it's coming together.

I smirk at them both and I'm sure my eyes are dazzling with unreleased glee. "I'll attend on your behalf. I have the perfect gown for it already."

Every inch of my outfit is a very careful choice, ones that I made with Lips over a coffee and plate of pastries while all of the men in the house slept in. It's floor length even with my new Louboutins, one of the requirements of this event, and strapless, lacing up at the back.

It's also black.

I have forest green diamonds in my ears, a halo setting with smaller diamonds surrounding them, but I also felt wrong without some sort of nod to Aodhan in the moment. The entire outfit is a statement, a very clear sign of my allegiance for the evening, and Lips grins at me when I finally walk down the stairs to meet with her.

She's wearing black as well.

I already know that Ash helped her pick out her outfit, the lace is an obvious tell, but the slit up her thigh that makes underwear impossible to wear with it is also a huge indicator.

The heels she's in are probably going to land her in hospital with a broken neck, but Harley has a strong arm around her waist and a very smug grin on his face.

When I raise an eyebrow at him, he smirks and drawls, "All I have to do is put on a monkey suit and I get to spend the night with my girl wrapped around me looking like that? There's no downsides here."

Lips elbows him and snarks, "That's until we get stuck talking to some rich asshole with a stick up his ass while he leers at my tits. We're the slum kids walking into rich dickhead territory, remember?"

He scowls at her and snaps, "Anyone looking at your tits is going to die tonight. That's all I've got to say about that, babe. Besides, we're there to keep Floss safe, we don't have to talk to anyone. Aodhan's the sucker who's gonna have to get social."

As if called, the front door opens and Aodhan steps in, already wearing the stunning Tom Ford that I had tailored for him. He looks amazing, smells divine, and when he very carefully kisses me so he doesn't smudge my makeup, I want to eat him alive.

"Gross. Fuck, I'm not gonna get used to seeing that shit," Harley snarks, and I roll my eyes at him.

"Try living in a house full of you all pawing at each other!

It's fucking disgusting," Noah snarks, stomping past us all on his way over to the kitchen to make a mess in there, I'm sure. I don't understand how there's always crumbs everywhere. What does he do in there to make such a fucking mess?!

Ash follows him down, scowling like he's about to destroy something, and Morrison laughs as he trails after him, a bottle of whiskey in his hand and a dumb grin on his face as he leers at Lips.

I'm surprised they aren't dressed to come with us and I share a look with Lips over it.

Aodhan shakes his head at Noah and then side-eyes Lips hard. "The Bay isn't big enough for all that fucking attitude, does he have any idea of who he's snapping at?"

She shrugs. "He doesn't give a fuck. I'll sort him out eventually. He either learns how to shut the fuck up and follow instructions, or he goes back to Wyatt's basement."

Ash snarls something and Noah is off, running down the hallway as though the hounds of hell are chasing him. I raise an eyebrow at him and he snaps, "It's bad enough that I'm stuck here with him tonight, I don't need to be dealing with his pissy mood too."

I fuss with my purse for a second, checking it for everything I need. "Why are you babysitting him? We've left him here before and, other than the fucking crumbs, it wasn't a disaster."

Ash kisses Lips with too much tongue and a complete disregard for her lipstick, and Harley huffs at me. "Oh, you mean that time that Jackson called us to say that the little fuck had taken the bus for a joyride to try and find some weed because he'd made it through Blaise's stash and wanted more? Yeah, he needs a fucking babysitter now. I'm not sure he's figured out what 'in hiding' really means, the fucking dumbass."

It's all too confusing for one evening and I shake my head at the lot of them. "Shall we head off, then? It's been too long since I had people shaking at my feet and the sadist in me craves it."

Aodhan chuckles at me, tucking me into his side carefully as we walk out to the sounds of Harley mumbling, "Fucking Beaumonts."

The gala is being held in one of the oldest and grandest ballrooms in the country, that also happens to be an hour's drive from Mounts Bay. I let Harley sit in the front with Aodhan so they can talk all about their favorite topics of cars and family politics while I sit with Lips in the back and work on more important things.

Like telling her to stop fussing with the lace neckline of her dress so she doesn't stretch it.

"I feel like I'm being strangled, what is your obsession with going to these things? Gimme a lingerie party at the docks any day of the fucking week."

Aodhan's head snaps around. "You guys went to that? Jesus fucking Christ."

Lips blushes and shoots Harley a scathing look at his very self-satisfied smirk and I attempt to keep the details to myself, even though this is prime shit-talking material in our family.

"We all went. Harley and Ash had a point to prove with the Jackal and certainly got it across. It was a very... exposing night for us all."

Lips groans and slaps a hand over her face. "Stop. Honestly, it's fucking weird enough that you were there, we don't need to talk about it all over again."

Harley throws back his head and roars with laughter, that infectious joy of his, and Aodhan meets my eyes in the rear view mirror. I shrug at him. "Lips will throw herself into oncoming traffic if we talk about it too much, she's very shy about all of the public sex acts she keeps getting talked into."

"Fuck this," Lips mutters, trying the door handle like she's actually feeling like throwing herself out.

When the guys get lost in conversation again, I check the security footage of Atticus again, just to ensure he's still in his bed resting like he's supposed to be, and when I'm satisfied he's not going anywhere, I glance back over to find Lips on her phone.

"Everything okay?" I murmur, a gentle prod to see if she's working on anything that needs my assistance.

She blows out a breath and murmurs back to me, so quietly that I can barely hear it over the guys talking, "Colt is in trouble. Chance too. I'm trying to figure out a plan out for them both but it's… fuck, it's nearly impossible. I'm sending Harbin out to meet them and arrange a meeting, but Chance is twitchy as fuck and, fuck, Aves, everything to do with the MC is a mess."

I nod slowly.

I've been ready for this, for the inevitability of her blood relations causing her stress and heartache, but meeting Colt has made me also feel responsible for him.

He was trying to get Poe clear of Grimm. That makes him one of the good guys.

"What can I do? Name it and it's done, Lips. We're in this together, your family is mine too."

She smiles at me, her eyes still sad, and the strain there is heartbreaking to me. We're supposed to be in the clear now, goddammit. She was supposed to come home to a city that had been wiped clean for her.

She waits until the guys are loudly arguing over something pointless before she says, "Grimm is trying to kill him. He's put in safeguards to make sure Colt couldn't just kill him and take his place. There's rats in with the Unseen, the Serpents—he's like fucking poison spreading everywhere. I can't let them die, Aves. This is my chance to have siblings and… Colt doesn't deserve this shit. He's got a girlfriend. A *pregnant* girlfriend."

Jesus.

Okay, new priorities.

It's not a huge shift, we already knew that Grimm and the Graves kids would have to be sorted out at some point. We might've been monitoring them for Poe, but Lips was always going to be hopeful to get to know them.

We need a plan.

"Tomorrow. We'll get up and start a plan for them all. We can do this, Lips. We can get him out of there alive."

When the car pulls up to the ballroom, I look around at the exterior of the building with disinterest. If you've been to one of these things, you've been to them all. There are screens set up everywhere with reels of dresses and fake smiling faces showing on them. As much as I love looking a certain way and finding all of the best fashion, this feels so empty to me.

Aodhan parks the car himself, not trusting the valet at all, then comes to open my car door for me. The predatory look in his eyes is perfect, the exact reason I went with the strapless option, because there's something he loves so desperately about the exposed skin of my shoulders.

I'm sure it's all of the dirty thoughts of marking me up, biting and grazing with teeth until everyone knows just how good he's fucked me into my sheets.

I grin back at him like the lovesick idiot I am.

It almost feels like a double date as we walk down the path and up the grand steps to the front entrance together. Never mind the fact that I have a list of men to speak to about business with the Crow, because Harley and Aodhan are doting and loving to us both, and Lips blushes enough that it really looks like a sweet little getaway for us all.

When we get up to the doors, the screens all turn black at once.

There's a moment where I immediately think we're about to be murdered, a spray of bullets into the crowd and good night for us all, but then the video starts.

The video.

My eyes squeeze shut as I clench my jaw tight, desperate to keep the bile creeping up my throat from coming out.

Oh God.

There's sound too.

I don't care that there are people standing around everywhere waiting to get in, looking and watching and seeing this nightmare happen to me, my hands cover my ears to attempt to block out the sounds because this is my worst fucking nightmare all over again.

The Jackal's taunts.

Aodhan telling me to sit back down, the cavalry's here.

My snapping retort, the grunting, the straining, every little part of that moment is playing on dozens and dozens of screens around the ballroom.

And then it's not.

Hands cover my own, a low and raspy murmuring instantly has my heartbeat slowing because even if my mind is gone, my body knows that Lips is safety, love, and family.

"Head back to the car, Aves. I've got this under control."

Aodhan bundles me into the car, snapping at Harley in his

rage, but Lips is already up the staircase, her back straight as she stalks through the crowds. They can't know who she is, there's no indication on her that she's the Wolf, but instincts have them scrambling out of her way anyway.

Harley's hulking frame charging in after her probably helps with that.

"Thank God Ash wasn't here," I mumble, and Aodhan threads our fingers together.

"I'm getting pretty fucking tired of that tape being used against you, Queenie. Whatever your plans are to deal with Amanda, we're moving on it *now*."

I want to agree with him but that's not how this life goes.

No matter how badly we want it to.

Queen Crow

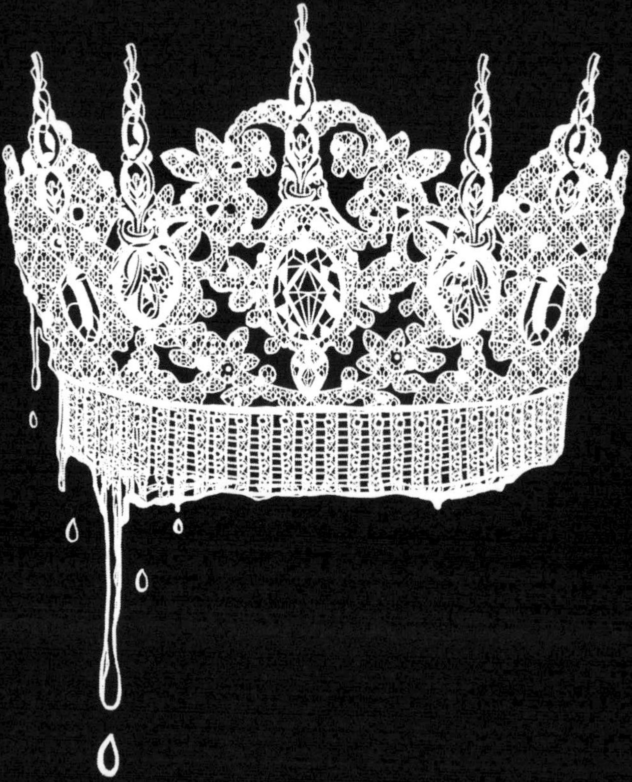

Chapter Thirteen

Lips must've called Ash to warn him about what had happened, so when we arrive home, he meets me at the door. I'm shaken but ready to throw myself between him and Aodhan the second the inevitable fighting starts up, so I'm shocked when he just steps forward and wraps me into his arms.

"It wasn't the edited one this time around. It was the original," Aodhan says, and I press my face into Ash's chest a little harder.

Harley steps up behind us and snaps, "With fucking sound too! There's a whole new layer of 'no fucking thanks' to the entire situation. Lips dealt with it."

Ash tenses and then curses, and I pull out of his arms a little to glance at whatever has upset him.

Lips is covered in blood.

The black fabric hides most of it but there's droplets and smudges on her cheeks. I can smell it now and, God, I must have been out of my mind completely to not notice it in the small confines of the car. I glance down and there's a smudge of red on my hand from where she'd held it on the way back.

When I glance back up at her, she cringes at it. "Sorry. I tried to warn you, but you weren't yourself. I thought it was better to give you comfort until we could get you a shower. I'll—I need to get your car cleaned too. Sorry, Aves."

I shake my head at her and then shock everyone when I lurch over to her and hug her tightly, blood be damned.

I hate it, I hate everything about the blood, but there's never been a time that this girl has let me down. Not once in our years of friendship, and once again, she's here, doing her best for me and apologizing for her trauma-inducing methods.

I'm a different girl now.

I can hate this and still function now.

"I love you. Fuck the car, I'll get a new one. Do we need a cleanup crew? What… what can I do?"

She shakes her head as she hugs me back even tighter. "I'm good. I already called it in and got it taken care of. Let's just get Amanda six feet under and then move the fuck on from some stupid tape. You hear me, Aves? Stop freaking out about something we all know about. I don't give a fuck what you did back then. You're alive, you're whole, and Aodhan is fine too. Who the fuck cares about any other part of it? Not me. Not Ash, not Harley, Blaise, Illi, Odie, no one. No one cares."

I swallow roughly but no one argues with her, no one starts yelling or fighting over it. No one tells her she's wrong and that

I was a monster.

I want to cry all over again but for very different reasons.

"C'mon, Queenie, you look like a fucking bloodbath yourself. Shower and get something fucking strong to drink," Aodhan murmurs, prying me away from Lips with a look over our shoulders at Harley.

He's already worked out their secret language, speaking with nothing but a look and some eyebrow action, and he directs me back into the house.

It's like the final exoneration.

No one cares about what happened.

Aodhan immediately steers me upstairs, waiting until the bedroom door is locked behind us before he strips the dress off of me and throws it into the trash for me.

"Such a fucking waste," he mumbles as he slowly slips my lingerie off as well, his fingers slow but respectful of the fact that I cannot think about anything even remotely sexual until I'm clean.

Someday that might change, but today is not that day.

When I step into my shower, I get the water as hot as Aodhan will allow it to be, grabbing the soap and attempting to be subtle about how much I'm scouring away at myself. There's not a lot of blood and it only takes a minute to get it off, the rest is just the act of scrubbing the night away.

Scrubbing the shame of the tape away one last time, because it no longer owns me.

"I will tan your ass if you keep that up, Queenie. We've talked about this."

I roll my eyes at him and then smile playfully. "Instead of just standing around critiquing me, you could come help out."

He doesn't need any more encouragement, the suit sliding off of him faster than lightning, and I giggle when he throws it dramatically in the direction of the bin as well.

"The suit is fine, no need to throw it out."

He huffs and steps into the shower with me, both hands cupping my face and bringing me in for a wet and slippery kiss. "The suit makes me look like something I'm not. I'll play that part for you, but it ain't me, Queenie. Fucking you against the glass in here is more my speed."

And then he makes good on his word.

His hands are everywhere on my body, in a rush to touch everything, fingers tweaking and pulling at my nipples, and he's groaning into my mouth as his hips jerk and rub his dick against the soft skin of my belly.

When one of his hands slips down to my pussy, I gasp into our kiss, desperate to come, but also needing more right now from him than just this. More than the firm and gentle ways he gives me pleasure.

I want more.

I slide down his body until I'm on my knees at his feet, his hand fisting in my hair as he guides my mouth down the length of his cock, his hips thrusting as he grunts like a dying man.

There's something so powerful about having him at my mercy like this, the ways that I control his pleasure even with his hand guiding my head.

I draw it out, teasing him and lapping at the head of his cock until his legs are shaking. It's like I'm taking back the night on my own terms, and when he jerks my head back to stop me, I grin up at him.

"You enjoying yourself down there? Teasing me with that mouth of yours, I should cash in my offer of anything I want."

I swallow, excited but with a little edge of dread in there too, but before I can ask for some details on what exactly it is that he wants, he grabs my arms to haul me back up onto my feet, spinning me around to push me against the glass.

The way he moves me allows my brain to just shut down, to let him take over for a little while and just enjoy the ride. He presses a hand against my back to bend me over, my hands bracing against the glass as he kicks my legs open wider before I rub his dick against the seam of my ass.

I feel very unprepared for anal but, again, he moves too quickly for words as he shifts and plunges his cock deep into my pussy. I moan so loud that the neighbors probably hear it, and he chuckles at me, his hips shifting and grinding into me slowly.

He's the expert at finding my G-spot at this point, shifting us little by little until he hits it, his cock dragging over it again and again, and another low moan tears out of my chest. He rubs my ass with one hand, murmuring in a soft rasp, "That's my girl."

My legs shake so badly when I come that I think I'm going to collapse, but his hands band around my hips to keep me upright, and he steps forward to press me fully into the glass again and the cold is like a slap against my sensitive body.

"Come again, Queenie. Come one more time for me."

His hips slow down again, a slow drag of his cock inside me, but it feels like fucking heaven against my oversensitive pussy. When he's sure my legs are steady again, he leans back and messes around with something on my shower caddy.

I'm too busy chasing after my next orgasm to take notice, my eyes shut and my own hand on my clit, circling around it in the most overstimulating, delicious torture.

Then I feel the slick, cold slide of lotion against my back and Aodhan's hand rubbing it in, and I sigh. He's too fucking good to me as he massages the tense muscles there, his hips still pumping slowly into me.

When he works his way down to the globes of my ass, his fingers dig in as I come again, my pussy gripping his cock and milking it.

"On your knees, Queenie. Open up wide."

I drop back down, not at all graceful or ladylike, and when he shoves his cock back in my mouth, I swallow around it until he's shooting down my throat.

I arrive at the hospital two days later to find Atticus dressed and perched on the seat in the corner of the room. He looks very gray. His suit, his shoes, even his face as he swallows roughly, every part of him looks absolutely lifeless.

I want to scream but I keep my tone as level as I can. "Why are you doing this? There is absolutely no reason you need to leave here today. You have the best doctors and nurses in the country looking after you. I know for sure because I spent days vetting them all and then watching them take care of you."

He doesn't reply, instead he takes a deep breath and then bends down to finish tying his shoes.

It takes every inch of my control to stop myself from walking the four steps it would take to reach him and punch him in the throat for not just letting me help him.

Typical male bullshit.

"You're not going back to your house like this. I highly doubt you'd let Luca help you with anything in your current state, let alone one of your staff. You've barely let the nurses touch you. This is utterly ridiculous."

He ignores me, his eyes shuttering closed as he sits back up and takes some slow, deep breaths. He looks exhausted and half dead, the panic in me that had dropped back to a simmer flares back to life at the sight of him.

Why am I doomed to deal with stupid, proud men who can't admit when they desperately need help?

"You're coming back to the ranch with me for a few days to get your strength back and then you can head home to pretend

I don't exist all over again."

I can't help but get the little dig in and his teeth clench, his words ground out from between them, "You want me to go back to your place to share a bed with the Stag? No, I won't be doing that."

My eyes roll upward as I talk myself down from the ledge, I'm starting to understand my best friend's dramatics at men now. "No one said anything about the two of you climbing into bed together. He's actually on a job and won't be around for a few days, but even if he was still in the Bay, I would want you to come home with me. He understands that."

He scoffs at me, his hand trembling just a little as he shakes it out, another sign that he's nowhere near ready to be leaving this hospital room. "I'm glad your boyfriend is so *understanding* of your other affections."

That's about all I can take of this pity party.

I step forward and grab his chin, something he's done to me a lot in the last year, and pull his head up so he's looking at me. "Don't you dare treat me like that, Atticus Crawford. Don't you dare treat me like some harlot for finding someone else while you were so busy with your secrets that you couldn't even tell me what was going on. Aodhan is understanding. He gets that he's got my heart just as much as you do. You're the one who won't compromise here, not us."

His eyes are the same steely gray that slices me open until I'm bleeding out everywhere. "That's not how the real world works, Avery. You can't have everything you want."

My eyes narrow at him, disregarding the fact that he looks like death, because he's being impossible. I understand on a cultural level that these sorts of relationships aren't the norm, but I've also never given a *fuck* about what any level of society thinks of me… only my family.

It's my greatest shield.

I've used that sort of public shaming to manipulate and blackmail, I've used it to fill my black book up with hundreds of names, and I will never leave myself open to that sort of attack. The fact that the stupid tape keeps showing up isn't about everyone else, it's about all of the people I love who will be hurt and disgusted by what happened.

I couldn't give less of a fuck about anyone else.

I lean forward until our faces are close again, his eyes closing at the feel of my breath fanning on his cheek. "Why not? Why shouldn't I have every single thing that I want? You told me you wanted to give me the world. Well, this is the world that I want to have, the only one I'll accept. Give it to me."

"Avery—"

"No. It's that simple, Atticus. I want it, I've never wanted anything more in my life. Give it to me."

He doesn't.

He doesn't utter a word to me… nothing.

Silence falls over the hospital room again and I refuse to let him know just how much this is killing me, just how deeply he's shattering my soul right now.

I've said all I can. There's no argument left to make, so I step away from him and turn back to the bed to fold up the small pile of his clothes there. It'll all be getting washed at my house, but my hands need something to do. I get everything packed away and then lift them from the bed. It's not heavy, even with the laptop bag in my other hand.

I glance around the room to ensure we're not leaving anything behind and even though I can feel his gaze on me, a hot and possessive branding, I don't attempt to catch his eye.

I need to get him tucked into a bed back at the ranch and then I need to call Lips to drink our body weight in cocktails together, enough that I can forget all about this shit entirely.

A nurse steps into the room with discharge papers and Atticus turns his glare on her, terrifying the poor woman. I want to snap at him and remind him that she's been the one here giving him drugs and cleaning up after him for weeks. She's a goddamn saint in my eyes and doesn't deserve his pissed off mood.

When it becomes clear that he's not going to help her out, I take the papers and sign them for him. "You've all done an amazing job. We're very grateful for everything you've done."

She smiles back at me, taking the papers and making herself scarce. I make a note to bump her bonus money up, throw in a little extra for her for dealing with us without snapping back.

When I turn back to Atticus to ream him a little for his poor attitude, he pulls himself to his feet, his teeth clenching together, and my heart skips a beat. He's standing for the first time since the bullet ripped through him.

Okay, he's wearing clothes so obviously he's been on his feet already and that statement isn't entirely accurate but still, every fiber of my being is so grateful for this moment.

Even if he has chosen not to have me under my terms.

I grab the bags again, offering him my arm in case he's too unsteady on his feet, which he stares at like I'm insulting him greatly. It's stupid and I'll bitch him out for the rest of time if he ends up on his ass.

When we get out to the hallway, his men all fall into formation around us without a word, their relief at seeing him up and about is palpable. He might not count them as friends or more than employees, but he has their respect.

We enter the elevator with three of them, the others waiting for the next one, and we make our way out of the hospital without any troubles or resistance. Atticus is sweating by the time I help him into my Rolls Royce. I pack the bags into the trunk and then I direct his men to meet us at the ranch to take up a security detail there for the next few days.

When I slide into the driver's seat, I'm so busy categorizing and planning out what needs to be done that I almost miss his words, quietly muttered under his breath.

"I'm marrying you. You'll carry my last name, not his."

I freeze and there's a sort of careful silence for a second

because this is as close to an agreement as I've ever gotten from him. He stares over at me with his head pressed back into the seat, still as angry as ever, but there's a resigned air about him.

I have to give myself another second before I speak because I don't want him to see just how relieved and happy I am. "I will have a conversation with Aodhan about it, but I'm sure we can reach an agreement."

His eyes drift shut for the rest of the drive home and I try not to wake him up with my glee.

Queen Crow

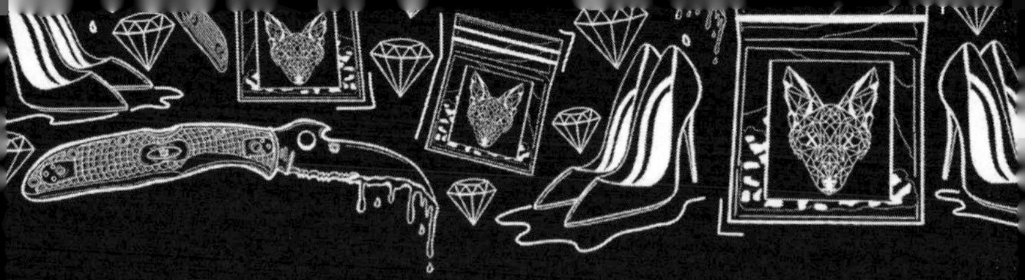

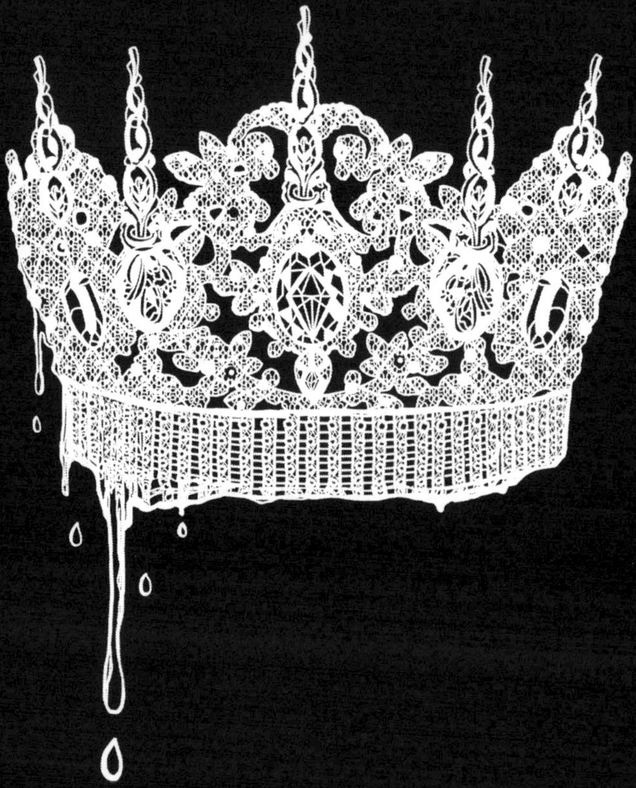

Chapter Fourteen

I get Atticus settled into my room at the ranch and even though he snarls and rages about it, I spend most of my time watching him sleep. I suddenly have a much better appreciation for how Lips reacted when Harley was drugged back in high school and spent some time in a hospital.

She'd followed him around and bugged the hell out of him for days, watching all of the food he ate and every move he made, just to be sure that he wasn't about to drop dead on her.

I would also like to monitor Atticus' every move for the rest of our lives.

One of the many amazing things about having the Wolf of Mounts Bay as your best friend and partner in all nefarious things is that while I'm fussing with Atticus and his savage mood, Lips goes on the warpath for Amanda Donnelley. She locks herself down in my panic room with nothing but coffee and a variety of snacks until she's read every little thing that Jackson gave us on the bitch. She texts me things as she finds them, little coded snippets of information that she thinks might be helpful, until finally she messages with with, 'Got her.'

I'm busy trying to stop Atticus from going home when it comes through and when I squeal happily, he drops his sour attitude for a half a minute to ask, "What's happened? Avery, what is it?"

I tug the blankets back up his chest, ignoring his snapping. "That was the sound of victory. If you promise to stay here for the rest of the week, I'll tell you what we've won... when it's done."

He's less happy about that option.

When I sneak back downstairs to put together a tray of lunch for us both, Lips meets me there, slapping Noah on the back of the head as we pass him when she sees the mess he's made of my pastries drawer. I'm too happy about *finally* dealing with Amanda to care too much.

"So? Tell me. I need to gloat over whatever you have on her."

She chuckles under her breath and grabs a broom to sweep up her brother's mess. "She's a traitorous bitch. The big and bad she's held over the Crawfords' heads to keep herself safe? Yeah, the bitch has been selling out her own blood and we're going to drown her in it."

Victory has never tasted so sweet before.

"How's grumpy-ass Crawford doing up there? Do you need me to kill him yet? Knock him out a little?"

I laugh at her. "A light stabbing, maybe? You always did say you could do it without permanent damage."

She finishes up with the floors and then starts wiping down the countertops. "And I stand by that. I could definitely bleed him out some for you."

I finish up with the cheese and meat selections on the tray, thanking Lips for cleaning up after her idiot brother, and then I go back up to my room to force feed Atticus.

"If this is about Amanda or my father, you need to tell me about it," he says, accepting a plate from me with only a slight grimace as the movement pulls on his chest.

I take one of my own and start piling on all of my favorite cheeses. This is the perfect light lunch and while the heathens in my family might not appreciate it, there's a very arrogant and spoiled part of Atticus that does.

"Your informants differ greatly from the Wolf's, did you know that? Not just who they are, but what they know... their loyalty, what they have access to. There are many things that Lips can find out that you just can't."

He raises an eyebrow at me. "You're really not going to tell me? Is this some sort of punishment for the times I've kept you out of business for your own safety?"

I roll my eyes and lean back in the seat I'm perched on, my phone is buzzing in my pocket and I answer as I dig it out, "I don't believe in punishments, Atticus, but I do see some validity to your methods. You're being kept out of this for your own safety. Your only job right now is to heal and be well enough to deal with your own interests again because if I have to listen to the Viper whine about his stupid fights one more time, I will have us running the Game again, and *no one* wants that."

There's a message from Lips waiting for me, just informing me that she's already reached out to her contacts about getting a meeting with Santiago Arias set up. Efficient, effective, and with zero attitude. Eclipse Anderson is my soulmate, and it's a tragedy that we're stuck pining after all of these stupid men.

"If you don't believe in punishments, then why are you sitting all the way over there? Is this the world you really wanted, one where you're bossing me around and keeping yourself as far away from me as possible?"

I drop my phone back down into my lap as I look him over. His words are delivered in a very even tone, no signs of a sullen undertone, and his face is passive. I see through it now, it's a whole new side of him I've never been allowed to witness.

The side where he wants me enough to let me in.

I stand up and move the chair back into the corner, ducking into my closet to find something more comfortable to lie around in. "Is that why you're being a nightmare? I thought it was pride, but really it's just… sulking? Lord have mercy."

He scowls at me but when I climb up onto the bed with him, his arms open for me to lie with him. I try not to lean on his chest, which pisses him off, but when we've wrestled a little, we find a spot we're both comfortable in, wrapped up in each other.

He mumbles into my hair, "I've spent a week with you trying to be as close to me as possible without actually touching me. It has definitely felt like torture, especially after you told me just how much you wanted me."

I sigh back, burrowing deeper into his arms. "I thought you were dead. Luca had to yell at me to move off of you because I thought I was crying over your corpse. I'm trying not to coddle you, but you don't know how that felt, what that did to me."

He pulls me into his body tighter, gasping a little at the pulling against his chest again but I let him, mostly because I know there's no use fighting him.

This is where I belong.

I decide to only take Ash with me on the cross-country flight to New York to meet with the Colombian cartel.

Lips was obviously my first choice, but there's no way we could've taken the flight with just the two of us, there's no way our family would let us go alone, and I need someone to stay with Atticus until he can get dressed without having to sit down halfway through the experience to catch his breath from the pain.

Aodhan is still busy on his trip to sort out the dock issues, so my next choice is to take Ash. He's not happy about leaving Lips behind, but he also trusts Morrison and Harley to keep an eye on her, so we take the Beaumont private jet and enjoy a quiet flight together like old times.

Except without Joey we do actually enjoy it.

The car that Arias sends to pick us up from the airport is manned by two heavily armed men who walk around the city as though no one will care that they're carrying enough ammunition to take out a mall full of people.

Ash doesn't react to them at all, his entire body is casual and carefree as he helps me into the car and then settles in after me. I keep my phone in my pocket and my eyes on the streets as we drive, confident in everything that we have prepared for today's meeting. Lips and I have spent too much time prepping together for this and she's back at home right now dealing with more than enough bullshit.

All I have to do is meet with this man.

It's nothing really.

We're driven for over an hour through the streets of the city until we arrive at the harbor full of million-dollar yachts and catamarans. There could easily be a billion dollars' worth of vessels here, all of them with full-time staff members and the annual spending of a small country in upkeep.

"We need a boat."

Ash follows my gaze to the catamaran on the end with the hammocks on the front. I can see him imagining Lips lounging there in some tiny bikini, it's easy to spot with the unchecked lust filling his eyes. "Get one then, but you should check that no one in the family gets seasick first. It might ruin the getaway if our friends are puking off of the sides while we're trying to anchor for the night."

It's a possibility.

I start to have my own little fantasies of fucking Atticus on one of those hammocks too, or riding Aodhan's cock on the main deck under the night's sky, and it's all very enticing.

Also a complete dream because there's no way that I could get them both on the boat at the same time… or get Ash to disappear for long enough for me to fuck them in all of the places I want to fuck them.

I still want a boat though.

The car pulls up and parks in front of the yacht at the end. It's a super yacht, the biggest one here, and I immediately want it. There's some Spanish words on the side of it, I memorize them to Google later, but no nuclear weapons are strapped to the side or any other warning signs.

I'm not stupid.

I know there's a danger to being here, I'm well aware that we're here to meet with a Colombian drug lord and that he could murder us both without any repercussions.

I also know the information we've sent ahead of ourselves will buy us enough time to convince him not to kill us.

"This is it. Señor Arias will see you here," the driver says, and the guy in the front seat chuckles like they really think we're children here to die for stumbling into something much bigger than we are.

Typical.

I wait for Ash to get my door for me, taking his arm when he offers it because the dock is slippery underfoot. Both of the men make faces at his chivalry, joking in rapid Spanish with each other as they lead the way.

We walk up the ramps and board the super yacht, finding the main deck full of more armed men standing alongside the crew and watching us like we're prey.

If there is anyone on this Earth with an icy cold poker face as good as my own, it's Ash. I watch as they all size him up in that ultra-masculine and completely bullshit way that all gangsters have, their chests puffed out and hips tilted like they want you to think their dicks are huge.

Ash doesn't flinch or react, the aloof and bored look still fixed to his face, and when he undoes one of his suit jacket buttons to comfortably slide his free hand into his pocket, their eyes all drop to the guns strapped in holsters at his waist.

There's three others hidden expertly on his body, thanks to Lips and Illi's fussing before we'd left.

I also have quite the arsenal strapped to me and, once again, I'm wearing bulletproof body armor under my sleek white coat. The wind here is cold enough that it doesn't look out of place and, paired with the right shoes, I just look like a wealthy socialite out for a nice stroll on a friend's super yacht.

It's all about smoke and mirrors.

"This way, Miss Beaumont. It's been some time since we've

enjoyed the company of a Beaumont onboard. Your father was once a very welcome guest," the captain says, his lips turned down in disapproval, so it's very clear that Senior did something to get himself removed from the guest list.

I wonder if it was murder or fucking the Señor's daughter?

I smile prettily and thank him anyway, playing along perfectly. Ash remains very calm and stoic. Whatever conversations Lips has been having with him, they're working, and I owe her something magnificent for them.

We're led through a grand dining room with chandeliers overhead and fine china on the tables, regardless of the lack of patrons sitting down to eat. There's only one occupied table at the end of the room and there's no doubt in my mind of which one Santiago Arias is.

He's sitting in the center of the table with a cigar in between two of his fingers, old and faded tattoos on display on his arms and even some visible curling up his chest, thanks to all of the open buttons on his white dress shirt. He's older than I was expecting, older than Senior was, and when he smirks at us, there's a gold tooth shining in his mouth.

He's not as clean cut as I was imagining. Even as a cartel boss, to rub shoulders with the level of society that he does, I was expecting more from him.

I'm oddly disappointed.

"You look too much like your bastard father! I was willing to meet with you just for the chance to tell you he's a cunt and I'm glad to see him dead."

His accent is strong but his English is very good; he's spent a lot of time in the country. I gesture at the seats on this side of the table as though asking if we can join them as I reply, "I'm very aware of his failings and I was very glad when my dear friend decided to pay him a visit."

Arias eyes us both for a moment longer before flicking his wrist at us to sit down. "I heard rumors that you paid the Wolf to do it. I did not think she worked for free."

He knows nothing about her because she mostly works for favors, only taking money when she needed it for school and, later, for Harley.

"She is a close friend, we do many things for one another. Including coming here to speak with you."

He brings the cigar to his lips and takes a puff, blowing the smoke in our direction without any attempts at civility or respect. I hate men like this more than most, but I keep my face clear.

Ash does too.

"You let her fuck your brother, eh? Is he the price you pay? Your father did always say he belonged to you, disgusting for men to act this way."

I look over at Ash as though I'm considering his words and then I turn back to him. "If my brother chooses to crawl into bed with the greatest assassin the Bay has ever produced, then that's his business. Did you also pay that price to my father? Let him fuck your daughter for… what was your business with him?

I can't imagine he was a good man to have around."

His lip curls and I enjoy it a little too much, almost forgetting that I'm here to impress this man and get something from him, not tear him to pieces verbally because he's a complete misogynist.

"He was useful for a time. You could be too but I think you'd break too easily. Little girls do not belong here, Beaumont. Little girls belong with men who will fuck this sort of ambition out of them."

Gross.

I incline my head to him. "I've found one of those already, but thank you for your concern. Should we move on to the real reason we're here today? Because I don't want to take up any more time than we have to."

He takes a drink from the glass in front of him, not offering us anything, and then he shrugs at me. "I looked over what your little friend sent me. There is a spy amongst my men. I will have it handled. Rule number one of business is not to give anything away for free. You need to work on that, little girl, because I have nothing to give you."

Ah, of course.

When *don't* these men resort to infantilizing me? "You mistake me, I'm not here to do business or ask for your help. I am more than capable of taking care of the problem. I'm here to see if you are going to be my next issue to deal with once this one has been moved from my planner."

The cigar burns in his fingers as though he's forgotten about it, the smoke curling up toward the ceiling and I force my eyes not to stare at the large brown patch up there from his disgusting habit, the only sign in this stunning room that a cartel owns it and does business here. His fingers are stained as well, filthy under the countless rings with giant precious rocks in them.

He's old and fat, tattooed and balding, a plethora of things that seem completely unrealistic for a Colombian cartel to be.

I pull my phone out of my pocket, moving slowly so they can all see exactly what I'm doing. I use the phone number Jackson had given me for Arias and send through the security footage Lips had found of Amanda Donnelley snitching on her father to the FBI.

Complete with subtitles and timestamps.

I glance over at Ash to check in with him as we sit through Arias watching it. His fingers tighten on his phone and his mouth pulls into a tight line.

"I think you've been protecting a daughter of your own out of loyalty... loyalty she doesn't share with you. As I said, I want nothing from you. I'm going to deal with your daughter for another error of judgment she's made, and if you understand how things work, you'll stay away from the Bay. You'll accept someone else doing your dirty work for you because there is a lot of chaos that my family can bring to you if you don't."

He starts the video over again as the door at the far end of the room opens and one of his men calls out in Spanish, but I catch a name. Nicolás.

Arias looks up immediately, waving them into the room, and I catch a little more of his words and their meaning. His son is here. Ash's eyes stay on Arias, but I glance over my shoulder to get a look at him.

He's a child.

Barely a teenager, he's that gangly sort of tall where it's clear he hasn't figured out how to operate all of his limbs properly yet. His father watches him with a possessive sort of pride. This is his son and his legacy, a boy who was never given a choice about who he is destined to become.

There's a fear in him as his father addresses him, one that Ash and I know intimately as the children of Joseph Beaumont Sr. I realize that if I were a normal human, it would be appropriate to feel some empathy, to wish that this teenage boy wasn't living in this way and to want to do something about it.

If there's one thing you could never call me, it's normal.

I smooth a hand down the rich silk of my coat to remove the creases, enjoying the feel of the luxurious fabric under my fingers. It's an old habit of self-soothing, something I can do that doesn't look nervous to anyone around me, but gives my brain a great dose of dopamine all the same.

I'm perfectly put together. I look as though I'm here to make a deal they wouldn't ever dare to back out of. I look exactly the way I should for this moment.

"Daughters can have uses. Sons are better though, they

have a lot more to offer a father." He grins at me and shrugs. "No hard feelings, Queen Crow, but I'm sure your father felt the same way."

Finally, a reaction from Ash as his eyes narrow just a little, but I don't need him running to my defense here. This kind of verbal sparring is what I truly excel at, what my entire childhood was training me for.

"It doesn't really matter what my father wants, he's rotting in a hole somewhere right now. You're right to look the other way here because sons will always look back on their fathers and crave their approval, hoping that they can live up to some ridiculous standard that was set for them."

I stand up and smooth down my skirt, taking the arm Ash holds out to help me out of this stupid room on this awful yacht.

"What about daughters then, Queen Crow? What's your assessment there?" he calls out to me.

I pause long enough to turn back and say, "All daughters know what their fathers are capable of and we don't just sit around, waiting to be found redundant. We wait and we plan, until we're ready to strike. I came here to get rid of Amanda and in doing so, I have saved your life. Remember this life debt you owe me. I'll be calling it in soon."

Queen Crow

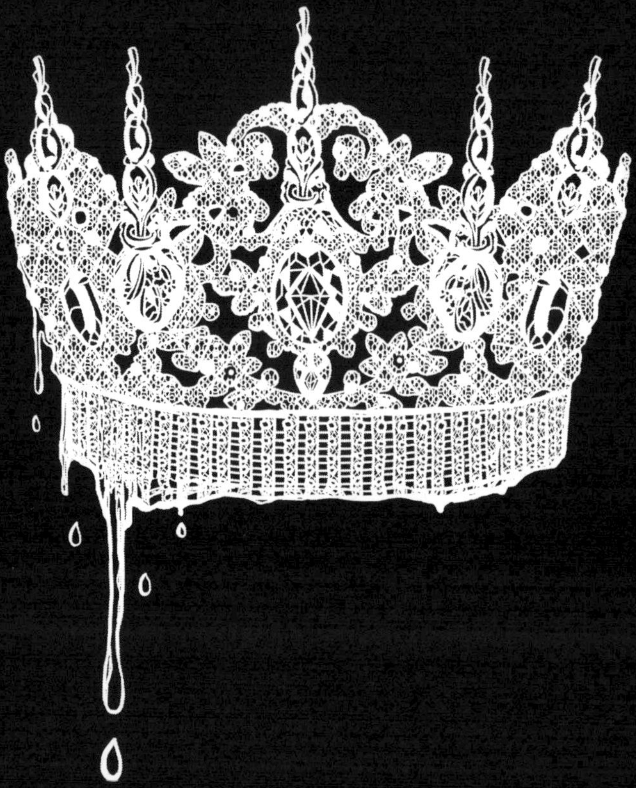

Chapter Fifteen

When we arrive home from New York, we find Aodhan home from his trip to sort the problems at the docks out, already down in my panic room with everyone, and I mean everyone.

Atticus is on the couch, scowling like a surly asshole, but when I start down the stairs and he moves like he's going to get up, Lips points a finger at him and snaps, "You're already on thin fucking ice, Crawford. I will put you down if I have to and we both know I'll enjoy every second of it."

Harley and Aodhan snicker together like children while Morrison roars with laughter, all of them a little too comfortable together for my liking.

Noah rolls his eyes from where he's starfished out on the floor in front of the Graves section of the wall, staring up at his siblings with a very blank face.

When I get to the bottom of the stairs, Aodhan steps over to give me a quick kiss, ignoring Ash's derisive noises in his direction.

"How was the flight?"

I shrug. "Uneventful. How was your trip? Did you figure out the cargo issues?"

Harley scoffs and flings an arm at the wall. "If by 'figuring it out' you mean finding more shit for us to sift through, then yeah, he did a great fucking job."

I want to sigh and possibly scream until my lungs give out, because when am I ever going to clear something off of this freaking board without ten more things being added?

I hold it in. I might end up with a fucking stomach ulcer, but I hold it all in. I give Aodhan's hand a squeeze and then step around him for the coffee machine, thankful there's one down here. "Right, what is it? Just tell me now so that I can figure out where on the planner it goes."

Aodhan glares at Harley and snaps, "It doesn't have to go on your planner, I'm sorting it out with Lips. It's a Graves issue and you've got enough going on."

I pour a large cup, the largest one I can find, and then perch on the couch next to Atticus, checking him out from the corner of my eye so he doesn't get pissed off that I'm fussing again. He doesn't attempt to kiss me in front of everyone, but I'm willing to take the baby steps with him.

When I offer him my coffee, he takes it, taking a sip and handing it back.

Again, it feels like a win.

Lips sits down near Noah, pulling one leg up to her chest,

and says, "Aves is never going to just take the sidelines. Grimm is smuggling through the docks. Half of the cargo down there has shit in it for him and the Demons. Aodhan noticed shit was wrong, and between the two of us, we figured out who it belongs to. So… either the Boar has no idea and there's some MC members pulling this shit without his knowledge, or he's betraying his own club. I spoke to Harbin about it… he gave me the long and very blood-soaked history between the Demons and the Unseen. There's no possible explanation for them to be smuggling for Grimm."

Harley scoffs again. "The explanation is that your uncle is a cunt, exactly what we've thought all along. Call Nate and get the fucker dead already."

I don't like how casually he says that, especially since I haven't warned Aodhan about him. If he finds out right now, in this room, I might kill Harley for his big fat mouth.

Noah blinks slowly, glancing over his shoulder. "Uncle? What's his name?"

Lips chews her lip and stares at him for a second. I get it, it's the first time he's shown any interest in any of the family and that in itself feels suspicious.

"Daniel. Poe calls him Uncle Danny, it's fucking weird."

Noah pulls himself up so he's sitting with her, propped up on his arms as he leans over. "Uncle Danny. You trust him? You guys are friends with him?"

There's a moment of silence because every person in this

room has an opinion on the Boar and I'm not sure any of them line up fully, but I'm interested to see what Lips tells him.

I should've known she would only ever go with blunt honesty with him.

"No, we don't trust him. He knew who I was related to for a very long time before he ever told me. He watched me starve and be abused for years without a word. I'm not sure whether he's evil or just a really shitty uncle."

He nods and looks up at the wall again. "Why isn't Poe up there? Where's the other brother?"

Atticus tenses next to me and I hand him the coffee cup again as a distraction. There's no way it'll actually distract him from this, but there's not much I'm working with here.

"Poe and Nate are both family. There's no need for them to be up there—we trust them. We know everything we need to about them, nothing else matters."

Noah nods and takes another second to look at each of the photos again, including the ones I'd been sent of Senator Blakeley and his kids with their eyes crossed out. "Whoever did that to the kids' photos needs to die. Bringing kids into this ain't right."

There it is. There's the little glimmer of hope that he's going to grow up a bit and turn out halfway decent.

I take the coffee back and grumble over the rim, "Agreed, but the senator could be knocked down a peg or two. Nothing serious, just a light maiming to shift his thinking a little."

Atticus scoffs at me. "Not a fan?"

Aodhan grimaces at him. "He was a complete fucking asshole to her, even after she saved his ass."

I shoot him a look because there's way too much testosterone and chaos in this room for him to be making those sorts of statements without thinking it through first. He smirks at me, completely unrepentant.

"I'll kill him. If he's going to talk to you like that, then what the fuck is he going to say to his little Mounty sister? Fuck that," Harley snaps, and I hold out a hand at him.

"He wasn't that bad and, besides, his problem with me was my assumed allegiance to Grimm. A man that high up in Congress that we could get on our side if we prove we're firmly anti-Grimm? That's too good of an opportunity."

Lips stares at me for a second and then nods slowly. "Plus, we need to think of the kids. We're not taking out a father just because he doesn't like his criminal bloodlines."

I nod, she's always far more pragmatic than anyone else, and I add, "He's a great father. He's surprisingly present for his kids, even with his aggressive political scheduling. I've trawled through his underwear drawer at this point, those kids know nothing in their lives but love and support."

Aodhan's eyes flick between us both before he says to Lips, almost hesitantly, "The kids both look like you, the girl especially. The pictures don't do it justice, she even moved like you. It was fucking weird."

Lips shrugs and glances at Noah again. "Maybe Jackson is right. Maybe Grimm really does have super-villain DNA. It would explain a lot."

When we finally leave the panic room to head back upstairs, I'm surprised to see how easily Atticus is moving now with only a few more days of rest here. I shoot Lips a look and she shrugs. "I let him roam around a bit while you were gone, maybe the movement helped him out."

Ash clearly doesn't want to look at or think about Atticus in any way and hauls Lips against his body, murmuring something in her ear that turns her eight shades of red as he drags her away from us in the direction of the pool.

I'm going to have to get it cleaned out again, goddamn him!

Aodhan stops me at the foyer to say goodbye, still completely unconcerned about the rest of the family around us, and kisses me like he's been poisoned and I'm hiding the antidote somewhere around my tonsils.

I don't hear anything else until he finally pulls away from me, smirking and biting his lip in a way that is far too tempting. My eyes are glued to it as he leans forward to whisper, "I have to make sure you still remember me now that he's been up there in your bed all week, Queenie."

My heart clenches in my chest and I whisper back, "There's no forgetting how much I love you. Once he's healed, we can…

work this out."

He grins at me and flicks the little caged diamonds around my neck. "I want a fifty-fifty share. Every other weekend, we can split the holidays."

I shove at him for the sass in his tone that's so unlike him, but he's an immovable wall when he wants to be, chuckling as he catches my hands and kisses me soundly on the lips again. "I love you too, Queenie. Don't worry about shit that doesn't fucking matter. I can see it all over you already and I'll see you after I'm done with this shit at the docks."

I press my lips together and wave him off, glad no one is here to see me holding back the tears at him leaving.

I need to get Atticus comfortable cohabiting with him right the hell now, before I become a basket case over it. I check the time and it's a little early for bed but there's nothing else I need to do, so I head up there anyway. Maybe it's the kisses from Aodhan, but I feel like I need to confirm that Atticus hasn't changed his mind.

That seeing it up close hasn't stopped him from wanting me.

I pass Noah on the stairs and I try not to get pissed about the bloodshot look of his eyes. I'm going to have to speak with Morrison about cutting down his supplies, he can't just spend all of his days here moping and high.

We already have one of those, I can't take two.

When I get to my room, Atticus is waiting in the armchair there, his shirt unbuttoned and a hand rubbing over the mottled scar tissue of his chest. It looks as though it should have killed him and, though I don't find it offensive, I glance away quickly.

I can't take any more panic right now.

"Are you feeling okay? Are you up to date with your medications? I should call the hospital, check in to see when you're next due for a checkup. We should pick out a physician too," I say, moving over to my closet and stepping into it without shutting the door.

I can practically hear his teeth grinding from here but that's kind of the point. Soon he'll be healed up and snarling demands at me for my own safety. I'm milking this moment for all it's worth because I'm also going to do everything in my power to ensure it never happens again.

I will wipe our enemies off of the board through whatever means necessary.

"Forget about it, I'm fine. There's more pressing issues that we need to talk about, Avery."

This is it.

This is where he ruins it all over again, I've been through this with him a dozen times already.

I slowly strip out of my jacket and blouse, standing in front of him in my favorite bralette. One of the many upsides of having a smaller cup size is how versatile the lingerie options are.

Lips struggles a little more.

His eyes don't drop down to the skin I'm revealing, which feels a little insulting but I don't let that show. "Like what? Which parts are so important that we need to talk about them right now instead of just enjoying each other for a minute?"

"Holden. Bingley. You running off to cut deals with Arias that will have Amanda gunning for us all."

I hold up my hand as I tick a finger off for each solution. "Holden is dead, thanks to Lucy's show of loyalty. He was a rapist piece of shit, so no skin off of our noses. Bingley is dead, thanks to the knife I pushed into his gut. Again, pedophile piece-of-shit rapist, so another job well done."

His jaw flexes and then he grinds out, "And Amanda?"

I smile at him as I unzip my skirt, letting it drop to the floor and leaving me standing there in a simple black thong. "She's a little tied up right now. So tied up that I don't need to think about her until tomorrow, when I've had enough sleep to look her in the face again. You should know me better than to think I'd just leave her to chance—she was dealt with before my plane landed in New York."

He stares me down for a minute and when it's clear he's fuming and not going to have any input any time soon, I bend over to pick up my skirt, folding it and stashing it away and when I step back into the room he's standing, stripping out of his button-up shirt efficiently.

He's still too injured for sex, I'm sure of it, but I wouldn't mind lying around with him for a few hours and enjoying being together. I'm a glutton for it now.

When he moves to drop the shirt down onto the seat, I head

for the bed, ready to lounge around and bicker over the deaths we have lined up a little more, but Atticus steps into my path.

He's spent too long stuck in a bed, so I've forgotten just how much bigger than me he is, his shoulders are close to twice the span of mine and when his hands come up to grasp them, there's a tiny moment of softness, his fingers caressing the skin there in a loving gesture.

His eyes are still hard and unforgiving.

"Atticus—" I start, but he swallows my words with a kiss, pushing me backward until he's pressing me into the mattress, following me down until his body is covering me.

I kiss him back, wriggling underneath him in an attempt for some friction, but with his legs on either side of mine and his chest pressed against mine, there's no room for me to move.

Then his hands take my wrists and pull them over my head, his weight on his knees so he doesn't crush me. I gasp for air, trying to force my brain to work, but he's unrelenting, using a low tone as he drawls at me, "Maybe once I'm done with you, you'll stop fussing after me as though I'm on death's fucking doorstep."

His fingers bite into my wrists from where he's holding them but I don't attempt to pull away because, for one, I don't want to hurt him.

I also desperately want him, however the hell I can have him.

When he fusses with my wrists for a second, I move a little

before he takes my lips again in an obvious distraction, but it really does work. His kiss is unforgiving, his teeth taking hold of my bottom lip and nipping it so sharply that I taste blood. My thighs clench at the pain, my brain is wired for the pain-pleasure and all of the blurring lines that he has for me.

I need him to fuck me so hard it hurts. I need him to want me so desperately that he's more beast than man, because that tight control he has feels like an insult right now.

When his hands come back down to stroke down my throat, I find that he's tied something around my wrists, effectively stopping me from fussing, or even being involved.

"I've had weeks of listening to your commands and being forced to submit to them. Avery, you're going to listen very carefully and do exactly what I say. Don't move. Don't say a word, unless it's begging for mercy or my name. Be a good girl and I'll let you come."

Somehow I've developed a praise kink and they've both figured it out. because even though his words are arrogant and entitled, I'm desperate for him to praise me, to think that I'm doing a good job.

It's a little terrifying to hand over that sort of control.

When I seal my lips shut and stare up at him obediently, he reaches over to my bedside table, takes my knife, the one that Lips got me, and unsheathes it. I swallow, but I trust him enough not to start screaming and thrashing around.

I can bleed a little, right? Right. It's fine.

He slices through the straps of my bralette, then through the center between the cups until it falls away from my body, my nipples already hard and straining for him as the adrenaline takes over my body. I feel as though I'm about to shake apart underneath him and he hasn't even touched me yet.

He puts the knife back, then strokes his fingers down my body intently, like he's looking for something. I'm not sure what, but there's a focus in him that is usually reserved for his business. The attention to details he shows while destroying men and their livelihoods is now aimed directly at me as he works his way down my belly before tugging my panties all the way down my legs. Instead of letting them drop to the bed, he loops them around my ankles, binding my legs together in a way that seems very counterproductive.

I keep these comments to myself.

He rewards me by kissing his way up my belly, stopping to lick and suck at each of my nipples as his fingers slip down to tease at my pussy. I let my eyes drift shut, holding in the moans and murmurs of pleasure I want to let out, and Atticus takes that as a challenge. His fingers drive me higher and higher until I come, the wet sounds of my pussy the only noise in the room.

My pussy is still throbbing around his fingers as he leans down and licks my clit, my legs are shaking as I try not to move and break his rules. I've never wanted to wrap them around his head so badly but there's something so addictive about his words, like a shot of dopamine directly to my brain.

Good girl.

He's merciless as he strokes my G-spot with his fingers, his tongue lapping at the juices sliding down my thighs before he works back up to my clit and he teases out an earth-shattering second orgasm, more intense than the first, and I scream until my ears are ringing.

With my eyes screwed shut this tightly, I can only tell where he's moving by the feel of his fingers slipping out of me and then his thighs moving slowly up my body until he's straddling my chest.

"Open up."

My mouth is falling open before the words are even out from between his lips, his cock sliding back deep into my throat as I swallow him down. There's no way for me to move or do anything but just take it as he fucks my face, hitting the back of my throat until tears stream down my face.

I fucking love it.

The sounds he makes go from controlled gasping to uncontrollable grunts and cursing, his hand gentle as he strokes my hair away from my face. I'm expecting him to come in my mouth, shooting down my throat and forcing me to swallow it all, but then he pulls back and tugs at the scarves around my wrists until there's just enough give for him to flip me over.

I want to complain about him doing too much, lifting me like he is, and I almost break, but then his words play over in my head and I clamp my lips shut again. He grabs a pillow to shove under my hips for a better angle and then my eyes squeeze shut as his cock slides into me.

The way my legs are bound together squeezes everything even tighter, until I feel as though I'm about to split apart. The feeling grows as he begins to move, the drags of his dick the most perfect torture. With every thrust of his hips he drives me into the pillow, my clit rubbing and grinding against the fabric until I'm coming again. My screams are muffled against my pillow as I break down into sobs, literally crying on his cock as he rides out his own orgasm, one hand on my back as he pushes my body down deeper into the mattress.

I'm grateful that I'm tied down because there's no way I can move and Atticus doesn't attempt it for a full minute, his breathing labored as he recovers.

When he finally loosens the scarves and lets my arms drop back down to the bed, I'm a mess. The wet spot is a lake and I have to crawl around it to where he's lying down to collapse in his arms.

I might die if the sex is always this brutal. I would die the happiest woman on Earth, but it'll be death all the same.

Atticus tucks me into his body, draping one of my arms over his chest and wrapping his arm around my shoulders. One of his hands comes up to touch my necklace, fingering the little cage as the diamonds clink together while it moves. My heart takes a second to slow down and return to its normal pattern.

"Where is it?" he mumbles into my skin, and I don't have to

ask him what he's talking about. Honestly, I thought he would've brought it up with me by now, it's been a miracle that he hasn't.

I pull away from him and walk over to the Monet on my wall. It's one of the very few indulgent purchases I've made, something I bought just to have because it's so expensive and rare.

I slide it to the side to reveal the safe there in the wall. It's an obvious spot for it but the MBPD hadn't found it when they'd trashed the place looking for Lauren.

It also only holds one thing.

I open it and pull out the small box Atticus had handed me on Christmas Day last year, trying not to let the emotion show on my face as I open it and stare down at the little black diamond there.

It's been cut into a heart.

"When I saw you wearing that little locket, I was furious. Enraged that once again, the Wolf was able to just have you on her side without repercussions, with only the Jackal giving a shit about it, and yet she handled him with ease. Everything I'd had to do to get you out of your father's house alive... all of it cost me you. I was jealous and couldn't stand that she had given you a favor as protection so easily."

I climb back into the bed to open the little cage up and add the diamond heart in with the others. All three of the members of the Twelve that I love, all of them hanging over my heart together.

He looks at it, running a finger down my collarbone gently until my body erupts in goosebumps. "If I would've befriended her… I would've gotten you and Ash out faster. I could've gotten you out of your father's house years before we did."

I hug one of my knees, resting my cheek on it in a very Lips sort of pose. "I don't blame you. I should've never put her through the hell I did in freshman year… I feel guilty about some of it now, even though I know we were testing each other. We wouldn't have been this close if we didn't, I'm sure of it, but there's still the guilt."

He leans back to look at the ceiling again, the mottled color of his chest stark in the low lighting. "I failed you. I failed your brother too. All I ever wanted to do was get you out and it took a little girl from the slums to get it done."

I reach out to trace one edge of the scar. I think I'm going to be obsessed with it for the rest of my life. "You can't be angry about not seeing through that. It's part of her superpower, no one ever expects her to be the most dangerous person in the room, and yet she is. Instead of being furious about it, just accept the past is done with. The Wolf is your ally, you're a part of the Family now and… I love you. We make our own choices from now on, together, and fuck everyone else. Stop playing other people's games and force them to play yours, Atticus."

Queen Crow

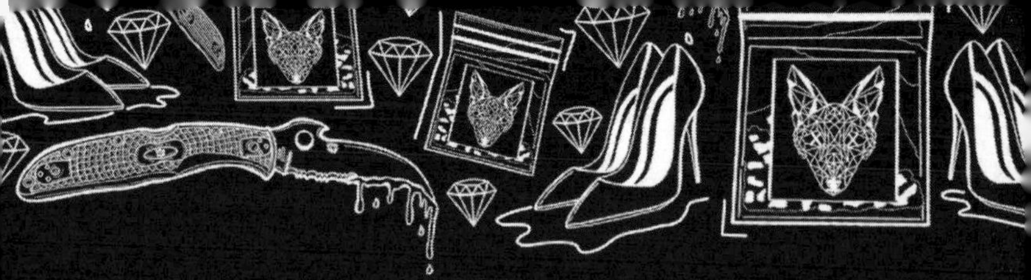

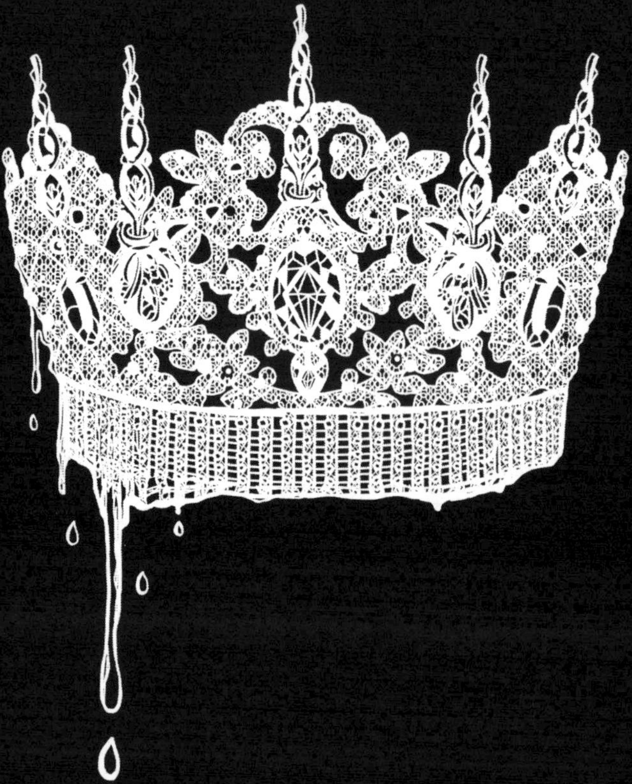

Chapter Sixteen

Atticus moves back out of the ranch the next day.

I'm fully prepared to have a mental breakdown over it, but I'm surprisingly calm as I help carry his things down to where Luca is waiting in the foyer, staring down the three idiots as they all glare daggers at him and make snide comments.

Lips is slightly more friendly about it, but she's still happily three feet away from him and draped in Harley's arms. I can't help but look between them after seeing the way he'd looked at her when she'd named him in the Game.

The guys all look like they want him bleeding out at her feet.

Atticus stops me at the steps and takes the laptop case from me, the only bag he'd allowed me to carry because his ego wouldn't let me touch anything else in his very manly presence. It's that old world gentleman in him, a complete departure from the man who was choking me with his cock only hours before.

I keep that to myself though, I'm sure our audience would have opinions on the matter if they heard about it.

"I'll deal with Holden and Bingley. I have access to some alternate disposal methods. It's best that Randy doesn't catch wind of this for as long as we can stretch it out."

I shrug and take his hand. "We already have him under control. I did have a question for you about him though… we've voted about how to deal with him, but Lips and I agree that you get a choice here. Do you want to kill him or are you open to the worst death possible for him? I vote worst death, and so did everyone else, but he's still your father. You're the one he hurt the most."

His eyes narrow at me and then flick back to where Lips is watching us both. "What exactly is the worst death? What danger does it put you in?"

I smile at him, the brightest one I can muster in an attempt to distract him a little. "None at all. Ash is home now, I'm barely allowed to leave the house for fear of splinters, didn't you know? I'm a damsel."

If his eyes narrowed any further, they'd be shut. "Avery, what have you done?"

"Nothing. I'm not involved with it at all. Lips came home and took over entirely. I swear."

He knows me too well and sighs at me, glancing over at Luca and directing him back to the car to give us some privacy. I'm not sure how their dynamic is going to change now that Luca has a seat at the table, but there's none I can see so far.

"The worst death possible. I don't need to be the one doing

it, I just need proof of death to be sure. Cutting the Jackal's head off was the smartest thing the Butcher has ever done because there's never been a doubt that he's really gone."

I nod, and with Noah wandering around my house right as we speak, it's not like we don't have evidence that deaths can, and do, get faked all of the time.

"We'll get the proof, don't worry about it. I'll see you at the meeting, we can have dinner afterward. We should just about be done with this mess by then."

He frowns at me again but then, with another sigh, he leans down to kiss me, one hand on my neck as he runs a finger down my pulse in his own little tic. A proof of life moment, a check that I am real and I'm here with him.

We're all a little damaged.

The moment his car disappears, Lips sidles up to me and jerks her head to the garage. "You ready to end this bitch? I thought he'd never fucking leave us to it."

I smirk at her and tuck our arms together as we walk. There's footsteps behind us but I always knew that the guys would be involved, so I don't bother to glance back at them.

The charred remains of the Mustang are littered around on the ground everywhere as we first step into the garage, but it only takes up two of the parking bays. There are dozens more, all of them containing Ash's collection. The custom Ferraris, the McLarens, the Porsche that he's trying out just for fun over some silly little comment Poe had made back in the hospital room when we'd met her—every part of this space is his pride and joy.

I was surprised when he'd offered to let Blaise build a soundproof room in the back for recording purposes, and I was even more shocked when Lips had told me that Morrison had helped her stash Amanda Donnelley in there after they'd hunted her down, killed all of her security, and dragged her back here.

It brings me so much joy to think that the fucking bitch had assumed she was safe from the Wolf, that no matter what the rumors said, there was no way Lips could actually get to her.

I never had a doubt in my mind.

Ash steps around us both and opens the door first, his gun in his hand in case she's managed to get out of her restraints overnight, but he drops his arm back down to his side and lets Lips slip past him once he's sure she's where he left her.

There is something truly satisfying about seeing her tied to the chair, a gag in her mouth as she screams and grunts while she throws herself around as madly as she can while being tied down. She's clearly gone off the deep end, because she doesn't acknowledge our arrival at all and her thrashing doesn't falter in the slightest.

I nudge Ash out of the way a little so I can step fully into the room. "I'd rather you not watch this. Lips is here; I'm safe."

He nods but doesn't step fully away, shutting the door behind me and then pressing his back against it. I shoot him a look but he waves me off without a word.

I'm not sure he'll be able to stop himself from interrupting the interrogation, especially not once he knows what I have planned for her at the end, but there's no real reason for me to stop him being here.

She sent him that tape.

He deserves some justice too, even if it's just being here to see her destruction.

When she finally stops thrashing around and notices the two of us, there's a glint in her eye, a little spark of hope that she'll be able to manipulate and talk her way out of this. She looks Ash over with that quick assessment of hers, takes in all of the ways that he looks like a Beaumont.

Too bad his appearance shows *nothing* about who he really is.

Lips steps out from the shadows, appearing as if from thin air thanks to years of being the Wolf. Amanda flinches at the sight of her and Lips gives her the smallest, coldest smile I've ever seen out of her before.

I adore it.

I take one of the chairs from the table and move it so I can sit in front of her, just outside of her reach if she were to break free of the ropes. Lips watches me settle in and then grabs one for herself, slumping into it like a true street kid, one foot propped up on the seat for her elbow to rest on. With the Docs, ripped jeans, and one of Morrison's old band tees, there's a lot of Noah in her look.

Even the sharp look in her eyes is the same as his, and another reminder that we need to stop ourselves from underestimating him because he's still a Graves sibling through and through.

Lips holds up the phone in her hands, Amanda's, and I take it, enjoying the fact that Jackson has already been through it and added my face to the lock so it just turns straight on for me. "What a lovely little black book you have here. Quite the list of men you own, I'll be sure to wipe them all out once your body is cold."

Her eyes flick down to the phone, the smudged eyeliner and matted hair around her face making her look deranged.

I come across my own phone number in the contacts list under that stupid little moniker she'd given me.

I smirk at her, a slow and dangerous thing. "It irritated me when you first called me little bird, you know. Well, it was your intention to demean and belittle me, that's why you've been sending out those pictures and the tape."

Her eyes finally snap away from Ash and zero in on me. She still feels like she's won here, it's as clear as day that she really does think her father will come and save her.

She's been outplayed.

"You were once a little bird, weren't you? That's what your father would call you whenever you'd be allowed to speak to him. You think I'm as naive and stupid as you were back then?"

She stares at me for even longer, the manic intensity in the room suffocating, and I nod slowly to her as though we've come to an agreement. "It's a valid conclusion to come to. You were only ever let down by the people who were supposed to take care of you. Hurt and abused by everyone in your life. It's almost... disappointing how banal and boring your story really is, Amanda. You're the same as hundreds of other little lost girls around the world with daddy issues, except that you found a serial killer to fuck through your emotions with."

Her eyes flick back over to Ash and the longing there sets my teeth on edge. The only thing that stops me from scratching those eyes out is the knowledge that it's not really my brother she wants. Just the father he resembles so much. The one we both resemble.

I lean forward in my seat to catch her attention again, enjoying the way she startles at the intensity and fury in both Lips and I at her actions. I don't have to look over at my best friend to know that she's livid over this woman's actions. Lips isn't a naturally jealous girlfriend, but there's also something about the way these women keep stalking and coveting her guys that forces her back into the merciless and cold Wolf.

"Last chance for last words, Donnelley. Any parting jabs you want?" Lips says, leaning forward to rip the tape off of her mouth in one brutal tug.

"You're all dead. When my father comes for you, he will wipe you all from the board in one swoop. Not even your little senator bastard brother can help you here."

Lips grins at her and gets up, pulling out sheets of plastic that Amanda watches with thinly veiled terror. She might be angry but she's finally understanding that she's going to die here, no matter what threats she throws at us.

I refuse to let her die with peace. "Your father chose his son. He doesn't care about his traitor daughter, fucking FBI agents and giving them intel on the cartel. It was a very simple transaction, but he owes me a blood debt now, so thank you, Donnelley. Thank you for your contribution to my black book. I promise I will squeeze your bloodline for all they're worth, and they will all know that it's your fault they belong to me. You better say your last prayer that there's no afterlife because they will hunt you there as well."

Her eyes are frantic but she has nothing left to say.

Lips hands me the knife and I take it, glancing back at Ash before I finish this. He doesn't attempt to stop me, he just watches as I slit her throat and bleed her out for daring to come after our family.

I take a two hour shower.

Ash had walked me back up to my room and waited at the bathroom door for the first half hour, calling out to me to reassure himself that I haven't just broken myself by killing that woman.

It's not the highlight of my life but there's a satisfaction to being the one to kill her. I never understood it before, but once you've been forced to kill the first time, the next time is easier.

He gives up after that and heads off to harass someone else

for a while, and I get to scrubbing every last inch of my body until I emerge buffed, polished, shining, and glorious.

I get into some casual clothes and throw a fluffy robe over it all, slipping into a pair of cashmere slippers as I head back down to attempt to cook something for us all to eat tonight.

I'm thinking... chicken parmigiana and salad.

The security alarm buzzes on my phone to let me know that Aodhan has arrived, so I stop at the foyer to let him into the house. He's freshly showered, his hair still a little wet where it hangs over his eyes, and he looks me over curiously.

"Harley said you killed the fucking cunt Donnelley, you okay?" he says as he swoops down for a kiss.

I hum against his lips, pulling away and murmuring back, "I'm fine. I'm taking the afternoon to cook and do nothing work related for a day."

He nods and runs a hand down my back, squeezing my ass when he comes to it. "You mean, I made it in time for dinner? Fucking perfect, Queenie."

I grin at him and lead him into the kitchen, enjoying the feel of his arm around my shoulders and his body against mine. It's perfect for exactly thirty seconds before we make it into the room and find my own personal nightmare happening.

Noah sits cross-legged on my kitchen island countertop and my eyes immediately narrow at him. I've tried to be calm and kind around the little asshole, no matter how much he tries to get a rise out of me, but sitting there on the space where I cook, in those filthy jeans of his, crosses a line.

"I walked in on your brother railing my sister on the kitchen table a few nights ago, I'm sure my celibate, clothed ass is the least of your worries here."

I will murder Ash in his fucking sleep.

Aodhan steps around me and smacks Noah in the back of the head hard enough that he actually yelps and jumps down. "This is her house, her food your eating, and her hospitality you're being a fucking nightmare about. Out of respect for your sister, I won't beat the shit out of you without a warning first. Consider this the only one you'll get."

Noah glares at him but he doesn't say a word as he stalks back out, slamming doors on the way.

"Pass me your cleaning bucket, I'll bleach everything," he mumbles, pressing a kiss to my forehead, and I shake my head at him.

"No, I'll be calling my deviant brother down here to take care of that. I shouldn't be surprised, he always did lean towards voyeurism. Disgusting."

Aodhan chuckles and pulls me into his body, pressing his lips to my ear and murmuring, "I'm sure I could convince you otherwise."

A shiver runs down my spine even as my eyes focus on the tiny thread that Noah's ripped jeans have left behind on the marble. I'm not going to be able to focus until I've scrubbed the entire house from top to bottom. "It's not about the act, it's the thought of my brother doing it. I'm finding there are some downsides to all of us living together."

Aodhan doesn't let me pull away from him, his arms tightening deliciously around me as he backs me into the countertop. "We both know you're not ready to be away from them yet, no matter how much the kid is pissing us all off. Fuck, I might even be able to deal with Atticus here full-time just to see how badly he handles Noah's ass. He's been too injured to really do shit about him."

I groan and Aodhan laughs at me, cupping my cheeks and bringing my lips to his for another blistering kiss. I've missed him so much, missed having him here every night and *goddamn* are we going to have to have some conversations soon.

I start pulling things out of the fridge and setting up my ingredients on a countertop as far away from Noah's spot as possible. Aodhan scrubs down the countertop and then heads over to do the same with the table despite my complaints, mostly because he can see how much it's affecting me.

Another reason I love him and need to talk with him.

"I need to talk to you," I murmur when he comes back to stash the cleaning supplies away, and he huffs at me.

"I saw the diamond, Queenie. I'm glad you're getting what you want. There's nothing to talk or freak out about."

I huff back at him, waving a spoon in his direction. "You haven't heard his list of demands yet, you can't say that! And they are demands, by the way, he's a tyrant."

He chuckles at me, kissing my neck. "Of course he is. Well, what's the list then? I'm imagining a whole lotta bullshit with scheduling and a dress code."

I sigh and put down the spoon, glancing around to make sure no one else is here to eavesdrop on this moment. I'd rather have it later in my room but now's the time.

"He wants to marry me. He wants to be my husband, which I know is a big deal, and I told him I'd have to speak to you. I wasn't just going to agree without… without your input."

He nods slowly and looks out at the dining room, the table still wet with the bleach from his scrubbing. I have no idea what he's thinking and that kills me.

"If that's what you want, then do it, Queenie. Marriage isn't a deal breaker for me, as long as you're still mine at the end of it."

My heart stutters in my chest. "How can you say that? How can that just be okay with you? I feel like a monster just for suggesting it."

He shrugs and leans against the countertop, crossing his arms over his chest and raising his eyebrow at me. "My Dad owned my Mom. I'm never going to treat you like that. If you love him and want to marry him, then do it."

"I can't believe how calm you are about this."

His grin is full of the O'Cronin charm, dirty and with an edge to it. "If he gets to call you his wife, then the first baby is mine. Those are my terms."

Jesus fucking Christ. "So this has become a negotiation? You're bartering for my womb right now."

He chuckles under his breath, like this isn't an incredibly offensive and childish conversation we're having, and I try my best not to stomp my foot like a child about it.

"Queenie, I'll do whatever it takes to keep you happy... and to keep you. If he wants to make demands, then I'll happily meet him in the middle. This is the middle—he'll either come to the party or miss the fuck out."

I'm still a little insulted. "I'm not marrying him right now and I'm certainly not having anyone's babies in the next ten years either. I have plans that don't involve being swollen and miserable."

He shrugs in that easy way of his. "I'm just letting you know that it'll be an O'Cronin growing in there the first time around. He doesn't get fucking everything just because he's the Crow."

This is how I imagine the rest of my life will go, these negotiations and little wars waged with each other... and I don't hate it.

It's exactly what I need and I love them both for it.

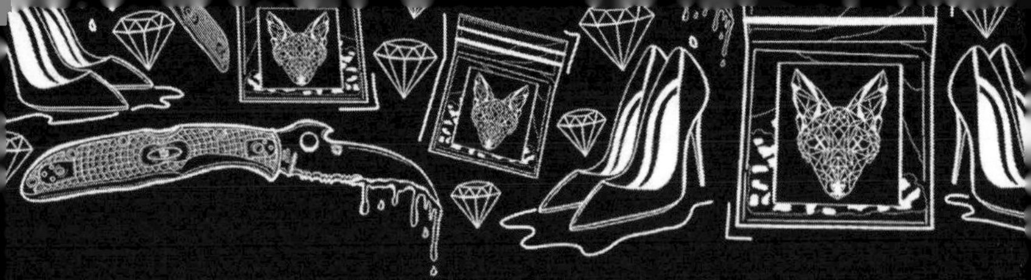

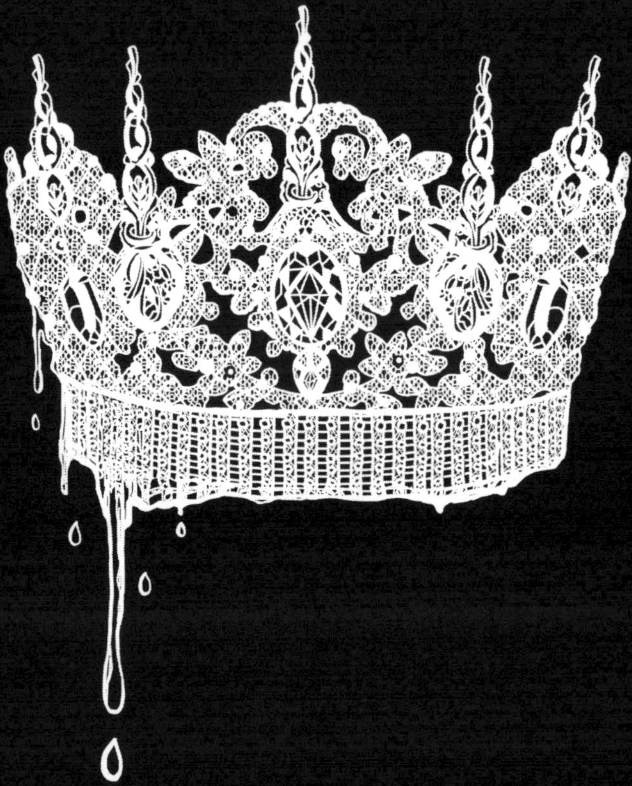

Chapter Seventeen

I ride down to the docks of Mounts Bay to the Twelve meeting in the Escalade with Lips and the guys, all together again just like old times. I get the front seat and Harley drives, still furious with Blaise over the incident that has the bus looking like a mess in my driveway. I don't comment on it, mostly because I'm sure some part of the story will infuriate me at how stupid they've acted.

Lips is silent in the back, her phone in her hand and her teeth gnawing at her bottom lip. Morrison is watching her closely, his arm around her shoulders as he leans in to kiss her shoulder and murmur quietly in her ear. Ash is surly looking, his hand tracing patterns on her thigh as he stares out into the city with a scowl on his face, deep in thought.

The Graves issue isn't going to just disappear and if we're not careful, it could take over our lives.

Harley directs the car down to the same parking lot that we'd parked at for the lingerie party, squeezing the car in between the

Rolls Royce and the Impala there.

We step out of the car together, looking like a very wealthy gang of deviants and playboys, and isn't that just the most appropriate thing? Aodhan steps around the Impala to hold out a hand for me, tucking me into his side as he shakes Harley's hand.

Harley smirks at him and then it drops away as he groans and mutters, "What the fuck is he doing down here? I thought we agreed to go to this shit without bringing anyone else in?"

I glance around and find Jack's younger brother Cian leaning against the car. He's not much younger than me, only about six months between him and Harley, but I know that Harley and Aodhan have worked hard to keep the other O'Cronins away from anything Twelve and gang related.

"He's here to find Patrick, who heard there was a party happening tonight and mysteriously disappeared. He's a fucking shit and he's going to end up dead if we can't get him outta this rebellious phase of his," Aodhan grumbles, and then there's a shout from behind us.

We all turn to find Atticus and Luca walking out of the huge warehouse, ten of their men with them, and one of them holding a very drunk and raging Patrick.

"For fuck's sake," Aodhan snarls, and lets me go to stalk over.

Harley takes off after him, the family ties between them are getting stronger the more time they spend together. Harley might have happily left the running of the O'Cronin family to his cousin, but now that he's had the chance to know his cousins, he's not just going to abandon them.

I'm waiting for Atticus to say something particularly asshole-ish to Aodhan about his cousin but he doesn't, they only have a few quiet words shared between them before Atticus waves at the man holding Patrick to hand him over.

Aodhan gets one hand under Patrick's arm and yanks him over to the Impala, snarling at him with a slew of threats and cussing that has Ash and Morrison snickering at the scene, as Cian opens the door and helps shove his little brother in. Aodhan slams the door after him and then hands the keys over to Cian and snaps, "Take him home, and if there is so much as a speck of dirt on this car when I get back, I'm throwing you both off of the docks with weights for fucking shoes. Leave. *Go*."

Cian is a little less jolly than his brother, his face a little pale as he glances around at all of the underground crime lords and members of the now- fabled Family standing there watching him ferry his drunk brother home.

I wouldn't want to be Patrick when he wakes up in the morning.

We stand there and watch the car disappear, the sound of the engine barely audible over the music of the party, and then Lips rolls her shoulders back and shares a look with me. "Ready, Queen Crow?"

I smirk at her for using that name and nod. "Let's go ruin some lives, Wolf."

She cackles and then glances at Atticus, wiping the joy from her face like a pro as she stalks toward the party. Ash shares a look with Aodhan as he passes him, but he waves him off.

It's a passing of the torch, Ash is handing me over to him for safekeeping. It's more than I ever thought I'd get out of my neurotic, overprotective twin and I smirk at Harley over it.

I slip my hand into Aodhan's and we step up to where Atticus is still waiting, clearly not happy going into the party or the meeting without us. His men disperse a little more, fanning out to cover us as well as their boss. Luca tips his head at me and I have to remind myself again that he's now an equal to Atticus, Aodhan, and Lips in the eyes of the Bay.

Aodhan glances at Atticus and then says, "Thanks for grabbing the fucking idiot boy for me, he's going to be led to hell by his fucking dick."

Harley scoffs from where he's following after Lips and calls out, "Aren't we all?"

He catches an elbow to the gut for that comment but Morrison roars with laughter like a child over it, singing some lyrics from one of his latest songs loudly, the words all dripping with obsession and love for his Mounty.

Aodhan shakes his head at them, grinning roguishly, and mutters to me, "Sometimes I think they don't all make sense together, then something like that happens."

I scoff at him, "They're all wildly co-dependent and obsessed with one another. You should ask Harley what he did to Morrison's stalker on tour… he didn't do that for the Mounty, that was all someone going after one of his best friends, and he doesn't deal with that well at all."

He shakes his head, and then Atticus is checking his watch like it really matters if we're late to this thing, so we get moving. It's very strange and oddly sweet the way they flank me, staring out at the drunk and high Mounties all writhing on the dance floor to the deafening music playing from the dozens of huge speakers set up throughout the warehouse.

The crowd parts like the Red Sea for us, the patrons already wide-eyed after the mythical Wolf and her pack walked through with their tattoos all glowing under the UV lights. My own tattoo of the Wolf insignia on my wrist glows as well, though Aodhan's arm mostly obscures it from view.

Once we make it up to the meeting room, we find everyone waiting for us, which is a nice change of pace. The Viper curls his lip at me and I smile back at him just to piss the asshole off. Ash watches the entire exchange with that very Beaumont sort of intent and I wouldn't be surprised if he's planning a trip down to the Dive to kill the man later.

I won't be even a little mad about it.

Lips takes a seat between Lucy and Jackson, greeting them both quietly. Jackson makes a shitty joke to break the ice and Lucy stares him down like she's trying to figure out if he's actually hitting on her or if he's just mentally deficient.

Thank God Viola isn't here to see it.

I take my place between Ash and Morrison, my phone in my hand even though we're not technically supposed to have them here. I want to make notes of the turf disputes that the Ox is once again having.

When Atticus starts the meeting, diving straight into the Ox's shit, Lucy looks around the room as though she wasn't expecting this sort of formality about the whole gig.

Lips looks at her with a raised eyebrow and murmurs quietly so she doesn't disturb Atticus and the Ox snarling at each other, but so I can hear her as well, "Welcome to hell. If you want my advice, keep your mouth shut until you know a little more about the lay of the land… it'll also get us out of here a little sooner."

Lucy still looks vaguely ill at the sight of Lips but she's not rude to her and answers her with a forced smile, "I have much better places to be than here at a fucking dock party."

From two seats down, the Fox's lip curls at her and he snaps, "Too good for them, eh? Another fucking wet blanket at the table, the whole place is going to the dogs."

The rest of the arguments continue around them as Lucy smirks back at him, not shaky at all when she's dealing with his crusty self. "Maybe if you cleaned the place occasionally, I'd come down here, but I've heard a lot of stories about girls getting chlamydia from sitting at the bar and that's not my idea of a good time."

I immediately look down at my shoes and curse under my breath.

Another pair of Valentinos to be burned.

I fucking hate this place.

Atticus is still attempting to mediate between the Viper and the Fox on some stupid issue with adding fights to the parties when my phone buzzes in my hand with an alert about my house alarm being turned off from the inside.

Fucking Noah.

I know it's him immediately because Lips had read him the riot act before we'd left and he stood there all surly and sassy, like he's got a leg to stand on with her.

And now he's sneaking out of the mansion.

"911," I murmur to Ash, and I flip the phone over to him so he can see the security footage of Noah sliding into one of his prized cars and driving it out of the garage like he wants to see it wrapped around a tree.

"*I will fucking murder that little cunt.*"

Okay, showing it to Ash wasn't the best idea, but at least I know where the little cretin is heading, because he's only ever shown an interest in leaving the ranch for drugs and most of the places to score easily in the Bay are within a mile of where we're standing.

I also have GPS on all of Ash's vehicles for this exact reason. It would be absolutely stupid of me to house hundreds of millions of dollars' worth of cars without being able to track them if they went missing.

I step forward to lean down and murmur to Lips, "Small emergency, nothing to worry about because I'll have it fixed before the meeting is over."

She tenses a little but nods, and I give Aodhan and Atticus each a look that I hope conveys my need for them to watch her back because all three of the guys are charging toward the elevator with a bloodthirsty air about them that spells real danger for Noah when we find him. I have a small moment of thanking my lucky goddamned stars that Ash now trusts Aodhan enough to be backup for Lips in this room, because I'm going to need all of their eyes on this hunt.

I try to look a little more sophisticated than the rest of them as I stalk out of the room, though I am pleased when they wait for the elevator to close behind us before they start up.

Harley runs his hands through his hair and snarls, "What the fuck did he take this time?"

"The McLaren P1," Ash grits out between his clenched teeth, and Harley almost *swoons*, the color draining out of him in horror.

Morrison shrugs. "Thank fuck it wasn't the bus."

"Are you fucking dense? It's a P1," Ash snaps back, and I start to think I'm going to be throwing myself between them in a freaking brawl before the doors open to let us out.

"Yeah, but I think we're all happy that the bus is safe. Lips would have a fucking aneurysm over the cleanup." It makes no sense to me, but I mentally give him a point for caring about his girlfriend's wellbeing.

If only he'd clean the *fucking* bus out and move it for me, then maybe he'd scrape his way out of the bottom spot in my ever evolving chart of favorite family members.

We walk out of the warehouse, past all of the mess of people, and at the doors one of Atticus' men steps up to me and says, "I've been assigned to protect you until you return."

Of course he has, I almost want to text Atticus a thank you because it'll get me out of this whining mess of car-obsessed guys.

With another check of the GPS to confirm he's still heading this way, I turn around to snap at them to stop them from squabbling like children, "All three of you are on my last goddamned nerves. Split up and head to each of the places you can score, we need to find the little shit as he arrives so this doesn't blow up."

Ash isn't ready to let us split up at all, but when I show him the gun I am not only trained to use but so ready to shoot someone with after tonight, he eases up a little.

It doesn't stop him from snarling threats at Atticus' man as he stalks off. The guy doesn't flinch. He waits for me to move without a word before he follows after me, his gun drawn and ready to fire.

We head toward the edge of the slums, the safest of all of the areas because naturally the guys all took the worst of the options. There's a dealer who does the best weed in the city, according to Blaise, who hangs out around the warehouses further up the coast, close enough to Illi's apartments that it's considered safer.

The Butcher doesn't allow rowdy neighbors near his home or his family.

It's a ten-minute walk even in my heels, and I start planning out all of the locks and chains I'm going to put on Noah's windows and doors because this is the last time I'm going to be doing this shit.

We make it to the first of the empty warehouses and, aside from a few homeless men sleeping among cardboard boxes, they're empty. I check the GPS signal again but, of course, it's gone out. There's only two reasons it would blink out like that, one being that the little shit found it and smashed it, which I'm really hoping is the case.

Because the other option is that he wrecked the car and he will be skinned alive if that's what's happened here.

When we get to the next warehouse, I pause for a second and text the guys, telling them about the GPS tracker, and then I nearly jump out of my skin at the sound of footsteps. I get my gun in my hand, the safety off, and point out into the darkness in no time at all and I'm once again quietly impressed with myself.

It doesn't last because there, walking through the filthy warehouse, is Noah.

I want to kill him.

I turn to the Crow's man and ask him to keep guard outside, not wanting a witness for the complete destruction I'm about to unleash on this asshole. He doesn't question it, just steps out with a curt nod.

Then I turn back to the sullen idiot scowling at me and snarl, "What the fuck is it about 'stay home' that you're struggling with? Because Lips was very clear when she told you to stay the hell home."

He rolls his eyes at me—they're already bloodshot and there's a scrape down his face that doesn't bode well for wherever the hell the McLaren is. "I'm not a fucking prisoner. I've done nothing wrong and you all treat me like you own me. It's disgusting."

Lord, give me the strength to get through this. "You're here under your sister's protection. If you won't give her any information about who tried to kill you, then how are we supposed to fix it so you can live normally again? Do you really think that Lips wouldn't kill for you? In a heartbeat, she would take out a whole city if they threatened you."

He rolls his eyes and snaps, "That's all well and good to ramble on about, but she's not going to do shit for me. None of you are."

I need to put my gun back in my purse before I shoot him for being a whiny little bitch. "I slit a woman's throat in the garage last week and watched her bleed out, you really think I won't kill someone who's threatening a member of my family?

You're Lips' blood, that's all I need to know. Now move your ass before we end up dead in a ditch just because you can't listen to simple instructions."

I text Ash and tell him to bring the car to us. It'll take him a little longer to get here but I need to get Noah out of the open in case whoever is after him knows literally anything about searching through security footage. With Jackson busy in the meeting, it's not like I can get the surveillance cameras around here shut off.

I send a message to Viola, just in case she's available and can do it.

When Noah tries to walk out of the warehouse again, I stop him, grabbing his arm and tugging him behind me as I murmur to the Crow's man still waiting for us outside.

"I have a pick up on the way, let me know when they arrive."

He nods again, his eyes sharp as he takes in the night around us, the sounds of the party still clear from here.

Noah isn't on board with this plan. "Why the fuck are we staying in this shit-hole? This feels like a trap, are you about to put me down because you're sick of me? I fucking knew it, you're so full of shit."

I roll my eyes at him as I slip the plastic booties over my shoes that I keep in my pockets for my trips down to the slums, ignoring the way he huffs and puffs at my obsessive need to keep my shoes protected from the nightmare that is the warehouse. "What would you know about traps? Keep your hat pulled down low, I don't want you getting caught on camera here somewhere and whoever the fuck is after you figuring out you're here."

He yanks on the brim, his curls squashing down a little more and obscuring his face. "I know enough about dodgy shit to know this is a bad fucking idea. Aren't you royalty or something? You shouldn't be wandering around like this."

His words are dripping with sarcasm but he's not too far off of the mark. On these streets, I am now the slum version of royalty—the infamous Queen Crow.

The part he's missing is the *ruthless* part of my persona, the part where I was forged in fire, over and over again, and there's nothing they can do right now that I can't get out of.

Because my night can't get any worse, that statement is going to be tested. Outside there's the sound of a gun going off and then a body hitting the ground.

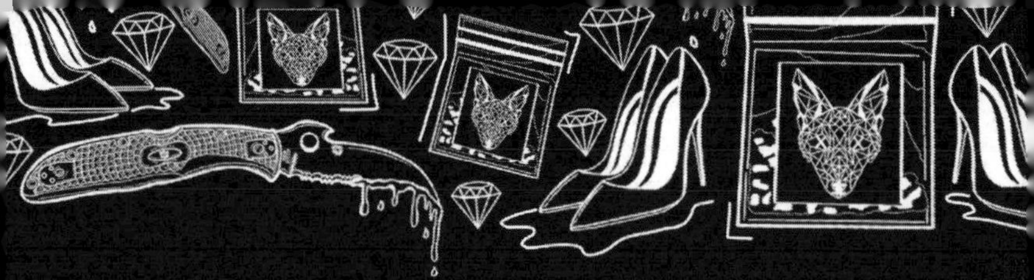

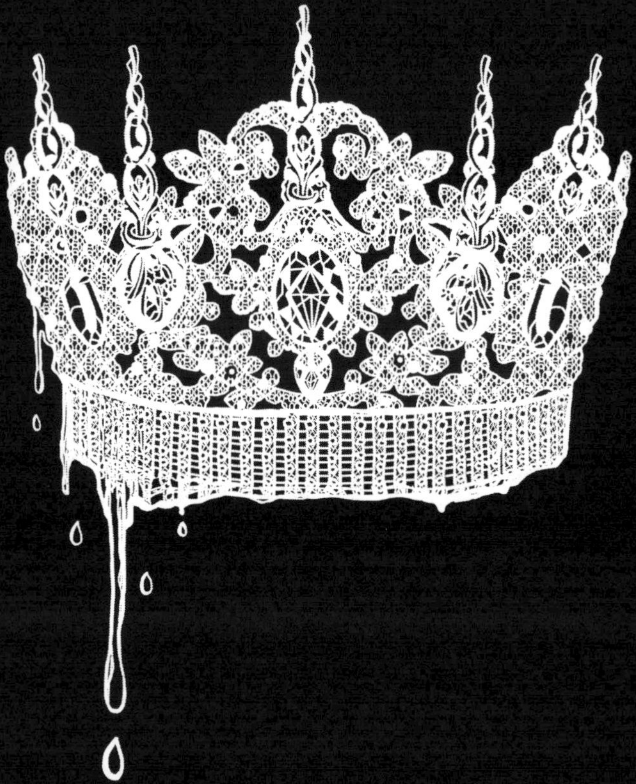

Chapter Eighteen

I immediately move into action, grabbing Noah's arm and dragging him as quickly and quietly away from the doors as I can. The warehouse was once a storage place for some sort of mechanic or construction company and there's still rusted-out pieces of machinery that we duck behind. I have a gun and two knives on me, and there's no way in hell that I'm handing Noah a gun without knowing that he can actually use it without killing us both.

He also just ranted about how much he doesn't trust me or his sister, there's every chance he'd use it against me on purpose, so instead I hand him one of the knives.

He stares at it for a second, blinking slowly like he's never held a knife before, and I accept that he's not going to be any use to me right now. Whoever is here to kill us—him? God knows—is my responsibility to take out until Ash and the others get here.

I'll be fine. Everything is fine.

I say it until my heart rate slows a little more and the gun isn't shaking in my hand. The last time this happened, Bingley was attacking me at Atticus' fortress-like mansion and I'd been forced to… disembowel him.

The only goals for tonight are to kill these men without traumatizing myself and to keep us both alive.

When the doors swing open, I can see Atticus' man is dead on the ground with a bullet between his eyes and I take a second to feel both a little guilty for not even knowing his name, and also very glad I left him out there alone. Callous and cold, but that's the way of the Bay and I'm not the same girl I once was.

Better him than me or Noah.

"I can smell her fucking perfume; she's a sweet little bitch."

Noah's eyes snap to mine right as I roll them because it's such typical male bullshit. Of course they'd be talking shit because even with the skin markets gone from the Bay, there's still more than enough terrible human beings out there.

I motion again for Noah to stay silent and then I watch as the men walk into the warehouse, counting them all and cursing in my head because three or four men would be totally fine. Eight? That's a bit much.

Ten?

We're fucked.

My gun has twelve bullets and I don't have a spare magazine. I wasn't even supposed to have to use the damn thing and now I'm going to have to start carrying my own arsenal like the freaking Butcher, because this shit just keeps on happening to me. I send Ash a message through muscle memory alone to get his ass here pronto.

Twelve bullets, ten men. I can't miss any of the shots and I also need to make sure I don't get shot myself. Can I talk my way out of this? Stall for long enough that backup arrives? Ash is five minutes away, ten at the most.

Noah tugs on my arms and points toward a side door, slightly ajar from where he'd come in looking to score, and I nod, motioning once again for him to stay low and quiet. It's like dealing with a child but his eyes are the size of saucers, so I'm really hammering it home.

I let him take the lead, covering his back because the thugs are all behind us laughing and joking about all of the things they're going to do to me when they get ahold of me.

The only guy that I can see carrying a gun calls out to the others, "Kill the fucking kid before he gives us shit for dealing with the girl. Remember, we don't get paid until she's dead. Crawford made that clear."

If I hadn't already guessed that this is Randy finally noticing that two of his three sons are dead, thanks to my involvement in their lives, his words just confirm it. I already knew that it wouldn't all happen smoothly, but the fact that they must have had eyes on us tonight pisses me off.

There's more yelling and jeering, one of the guys yelling back, "Like I'd be worried about some fucking queer, did you get an eyeful of him? Just leave him here to rot so we can get rid of the Queen bitch."

Ah, lovely. Homophobic, rapist thugs sent by Randy fucking Crawford. Just what my night needs. I'm suddenly filled with an immense joy to know that Nate is on his way to deal with this for us in the most horrific and blood-soaked way.

The concrete underneath us is cracked and reduced to rubble in some spots. I'm an expert at walking on any terrain in heels, they're all I wear, but this is probably Noah's first rodeo and when his footing slips, I know the moment we're made.

I turn on my heel and open fire, thankful that my eyes have adjusted to the darkness and for all of the years of Harley working on my marksmanship. I take out the guy with the gun first, aware that the others are probably carrying too, but I can only make the call with what I can see.

It takes two bullets to take out the next guy, but he's at least as beefy as Harley is and taller even than Ash, so it's not a shock to me. The guys start diving behind the machinery as I shoot at them all, hitting a few more. I'm not sure if they're dead, but when a bullet hits the door behind us, Noah grabs me and drags me behind another giant rusted hunk of metal.

"This is fucking crazy!" Noah hisses, and I roll my eyes at him.

"Welcome to Mounts Bay, Noah. This is how things go down here."

There's a moment of silence and then the door opens again and I hear the footsteps of some of the men leaving, fleeing as though they're facing an army and not two people.

Enough of them stay behind though.

I'm trying to decide if we're going to stay alive long enough for Ash to arrive, but when we start to move to the door again, the men left in the warehouse start to murmur together, noticing our movements and making another play to kill me.

Three of them rush us at the same time, two of them heading for me while the third takes his chances with Noah, probably aiming to have a human shield. Whoever they are, they did not think this plan through with the lack of firepower between them.

I shoot both men in the chest, the biggest and most effective target, and when I turn to the other one, he's already slipping past me for Noah, going for his arm. I swing out my hand with the knife, impaling him and losing my grip as he yanks away with a scream. Noah's eyes snap to mine, wide and startled, but there's too much happening around us to acknowledge the fact that my priority here is getting him out of here.

He's an asshole and a pain in my ass, but he's also my best friend's little brother, the same best friend who would die for me or my own brother without a second thought, so I'm getting him the hell out of here and then I'm going to kill the little shithead.

I move to shoot him from where he's groaning on the ground with the knife still hanging out of his arm. That's the last bullet, but it's worth using it because of how close he was to us and there is no time to figure out a plan to kill him otherwise.

There's still one man left alive in the warehouse, the rest have fled.

Randy really should have chosen his killers a little better—ten guys and only a fraction of them have a spine? Pathetic.

I carefully lean down to put my gun on the ground, pulling my knife back out of the corpse at our feet and spinning it in my hand to get comfortable with it again. Deep breath, this will be fine.

The problem is that while I'm psyching myself up at the thought of more disembowelments, the last guy creeps up on us, his feet unnaturally silent against the concrete. He could give Lips a run for her money, and he manages to get his arm locked around my throat. Before I get the chance to move into one of the defensive maneuvers that Lips has drilled into me, Noah lunges forward in a blur.

I don't see what he does, but the man holding me jolts and then collapses around me, almost taking me to the ground too, except that Noah catches me and holds me upright.

I look down to find that there's a knife hanging out of his skull now, a clean shot, straight through his eye socket and into his brain.

I glance up at Noah and his voice is steady as he says, "He's right. I am a queer, but I'm not a fucking pussy."

Jesus fucking Christ.

I pull myself away from him, wobbling on my feet for a second before I grab his arm again to steady myself. He might've been a complete brat to me all night, but at least he's figured out his loyalties. "If anyone demeans you like that to me again, I will put a bullet between their eyes. Either myself or I'll get one of the guys to do it, I'm still not the biggest fan of blood and gore so I save my heroics for special occasions."

He shrugs and leans over to yank the knife back out, chuckling at the way the body jerks as he does it, the nerves still firing even with his heart stopped. "I am a queer, no use getting mad over some ugly fuck commenting on it. I'm never going to be anything other than what you see."

I shrug at him and pull my phone out, finally pushing send on the text to Ash. "Why the hell would we want you to change? I care about loyalty and whether or not you're good to your sister. The guys only really care about that too. Ash is a little snarly at you, but that has everything to do with you being his girlfriend's brother and propositioning him, and exactly nothing to do with your sexuality. Lips cares about you because that's who she is. She likes you already, she just wants you to like her back."

He stares at me for a second before he wipes the knife off on his pants and then holds it out for me to take. "I don't need taking care of. I lived on the streets for years. If there wasn't all of this bullshit, I'd be paying my own way."

I nod my head slowly, years of being with Lips has made me a little more sensitive to kids with poverty issues, but there's also no getting around this. "Money is nothing to us. Sorry if that's too blunt but it's the truth. Keeping you safe is all we care about. No one is keeping tabs on anything… except that Ash will definitely have a lot to say if you touch his cars without permission again. Also, only Lips and I have free rein with them, so you're probably never going to drive one again."

He scoffs but takes it better than he has ever before, scuffing his shoe against the ground, his face serious again. "I've only trusted three people in my life. One betrayed me in the worst way and another is the guy who tried to kill me. This isn't easy because if my gut feeling is wrong about you all, then I just spent a year in a basement for fucking nothing."

I nod slowly. "And the third person? What did they do?"

"Wyatt gave me the basement. He's a cop who's as straight as they come, and he faked my death. He's the only person I trust."

The lights of the Escalade hit us and I use the seconds we have left in this moment to sway him. "I had the same thing with Lips. The moment I did trust her though, my whole life changed. I went from a terrible life of being scared and hunted to having a family, all of us safe, thanks to her. Trust her with this one thing and she will never let you down, Noah. She doesn't know how to be anything but loyal and ruthless."

The tires on the car screech as it comes to a stop, then the car doors fling open and Ash flies out of it as though the hounds of hell are biting his ass, bundling me into his arms and growling under his breath, "Can we be done with this phase? I can't fucking handle you being out here on your own and dealing with men yourself. It's fucking killing me, Floss."

I chuckle at him, glancing over at where Noah is staring at Ash like he's a piece of meat, still completely unrepentant in his obsession with his sister's boyfriend. "I wasn't on my own. Noah is a very handy young man in a fight."

Ash glances over at him, a frown still secured tightly over his features, and then mutters, "Good job. Now get in the fucking car."

I'm fairly certain Noah ejaculates in his pants at the praise, which is completely disgusting, and I wave him on in front of me to get him moving.

If I wasn't already a thousand percent sure of it, I definitely am now; we're going to have our hands full with him around.

When we're all back in the car again, Noah lets himself bask in Ash's approval for an extra two minutes before he pipes up in the back and destroys it all, "Was that McLaren P1 insured?"

Noah doesn't get a whole new personality thanks to our little adventure at the docks together, but he does suddenly become much less of a problem to handle. When Ash finds out the McLaren was stolen, not wrecked, he starts harassing Jackson to find it, scouring through security footage until it shows up.

In pieces.

Thanks to a chop shop run that's been opened by the Hyena,

who's taking over from the Bear's old businesses. Lips almost has a coronary when she finds out how much the car cost Ash, not that he can't afford to get a new one, but Mounties are all very neurotic about the prices of things, and for a moment I think that this might be the thing that gets Noah sent back to Wyatt's basement.

He does actually apologize for what he did and offers to work off the cost of the car. Ash refuses to look at him or acknowledge him, which is the real punishment here because for all his teasing, there's something about my brother that has Noah craving his approval and attention.

I don't bother telling Atticus about his father's attempt on my life, other than to apologize for the death of his guy, and he doesn't find out about it until days later thanks to our great job at the cleanup down there the next evening.

Aodhan could very well take over the business if he wanted to, arriving in the morning with a van and a handful of O'Cronin men, including a very green-looking Patrick who had the decency to look sheepish at us.

When we're done, we all head back to the ranch together, except for Lips who is meeting with Nate for dinner. For once, none of her guys argue with her or insist on riding along.

The true power of the Devil.

I almost think I've gotten away with multiple counts of murder without any complications when Atticus storms into the kitchen with an enraged look on his face while I'm busy making enough pasta to feed an army.

Aodhan slides in front of me immediately, ready to shoot Atticus for whatever has pissed him off and sent him to me. Sweet, but entirely unnecessary. He's not a threat to me, no matter what's pissed him off.

He doesn't look at or acknowledge Aodhan's existence, snarling, "The worst possible option? If I wanted Morningstar to come deal with my father, I would call him and pay the price myself."

Aodhan turns to stone, horror written over every inch of his face, and I have to step around him to level Atticus with a glare for dropping this bomb on Aodhan like that.

I still haven't worked out how to tell him about Nate. Does that make me a bad girlfriend? Probably, but I already know that the Devil is kind of a touchy subject to anyone even remotely aware of his history and what he is capable of.

"This is a freebie. Lips called in a favor."

And now Aodhan looks like he's going to vomit. "The Devil himself owes the Wolf a favor? Balls of fucking steel on her, that girl, but, Avery, you can't meet with him. I don't care what he owes her, you are not meeting him."

I cringe and Atticus snaps, "She's already met him. They're on a first name basis, he's a member of the family."

Again, I think Aodhan is going to pass out. I shove him gently toward a chair and then wave a hand at Atticus. "I gave you the option to kill him yourself, you chose the other option.

I can't really go back on that now because Nate is already here to see Lips. They're actually out having dinner together as we speak."

Atticus is still staring at me like I'm unhinged for trusting Lips' assessment and loyalty to her brother, but I agree with her.

He sent her the heads of her enemies. He answers all of her texts and phone calls and even though he doesn't really seem to understand human emotions, he asks about how her day is going. Whatever his life looked like before, helping raise Poe has humanized him enough that I'm not worried about my safety.

As long as Lips loves me, I'm safe.

"Lips is out to dinner… with her brother. The same brother you said you wouldn't put on the murder board downstairs because you're sure about him." Aodhan looks at me with a very appropriate amount of terror in his eyes. "Don't fuck with me, Queenie."

Atticus' lip curls at him and he shoves the file at him. "She's not. The Lynx was killed because she stepped out on the Wolf and her brother dealt with it."

I can see the cogs turning in his brain, everything sliding together, and he's turning a little bit green around the edges. "Lucy… she said she saw her aunt's death. She saw him and that's why she freaked out over Lips. Fuck me, fuck me, this is the worst fucking thing I've ever heard."

Atticus huffs. "I'm glad we can agree on the fact that the Devil is not an ally. He's a serial killer, and he's a danger to everyone who comes across him."

This is getting out of hand. "He is Lips' brother. She called him for help, and he came without question to fix the problem. When he found out she existed, he came and tore through the Bay for her. If you think for a second that you're going to convince me to side against a Graves sibling, you are fucking *dreaming*."

"Avery—"

I cut him off, "It's already done. The deal is signed, the payment waived, and your father is going to die screaming. Nothing else matters here. Now, are you joining us for dinner or not? I've made enough if you want to stay."

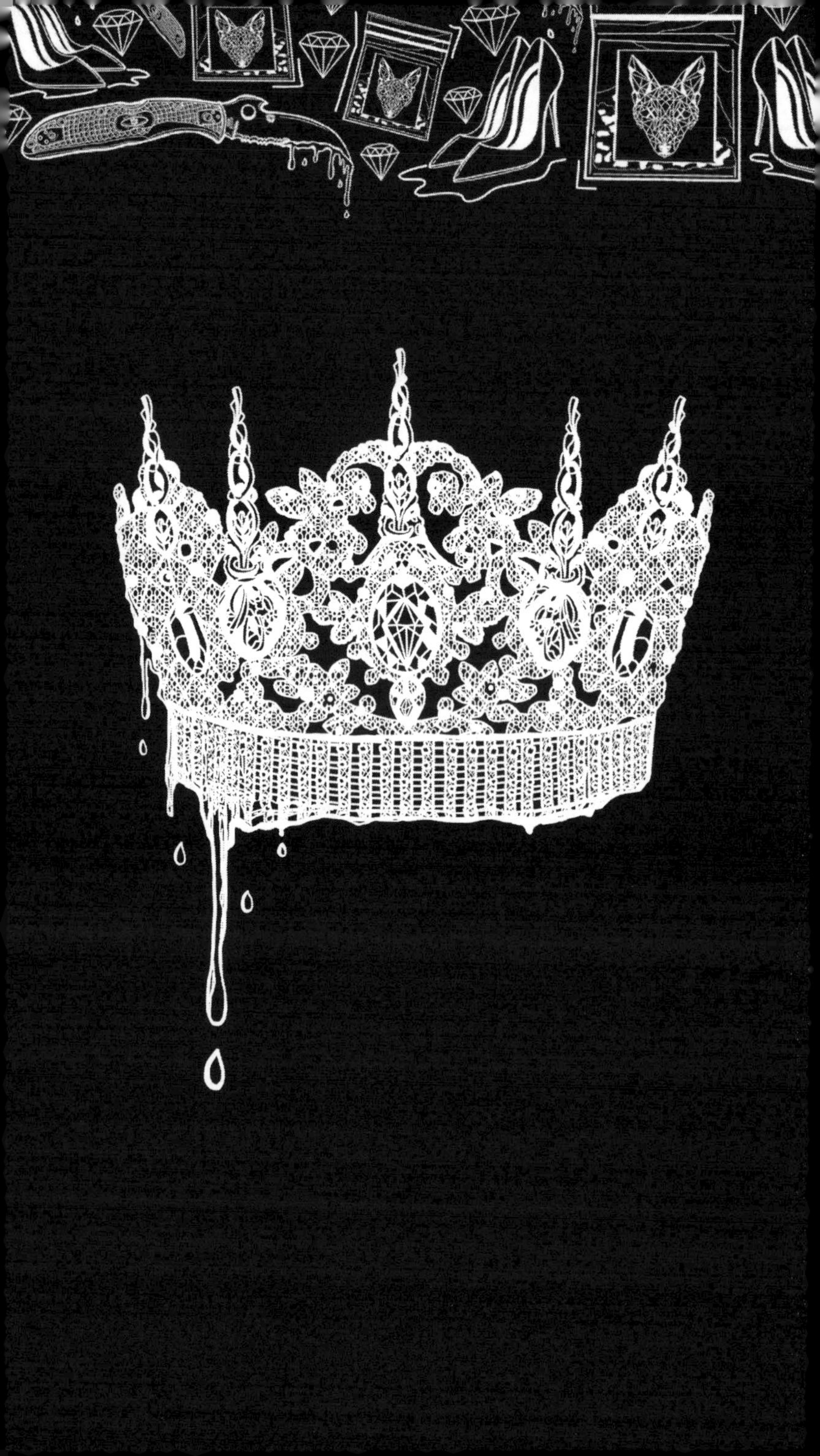

Chapter Nineteen

It causes the biggest fight I hope I ever have with Aodhan, but I convince him to stay at the docks instead of joining us to meet with Nate.

I have no doubt that the Devil will already know that we've told another person about his identity; his access to Lips' life and what happens in it is a little terrifying. I still haven't figured out his methods.

Lips and I are driven down to meet with him and deal with Randy once and for all by Ash, who isn't worried about meeting with Nate. I fuss with my outfit for an hour before we leave, mostly because I'm nervous about being around Nate again.

He really doesn't like anyone but his sisters, and while I'll argue in his favor with Atticus until the end of time, I'm still fucking terrified of him.

There's also the fact that there's no place I hate more in the world than the Vulture's skin markets.

They've been abandoned for years at this point, but the

building is still standing untouched. I think the entire Bay is leaving this cursed place be, letting all of the ghosts and bad karma lie because there's nowhere else that saw the same amount of pain, suffering, and devastation as here.

All of the women and girls who were sold and traded through this building, it's horrifying and incomprehensible.

I have to steel myself to walk in there, even with Lips at my side, and Ash's jaw is so tight that I'm worried his teeth might crack under the pressure.

"I got him down here a few days ago... he's a terrible prisoner. He really just hasn't figured out how fucked he really is," Lips murmurs to me, glancing over at Ash with a grimace.

I'm not worried.

If anything, I'm glad he's acting that way. I'm going to enjoy watching him take in his own death, seeing the horror dawn on his disgusting face when it all finally clicks together in that arrogant brain of his.

I can't wait.

Lips leads us through the building by memory alone, another thing that has Ash fuming, and when we make it down to the back rooms, the smells get even worse. I want to vomit, but this last year has strengthened my stomach a little. I can handle it just to get the victory of this moment.

The back rooms have cages lining one of the walls and jail-like cells, complete with bulletproof glass, for the extra valuable girls along the other. We stop in front of one of them to find

Randy standing in the center, his nose broken and both of his eyes black.

I pull out a handkerchief from my purse to grab one of the chairs without actually touching it, dragging it over to perch on the seat and stare into the cell. He stares back at me like this is nothing to him. A slow smirk, something I've seen my brother give out a million times, stretches over my face.

"Oh, this will not do at all. I think we need to find you some chains."

Randy sneers at me "I will enjoy breaking you, slave."

Lips and Ash stay silent, sinking back until they're against the far wall to watch how this is going to go down.

I raise my eyebrows at him, a smile flirting with the corners of my mouth, because he really has lost all sense of reality. "Randy, your sons are dead. The only reason you are still alive is because I wanted you to know the feeling of being trapped and having no control. I wanted you to know that now it's you who is the slave."

He scoffs and turns to face the wall, icing me out as though I'd care about this little show of his. "Your father should have dealt with you sooner. Spare the rod, ruin the slave."

I shrug just as Nate arrives, nodding at Lips as he walks in. I don't understand how he does it, but the entire energy of the room changes completely. It's as though the oxygen has been sucked out and replaced with an electrical charge, coursing through our lungs and into our veins until we're all running on a high.

It's terrifying.

The Devil himself steps up to the glass. Randy's eyes flare as he takes him in and finally, *finally*, he seems to understand the real extent of trouble he's in. The tattoos that Nate is covered in make it very obvious who he is, and the cold, dead look in his eyes is telling.

"How much did she pay you? I'll double it, don't kill me," he rasps out, and Nate doesn't react, just stares in at him like he's a bug under a microscope.

Randy's eyes dart between us. "Whatever she's paying you, I'll triple it, just—"

Nate steps forward and it doesn't matter that there's eight-inch-thick bulletproof glass between them, Randall's mouth snaps shut as he shrinks back.

It's intoxicating and I wish Atticus were here to experience it with me.

Nate turns his back on Randy, looking over at Lips as if for confirmation on something, but they don't speak a word between them.

Randy starts screaming, his fists banging against the glass until they bleed. "You filthy fucking beast! I'll kill you for this. I'll fucking kill you."

The Devil lifts his cigarette to his lips and inhales, the smoke slowly curling out of his lips as he exhales, staring at Randy Crawford like he's planning all of the places he'll slice him up once the murdering part of the job begins. I'm almost tempted to stick around to watch it happen.

Almost.

"You sure you don't wanna do it yourself?" Nate says, and it takes me a second to realize that he's talking to Lips.

She shakes her head. "No, I want him to suffer the worst death… that's what we all agreed on. I want you to have fun with it, really make sure he knows what those *slaves* he's been breaking felt."

The Devil nods his head slowly. "Why give him a decent death if you can make an example of him? I'll make it a good one."

Lips shrugs at him, pushing away from the wall to stand next to him. "This man hurt my family, threatened us all, and is a disease to our world. I can think of a lot of ways I could kill him, but I think you're a better fit for this one."

He lifts the cigarette to his lips again, watching Randy lose his fucking mind over the conversation happening around him with that same cold apathy. "Then so be it. The slowest, most painful death I can give a man."

We leave to the sounds of Randy's screams and for once, I don't think they'll haunt me. I'm pretty sure it'll be the sweet sound I fall asleep to for the rest of my life.

We sit out in the car together for hours waiting for Nate to emerge again. When he does, he's covered in blood and dragging a body bag out behind him. I wasn't expecting him to clean up after himself. I was kind of hoping that Randy would slowly rot down there in that cell, the most perfect ending for that man that I could think of.

Lips curses under her breath and climbs out of the backseat to go after him, grabbing the other end of the body bag to help him carry it over to his car.

I hesitate to go after her. Ash does too, his hand hovering over the door handle while he watches them both obsessively. I raise an eyebrow at him, surprised at this abrupt change in his attitude toward protecting his girlfriend.

He grimaces at me. "Lips asked me to back off a bit around him. I think she's worried that he'll think we're too controlling and come after us for her own good."

Jesus H. Christ. "That's a wise move... at least until he gets to know you a bit better."

He scoffs at me. "He has no interest in any of us except Lips, and that's perfectly fucking fine with me, Floss. I went through that shit Atticus left you about him; it's worse than Illi ever told us."

I look over to see Lips grin and duck her head, still quietly pleased to know that he'd come here for her with just a phone call. After the terrible childhood she had that only ever makes me want to scream the very few times that she's opened up to me, having a sibling who actually cares about her is a wonderful thing.

No matter how fucking terrifying he is.

"Look at him, he's obsessed with her, and not in a bad way. He watches her the way you watch me. I'm not going to get in the way of that."

He shakes his head. "I'm not saying we should. I'm saying we all need to stay out of it and away from him. Let them figure out how to be siblings and just… try not to get killed for breathing too close to her in his presence. Fuck, we're still trying to make sure he's never in the same room as Harley ever again."

I startle away from watching the siblings and hiss, "What? Why?"

Ash gives me a look. "He's obsessed with Poe being eighteen before she dates, right? Well, only one of us was with Lips before she was eighteen. What if he's adamant about that rule with Lips too? Harley is dead and buried."

I groan and slump forward in my seat. "Right. Of course. *Of course* that's a concern. Dammit, I should've been more of a nightmare to keep you lot away from her."

He chuckles at me. "You mean that's possible? Blaise still flinches around you and silverware. He's convinced he's going to wake up dickless someday with you grinning at the foot of his bed."

I roll my eyes at him, enjoying this moment even if we are both watching our favorite Mounty interact with the worst serial killer the country has ever known. "I definitely could've been worse about it. I was very mild on my true scale of power, you should all be very thankful. Ugh, I can't believe you keep fucking Lips on furniture in my house and I haven't bled you out yet. That's how good I am as a sister! I just spend all of my time bleaching everything."

He smirks at me and I shoot him a vicious glare back, smirking as I tease, "You know I could start telling you—"

"Nothing. If you want either of them to live, you will tell me *nothing*. If I find out you've fucked Atticus in the general vicinity of the public areas of the house, I'm going to show up to the next Twelve meeting and cut his fucking head off. There's at least three members who'll high five me—I'm safe."

A laugh bursts out of me, loud enough that Nate and Lips both look over at us, and Ash groans at me for getting their attention, even as his eyes stay glued to Lips as he fails miserably at not looking like a controlling and obsessive boyfriend.

Lips shakes her head at us both and then waves a hand at us, gesturing for us to join her.

"Well, I guess we better go make happy families. Try not to look at your girlfriend, it's the only way you're going to get through this without looking like the asshole you are," I murmur with a grin, and Ash rolls his eyes at me.

I wait until he comes around the car to help me out and I'm not at all ashamed to admit that it's because I want to walk over to them together, strength in numbers and all that.

Nate doesn't react to us joining them at all, and Lips

immediately pulls Ash into their conversation about Poe and their time down in New Orleans together. Nate listens to her without a word, but he also doesn't pull out a knife and stab Ash through the heart, so I think we're doing okay.

After a minute of this, once Lips finishes her story and gives Nate one of her trademark quick hugs, Ash slings an arm around her shoulders and walks her back over to the car, expecting me to be close behind him. He's aiming for casual and failing miserably, it's clear he's getting her away from Nate as quickly as he can manage.

I sigh.

And then I do something stupid by speaking to Nate without Lips present to mediate, but I feel like I should. "Thank you for coming. I know you came for Lips, but I still feel the need to say thank you for what you've done."

He is not impressed. "I'm not going to be manipulated. Not by you and not by anyone else in her life. If it's not about her safety, don't fucking call me."

I'm careful not to react in any way to him, even though I've never been so terrified in all my life as I am staring at the Devil himself. Every inch of his body screams death, pain, and destruction. Every inch of mine is desperate to get away.

"This isn't about manipulation. I understand that you don't give a fuck about anyone but your sister, but if this man dies, then three more will take his place. We'll never be free of it and Lips will always be in danger."

He pulls out another cigarette, placing it between his lips and lighting it up as he watches Ash help Lips into the car with that same intensity that he's had around her from the word go.

Then he looks at me again and shakes his head. "Last chance. No more warnings. I'll bleed every last one of you out without hesitation."

Queen Crow

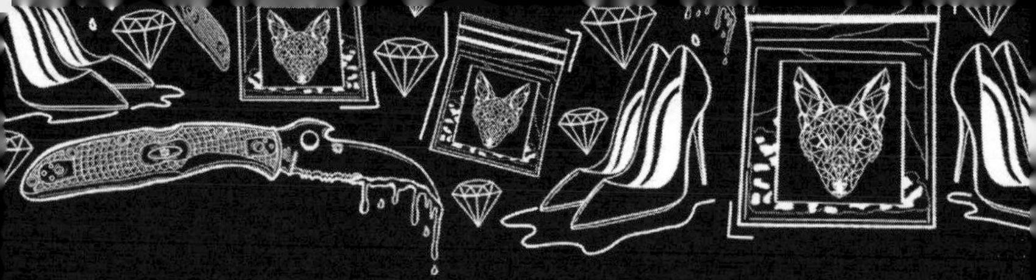

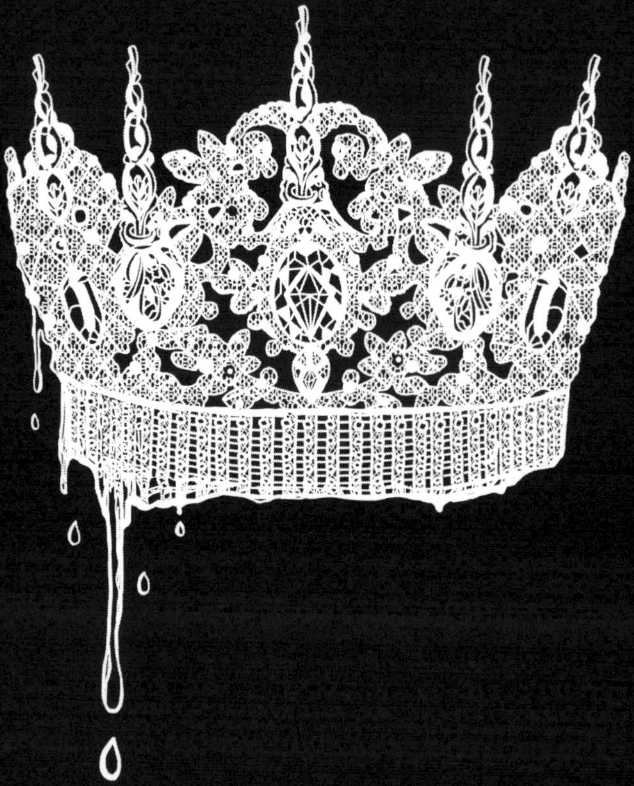

Chapter Twenty

Aodhan

Avery comes back from that fucking meeting with the Devil with a whole new outlook on life. There's some part of her that seems lighter, like whatever heavy burden she's been carrying around has finally been lifted and she's back to being her regular gorgeous, ruthless self again.

It's fucking intoxicating to be around.

I thought that the girl I've gotten to know over the last year was magnificent before, and she was, but this version is breathtaking. Vital to my survival. So earth-shatteringly perfect that I cannot believe she's mine.

When I talk her into dancing for me, I know I have to get to her before dinner because the chaos there always distracts her and gets into her head, so I seek her out and murmur into her ear, "We should have an early night."

The slow smirk that stretches over her lips is indulgent. "I don't think any of the things you're planning count as an early night."

"I'm not stupid, Queenie. I need you away from that scowling, snarling brother of yours and the studio is the perfect place."

I remember my promises of luring her into voyeurism, and her promise to me of letting me do whatever I want to her, and both of those things intertwine in my head until I'm coaxing her into her dance studio for my own private viewing of her latest dance routine.

She's been slow about getting back into it, not pushing herself too far too fast, but with Lips and the others back, and her plate a little less full, she's gotten back into being down here and stretching out her body.

The little outfit she wears each time is fucking obscene, and I decide that rich people are fucking weird because who in their right might would let their daughters wear those things in front of an audience? Ash let Avery walk on stage in front of hundreds of her classmates' families during high school in one of these and the moment I see her in it, my cock is throbbing in my jeans, weeping at all of the curves she's barely hiding under the stretchy fabric.

"You're not supposed to get hard over Don Quixote," she scoffs, her arms rising above her head and her tits bouncing with the movement.

"I know exactly who I'm getting hard over and it ain't Don.

Fuck, do that spin thing again. The bend too, do the bend—oh fuck. You better get that thing off, Queenie, before I rip it to shreds to get to that pretty pussy you're hiding from me."

She laughs at me, moving her body this way and that at my words, rising up to her tiptoes and stretching one leg out. I can't take anymore of it, grabbing her ankle and jerking her back into my body. She giggles, already prepared for all of my manhandling of her, and when I spin her around, she loops her arms around my neck, climbing up into my arms. She kisses me without hesitation, her tongue stroking mine the way I want it stroking my dick, and her hips grind against my stomach so I know she's just as primed for me as I am for her.

"Take me to bed," she murmurs against my lips, and I break away from her to drop us both down onto the ground, laying her out and covering her with my body.

"I'm not making it upstairs—where do I undo this thing? Queenie, I'm not playing around. I'll rip it off if I have to."

She laughs again, that breathless sound she makes while we're together has my balls pulling up tight with the need to be inside her. I have to ease back a little to let her shimmy out of the little outfit and I shove my jeans down my legs at the same time, rearing up to lose my shirt.

She looks so petite and perfect underneath me, her nipples hard and begging for my mouth and who am I to say no to them?

I work my way across her chest with my mouth slowly,

tasting her skin and enjoying the feel of her hands in my hair, tugging and pulling me this way and that. I want to drop down and eat her out, because her pussy is everything and I need her cum all over my face, but if I do it now, I'll never end up getting what I want from her today. So instead, I pull away and smirk down at her.

"I remember you telling me I could have anything I want, are you still game for that, Queenie? Or have you changed your mind?"

Her eyes are a little glazed over and she has to clear her throat to let out her usual sassy reply, "You do realize my best friend regularly has group sex, right? I'm not some innocent, I know all of the things you'll want from me."

I don't doubt that, but I also know that sometimes her head gets caught up in what's right and acceptable and not what feels good.

I'm going to push those boundaries tonight.

I lean down to bite at her throat and then I grasp her hips and flip her over. Fuck, her ass is just as perfect as the rest of her. Her legs are long and strong, shaped perfectly, and I lean down to bite the curve where her thigh meets her ass, hard enough that it'll bruise, but her squirming hips show no hesitation.

Then I straddle her hips, testing the slickness between her thighs and finding her already wet and sliding my cock down the crease of her ass.

Fuck I want that too, but for now I push my cock into her

pussy, groaning and thrusting a few times because it's too fucking perfect not to.

I didn't bring supplies down here but I'm not taking her too far tonight, just a little taste of the many things we have left to explore together, so I spit on her ass, running my fingers through it before I push my thumb into that tiny little pucker of her ass.

She gasps and wriggles a little underneath me, and I slap her ass with my free hand all while pushing my thumb in and out in time with the pumping of my cock in her pussy.

She moans, long and loud, every part of her body shuddering and squeezing, and I try not to crow in complete male satisfaction. She's mine and she's perfect and she loves what I do to her.

When she comes, gasping and moaning breathlessly, I pull my thumb out so I can brace myself properly and pound into her again, fucking her across the mats until I have to jerk her back down to where I need her. She's thrashing and groaning underneath me, writhing her way up to her next peak, and I'm just as desperate to get her there as I am for myself.

I see him before she does.

There's no possible way that I can stop, not a fucking thing on this Earth could stop me from pumping my hips into hers, my dick pounding into that tight, wet pussy of hers, but I also prepare myself for the fight that's about to happen because whatever he might've said to my girl, there's no way Atticus Crawford is going to just stand there and watch me fuck her.

Except that's exactly what he does.

I don't look over at him, but he's been too much a fucking dick about this to Avery for me not to fuck with him at least a little. So I shift my weight to one hand and then I grab her chin, turning her lips up to mine for one last reminder of who is fucking her, of who is breaking her apart right now as she moans and shakes beneath me.

Then I turn her head to face the doorway.

Her eyes stay squeezed tight for a minute longer, but I know the moment she opens them. A small gasping sound stutters out of her chest and her pussy tightens like a vise around me as she startles, ripping an answering groan out of me.

I have to get myself under control because even though she's already come twice, I'm not going to let him stand there and think that I'm a quick fuck and I don't treat my girl right.

So I fuck her slow and hard and deep into the mats of her dance studio while her other lover watches on in seething jealousy, and I don't let myself come until she's screaming my name again.

Avery

Aodhan smacks my bare ass as he wanders back off through the house, completely calm in the knowledge that I'm going to hunt Atticus down and find out exactly what dark pleasures his eyes were promising me.

I pull one of my robes out of the bathroom and head back up to my bedroom, deeply uncomfortable with walking up the stairs while everything still feels very… wet.

I'd wiped down, obviously, because I'm not a heathen, but all of the movement definitely means I need a shower, pronto.

Atticus is waiting in my room.

I smile at him but don't say a word as I walk straight into the bathroom and climb into the shower. I get through my first scrubbing down before he appears in the doorway, that same scowl still on his face. I try not to preen under it though because there's something deeply satisfying about his glowering when it's about Aodhan fucking me.

He notices because he notices every little thing about me, always. "I'm glad you're enjoying this, Avery, because I'm not going to back down."

My toes curl at the dark depths of his tone. "I'm fully prepared for the two of you to wage war across my body."

His eyes narrow and he snaps the shower door open. "Out. Get on the bed, Avery."

Goosebumps explode across my skin at the demand in his voice because there is no compromise there, no chance for me to say no to him. There's only submitting to every last one of his desires and trusting that he's going to make me enjoy every second of the ride.

I move to grab a towel and he stops me, his button-up shirt

half unbuttoned and the sleeves rolled up to his elbows. The stark difference between the two of us, him well-dressed and me naked and wet, is perfect, and it doesn't matter that I've already come three times—I need more.

I need more from him.

I also need to convince them to fuck me together, but that's a battle to be waged later.

I wait for him to take me into his arms or maybe to wrap a towel around me and dry me off himself, but that's not the man with me tonight. That's not who he is after watching me come apart on another man's cock.

His hand comes up to brush my hair away from my face, drifting down my neck until it comes to wrap around my throat.

My pussy throbs between my legs, my mouth dropping open as his fingers tighten and then he's backing me out of the room and up to the bed as his fingers flex around my throat in little pulses. I would've never really considered breath play on a list of things I wanted to try, but there's something addictive about the way that my brain just… stops.

There's nothing but the fire in his eyes for me to focus on when he's controlling the very air in my lungs like he is. The ultimate control, something I would never hand over willingly, to have him take it like this has my body just melting for him.

I want everything from him, every controlling inch of him on me and in me and destroying me. I want him with a desperation that rocks me to my core.

He takes me down to the bed, his hand finally dropping away from my throat as I gasp for air, stars bursting across my vision already. If this is the intensity I'm going to have from him tonight, I might die a very happy death.

"Close your eyes, Avery."

I whimper, mostly because I desperately want to watch him this time, and the molten look from the bathtub flashes into my mind. I want that. I want the controlling but the tenderness this time too.

"You'll come when I tell you to, and if you're good, I'll let you watch me come. Now shut your eyes."

I squeeze them shut, ready for him to tie me down or fuck my face, ready for whatever rough claiming he has for me, but I'm not at all ready for him to chase the water drops on my body with his tongue.

I'm not prepared for him to taste every inch of my skin, lapping over my nipples and the valley between my breasts, then working his way down my body until he's biting at my thighs, his tongue dipping into my pussy.

He's making me his all over again and the moment I feel his tongue on my clit I want to come, the words falling out from between my lips, "Please, please, I need to come."

He doesn't answer me, doesn't say yes to my begging, instead he slips his fingers inside my pussy as he eats me out, getting them wet before he slips them out and back into my ass like he's writhing with jealously that it was another first Aodhan got to have with me.

Still he doesn't give me permission to come and my legs are practically vibrating as I clench my teeth in desperation, every inch of my body tense as I hold it back.

He pushes and pushes, driving me higher and higher, and when he finally murmurs against my skin, "Come now, Floss," I shatter, my vision whiting out as I come so hard that I lose feeling in my toes.

Before I have a chance to recover, he climbs back up my body, one hand tweaking my nipple in a harsh pinch. "Open your eyes, Avery."

Tears I didn't realize were falling stream down my face and he watches them with that same dark pleasure he had when he watched Aodhan fuck me into the floor, a finger buried in my ass and his cock in my pussy as he stroked my orgasm out of me.

I gasp when his hand comes around my throat again and tightens. The deprivation heightens everything, his touch burning into my skin like he's branding me, his fingerprints covering me until there's no question of his claim to me.

It's as though he's trying to prove that to us both.

Then I watch as he wraps his other hand around his cock, stroking himself as his eyes roam over my body. I whimper, desperate to touch him and make him feel every bit of pleasure he has given me, but he shakes his head at me the minute my hands reach for him.

I cry a little more and he likes that, coming a minute later over my chest with a rough grunt as his fingers tighten a little more around my throat.

If I didn't already know it was a claiming, his fingers rubbing the cum into my skin are a dead giveaway and I wouldn't have it any other way.

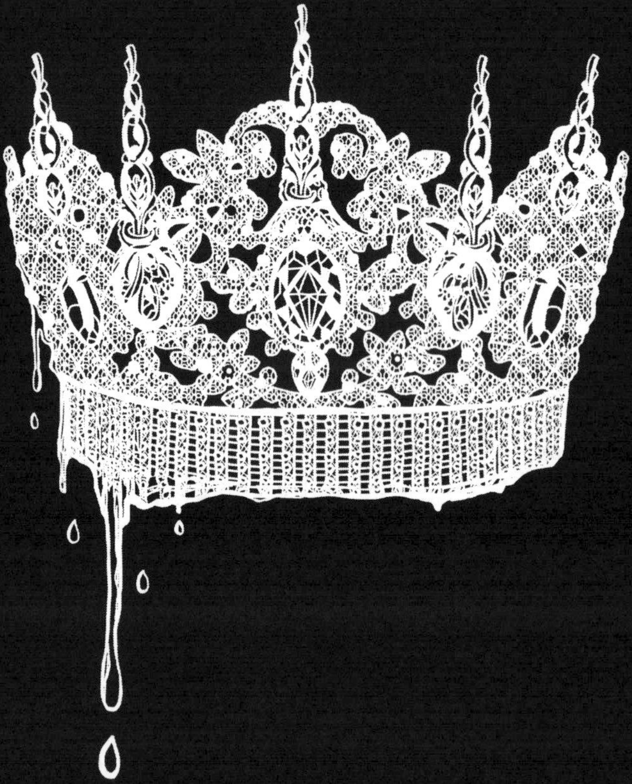

Chapter Twenty-One

I send out invites to a nonnegotiable extended family dinner.

I don't invite the out-of-towners but everyone else who matters to our family gets a time and date to arrive as well as a menu in case there are any allergies I need to contend with.

I should know better than to try for formality.

Roxas immediately messages back with critiques about the lack of red meat options, and I threaten to send Lips after him in the cold dead of the night if he doesn't just shut his mouth, sit quietly at my goddamn table, and eat my cooking.

Harbin is better about it. Jackson and Viola just send through their RSVP as though they had an option here, and Odie sends me a lovely reply about how much she can't wait to see us all and an apology for needing space to breastfeed so her husband doesn't kill all of the men attending.

I adore her.

I have the entire meal prepped and ready to go an hour before anyone is due to arrive. Aodhan is already here drinking with Harley and Morrison, all of them arguing over some fighter I've never heard about before, while Ash is muttering in the corner with Lips about something I can't quite make out.

Noah is behind the bar, mixing drinks with a little *too* much skill.

When he hands me a margarita that he's just poured, I eye him over the rim distrustfully. We might've come to an agreement, a peace treaty of sorts, but Illi's warnings of poisoned food and drinks ring in my ear.

"Just fucking drink it, *Aves*," he says, sarcasm at an all time high but I sigh and take a sip.

It's the best margarita I've ever tasted.

I take another gulp, looking like my brother sucking back the alcohol like I want to die, and Noah grins at me. "Mixing drinks is my specialty."

I finish the glass off and hand it back to him for a refill, fully preparing myself for a messy night thanks to his skills. "How? You look about twelve years old, who gave you access to enough spirits to learn?"

The grin dims a little but he shrugs and says, "You'd be surprised. The Bay isn't the only shitty city in the country, you know."

I can't argue with that.

I shoot him a look of camaraderie, because I also understand terrible childhoods, and Lips sidles up behind us as Ash moves over to join the guys' raucous argument. Noah holds out a margarita to her as well which she takes with a little cringe.

"Lips is a whiskey girl, straight and fiery," I murmur, and Noah gags dramatically.

"Of course she is, she's a better man than I'll ever be."

Lips rolls her eyes at him and takes a sip. "Not bad. I could drink these more often. I like whiskey because it's what was around, not because I have some refined palette."

Noah starts fumbling around with some of the bottles to mix up something else, and Lips glances behind us like she's checking the guys still can't hear us. "So, you're going to be a Crawford, huh? I would've guessed he'd be the stickler for marriage."

I groan. "Of course Aodhan and Harley have been gossiping. We're never going to get to tell each other anything anymore! Those two will spoil it all. Besides, it was a negotiation. It's not happening anytime soon."

She grins at me and shares a look with Noah, one that says they've managed to form some sort of bridge between them. "I'm surprised you didn't tell them it had to be a split down the middle. I thought Atticus would've loved a perfectly fifty-fifty split."

"What am I supposed to do, move to the Maldives so we can have a polygamist marriage?" Lips turns to face me, and I wave a hand at the look she gives me. "Of course I looked up legal polygamist marriages, Lips—it's what I do! Christ, I've known all about them since about ten minutes after you said 'I don't know, I like them all.'"

She scoffs at me, that lovely blush of hers back on her cheeks, and I try not to laugh back at her. I really should turn the oven on before the margaritas get to me but the moment I finish my glass, Noah is there refilling it.

He's not so bad.

After the arguing dies down a little, Harley stomps over to us and slings an arm around Lips, drawling at me, "Why the fuck do we have a seating chart for dinner? Is this a secret fucking wedding or some shit?"

I roll my eyes at Harley's dramatics and snap back at him, "Well, if you could all sit through an entire meal without threatening each other or risking damage to my good china, then we wouldn't need one, but unfortunately you're all unruly children."

Aodhan scoffs quietly under his breath but when I turn to look at him, he raises both of his hands with a grin. "I didn't say a word. As long as Crawford is on the opposite side of the table as Ash then I'm good. I don't really wanna listen to their bullshit the whole night."

Ash walks over and Noah hands him a bourbon obediently, looking positively gleeful when Ash thanks him directly.

This might end up a very messy evening.

I stumble into the kitchen to start heating up the dishes right as the doorbell rings and Lips skips off to start letting people in.

Illi walks in with Johnny's capsule in one hand and the other arm wrapped around Odie, a glare on his face like he's mad at the entire world for existing and dragging him out of his apartment to be here today.

It melts away when Odie smiles up at him, pressing a kiss to his cheek and then pulling away from him to hug Lips as she approaches them both. I head over to greet them and coo at the sweet little boy who is having a sleep, a little plush wolf toy tucked into his arms that I could die over.

I give Illi a quick squeeze. "I've packed up a month's worth of dinners for you both to take home tonight. I hope you enjoy vegan casseroles."

Illi scoffs at me, taking a beer from Harley with a nod. "I already know you wouldn't do that shit to me, Queenie. I get rid of the leaking, bloating, stinking bodies of your enemies too good for you to pull that shit on me."

He is absolutely correct, and I used the highest quality meats in all of the dishes. I also packed enough lactation cookies to keep that baby in milk for the next twenty years, because I'm sure Illi will end up digging into them as well and I wanted to make sure Odie had enough to keep her going for a few months.

Morrison comes over and snaps, "Thank fuck for that. When are you back on the streets again? It's been disgusting without you, I'm not gonna lie."

Lips rolls her eyes at them all, and then the doorbell goes off again and the house becomes a chaotic mess.

I get everyone seated at the dining table, dinner served, and everyone eating happily an hour later. I consider it a huge achievement but when I look around at everyone there laughing and chatting together, there's a swell of pride in my chest as well as an overwhelming sense of achievement.

We did it.

We made it through all of the trauma and the devastation, the lies and the testing loyalties, the betrayals and the heartaches.

We made it through with each other.

Atticus watches me watching everyone else and his hand slips into mine under the table, sipping at his bourbon and nodding along to something Luca has said to him. I glance down at where Harley is telling Aodhan some ridiculous story about a party they went to in Jersey while they were away, and I grin at them both.

Every part of this night is perfect.

Once dinner has been eaten and dessert has been annihilated thanks to Lips and Noah, the sweet tooth clearly a Graves thing, everyone breaks off to sit around and chat some more, the alcohol flowing and keeping everyone happily social. Lips and I have a cuddle with Johnny on the couch in front of the TV, cooing at his big blue eyes because someday this boy is going to break a lot of hearts.

I cover his eyes when the news comes on, the real reason we're sitting in here instead of enjoying everyone else's company by the bar area.

The cross is shown on the TV, heavily pixelated so there's no telling that it's Randy Crawford strung up there like that, but the Wolf insignia that's been carved into his flesh is shown in full HD.

We all know, though, and there's no better feeling than hearing everything the news anchors have to say about it.

"Gang violence is once again on the rise in Mounts Bay after a short lull following the massacre last summer. We have spoken with Police Chief Drummond but he has stated that the Mounts Bay Police Department has no comment at this early stage of the investigation."

I glance over to where Lips is holding Johnny, more comfortable now she has some experience with it, and I raise an eyebrow at her. "Well, that certainly is a statement."

She grins at me. "He's good at what he does, that's for sure."

The sounds of our family are loud around us, but no one is taking any notice of us sitting here quietly together. The margaritas are warming my blood and making me giggly as hell as I finally ask her, "Are you going to tell me what happened on tour yet?"

Lips groans and juggles Johnny in her arms a little, lifting her glass from the coffee table again to knock it back in one go. "I wish what happened on tour could stay there, but there's the small problem of dealing with the corpse in the freezer on the bus."

I blink at her.

Then again, just to be sure I'm hearing her correctly. "The corpse. In the freezer. On the bus. The bus in my driveway that

I've been trying to get Morrison to move for weeks. That bus?"

She pours another drink and finishes that one in a single gulp too. "That's the one."

Jesus fucking Christ.

Queen Crow

Also by J Bree

The Mounts Bay Saga

The Butcher Duet
The Butcher of the Bay: Part I
The Butcher of the Bay: Part II

Hannaford Prep
Just Drop Out: Hannaford Prep Year One
Make Your Move: Hannaford Prep Year Two
Play the Game: Hannaford Prep Year Three
To the End: Hannaford Prep Year Four

The Queen Crow Trilogy
All Hail
The Ruthless
Queen Crow

Unseen MC
Angel Unseen

***

The Bonds That Tie
Broken Bonds

About J Bree

J Bree is a dreamer, writer, mother, farmer, and cat-wrangler. The order of priorities changes daily.

She lives on a small farm in a tiny rural town in Australia that no one has ever heard of. She spends her days dreaming about all of her book boyfriends, listening to her partner moan about how the wine grapes are growing, and being a snack bitch to her two kids.

For updates about upcoming releases, please visit her website at http://www.jbreeauthor.com, and sign up for the newsletter or join her group on Facebook at #mountygirlforlife: A J Bree Reading Group

Printed in Great Britain
by Amazon